Astray in Arcady

Other books by Mary E. Mann available from the Larks Press

The Patten Experiment

Rose at Honeypot

The Parish of Hilby

The Complete Tales of Dulditch

The Novels of Mary E. Mann

Astray in Arcady

Introduction by Patience Tomlinson

Larks Press

*First printed and published in England by
Methuen & Company, London, 1910*

This new edition published in November 2009 by

The Larks Press
*Ordnance Farmhouse, Guist Bottom, Dereham,
Norfolk NR20 5PF
01328 829207*

*Printed by Newprint and Design, Garrood Drive,
Fakenham, Norfolk. 01328 851578*

A full catalogue of Larks Press books is available at
www.booksatlarkspress.co.uk

*British Library Cataloguing-in-Publication-Data
A catalogue record for this book is available from the British Library*

Patience Tomlinson has created a one-woman show about the life and work of Mary E. Mann entitled *A Tale That Is Told*, which she has performed in many venues in and out of Norfolk. A frequent performer on BBC Radio 3 and 4, she has broadcast several of Mary Mann's short stories and four of these are available on CD under the title *The Fields of Dulditch*. Further recordings will include more Dulditch stories and audio books of *Rose at Honeypot* and *Astray in Arcady*.
email: patienceacts@aol.com

ISBN 978 1 904006 50 3

Introduction

'Write a good book and you probably starve; write the rubbish the public will read, and rich is the reward.'

Mary Mann, who wrote the above words in a letter to her nephew, Thomas Ordish, was such a gifted writer that she was able to produce books that pleased all tastes. Her short stories, set in the fictional parish of Dulditch and recently republished by the Larks Press in a complete collection, are unquestionably her finest work, but *Astray in Arcady* combines all her powers in one novel and is a superb read. If you want to be amused and entertained, read this book, if you want to learn about life in a Norfolk village shortly before the First World War, read this book, and if you want to understand something of the personality and character of Mary Mann herself, read this book.

Charlotte Poole, the flamboyant narrator of this novel, is a delicious creation, undoubtedly something of a self-portrait by Mann. 'The insight and the literary gift of Mrs Mann do not, of course, fail her in the person of Charlotte Poole.' So wrote the reviewer of *Astray in Arcady* in the *Times Literary Supplement* in September 1910. Poole is the town-mouse reflection of Mann's country mouse, domineering, theatrical, self-important and falsely self-deprecating, with a brilliantly ironical sense of humour. How Mann must have enjoyed writing this book and allowing this fictional woman to voice her own feelings about living in 'Arcady.' It cannot have been difficult for Mann to project herself into the character of the more famous urban authoress. 'Do you observe,' she had written in frustration to Ordish in 1902, 'how with good notices in *The Academy, Spectator, Times, Telegraph, Globe* and so on Mr Fisher Unwin [her publisher] sticks my book at the bottom of the list with only a notice from a Norwich paper. A Norwich man - editor of a newspaper - says I should be raking in the shekels. But how?'

The Athenaeum review of 1910 appreciates the 'humorous satire' in *Astray in Arcady* but complains that 'there is virtually no story at all...unhappily there is so much truth in the picture that Mrs Mann makes one pause and wonder and question. It is enough to send true country lovers scuttling back to London.' In its condemnation, however, is concealed unwitting praise. If Mann was seen as telling the truth, she succeeded in her aim.

Charlotte Poole's Arcady, namely Dulditch, is based upon Mann's own village of Shropham in south-west Norfolk where she came to live in 1871 on marrying her tenant-farmer husband Fairman Mann. She lived there for 42 years, and despite the many claims on her time from farming and village affairs and bringing up four children, managed to write 39 novels and a collection of exceptional short stories. There must have been times when Mann had wished to do the reverse of what her character does and try living in London to see what inspiration that would give her. Her family tied her to the country but instead of letting that stifle her voice she turned it to her own advantage, saw with her own eyes the 'necessary fuel' to the writer of 'farce, comedy, tragedy all around' and used her remarkable skills to bring the dullness of 'stagnant Shropham' to vivid and rich life.

'I come from a family of readers rather than writers,' Mann said when asked about the source of her talent. She was born in Norwich in 1848 into the wealthy middle-class Rackham family - she was related to the well-known artist Arthur Rackham. Unusually for a girl of that period she received an excellent education – perhaps because her six siblings were brothers. She read avidly and widely, including European, American and contemporary English literature and there was plenty of what she called 'the stimulation of educated discourse.' She wrote to Thomas Ordish 'My mind is not a jewel to shine in a dark place, it is of a metal that requires friction in order to do itself justice, contact with other minds.' Ordish was her husband's nephew, an author and noted Shakespearian scholar only six years younger than her and a great admirer of her writing. He lived in London and helped her deal with her publishers, agents and business affairs, sent her literary magazines and periodicals and provided a constant source of mental stimulation which she could not find in Shropham. Her regular correspondence with him began in the late 1870s and carried on into the 1920s. 'For so long,' she wrote in 1906, 'your letters have given me such lively satisfaction.' As indeed hers must have given him, full as they are of Shropham, family, farming and particularly bookish, gossip. She often recommended books for him to read and once wrote, 'You are wrong not to read more women authors, George Eliot, Edith Wharton, Mrs Braddon, for instance - all very clever.'

In 1908 Mann was asked to write a short article for *The Bookman*, a well known literary publication of the period, on the subject of 'the disadvantages of working in London and out of it.' Other writers who were asked to contribute something to this 'Authors at Work' column included H.G. Wells, Jerome K. Jerome, W.W. Jacobs, E.F. Benson and Henry Rider-Haggard, which shows the high esteem in which

Mary Mann was held at the time. Indeed she had become a household name by 1906 when eighteen of her most popular novels were reprinted by Methuen. In her article Mann says of her writing:

I have sometimes thought it would have been done better if, instead of struggling against the sleepy influences of solitude, the torpor engendered by communion with the rural mind, I had rubbed shoulders with the world and enjoyed the advantages of those writers who complain that their moods are upset and their ideas unsettled by the noise and hurry of town. Brain must stimulate brain; wit sharpen wit; the perceptions must grow brighter by constant use... I should say, however, let the man who writes of town life live in towns, let him who would describe the country take up his abode there – a counsel neglected flagrantly by many authors, with results to be expected and deplored.

Perhaps thinking and writing on this subject gave Mann the germ of the idea for *Astray in Arcady*, which she began to write the following year. So she invents her narrator, Charlotte Poole, a very well known and successful London author, whose husband has recently died. Charlotte Poole's son, George, has advised her to 'Write a book of the country in the country... Have done with stage effects; the virtuous peasant of the footlights, the used-up pathos, and the second-hand scenery that everyone knows. Make your own observations, write of what you see and hear.'

So Charlotte Poole, 'seized with the desire to ruralize', rents a house in a remote village in Norfolk from where she intends to 'study the native at first hand and to wrench some of her precious secrets from Dame Nature herself' and from where 'she will send forth the new book for which her public eagerly awaits.' The book is written in the form of letters, which Poole intends to work into a novel.

In the first third of *Astray in Arcady* Charlotte Poole writes to a young woman, a widow, Hildred Valetta, whom she has more or less brought up as her own daughter. Hildred herself has a nine-year-old daughter, Nan, and Charlotte Poole invites them both to stay with her in Norfolk. When Hildred and Nan eventually arrive in Dulditch the rest of the book is made up of letters to Charlotte Poole's son George who is working overseas. Mann's own son, her eldest child, Rackham, was a naval surgeon, also working abroad at this time. Gradually, in the letters, we are introduced to the characters in the village through a series of finely drawn vignettes, which build up to give a broad picture of the village as a whole until the grand finale, the Rectory Bazaar and Garden Fête, where many of the characters and some new ones, come together. The main characters, Squire

Hobbleboy and his wife, Major Barkaway and the somewhat ineffectual Rector and his spinster sister Bertha, are ridiculously snobbish and narrow-minded, affording Mann much material for Poole's wry and ironical comments.

Poole retains the services of the previous tenant's gardener, Syers. The conflicting opinions of Syers and Poole on the subject of gardening are a source of great amusement, until the 'woodpecker incident' reveals something deeper in Poole's (and Mann's) feelings about the countryside and the creatures in it. So does the letter about Poole finding a hare in a gamekeeper's trap. There is significant contrast between Poole's slightly saccharine words as she talks about 'the incomparable Nan' or delights in the beauty of 'Dunn's Heath' (a real place in Shropham, though renamed), and the totally unsentimental description of the reality of the hare's pain, and Poole's anxiety to end it. There is something of the power of Mann's short stories here. Published in numerous magazines and periodicals over a span of twenty-five years they seemed to escape her agent's exhortation to 'only write cheerful stories.' Perhaps he failed to see the wit in even the darkest of them. They describe in matter-of-fact detail the terrible deprivations to her local village community caused by the agricultural depression of the late nineteenth century, which she experienced at first hand. They were collected together and published as *The Fields of Dulditch* in 1902. The style of the stories emerges again in Charlotte Poole's letter which describes the grief of a shepherd who, due to age and ill health, is no longer able to work with his sheep, leading to tragic consequences - and also in the unselfpitying conversation of a young woman she visits who is dying of cancer. Mann, through Poole, not gushing but writing sparely now, uses the matter-of-factness of the Norfolk dialect to great effect here. There are several examples of this style, and of Mann's talent for making her point by using humour in almost every situation.

Charlotte Poole says that all the people she has met in Dulditch 'accept me entirely on my surface merits, and have a well-bred way of seeming to ignore any of the things I have done.' She pretends to appreciate their 'delicate reticence' and assumes they are either ignorant of her best-selling novel, *'A Splendid Failure,'* or will not give her the satisfaction of asking her about it which makes her angry. Mary Mann well knew that situation in Shropham. In a letter to Thomas Ordish written in September 1906, when she herself was very well known, she remembers taking a trip to Loch Lomond where a favourite author of hers, Robert Louis Stevenson, 'was quite unknown in his own land. That,' Mann says, 'reconciles one a little to various experiences of one's own regarding the indifference and violent disregard of one's neighbours.'

Mann knew the local clergyman and historian, the Reverend Augustus Jessop who was the Rector of Scarning, near Shropham. His book entitled *Arcady for Better for Worse* (1887), like Mann's stories a realistic depiction of rural life, must have given her inspiration. In another letter to Ordish she describes attending a village wedding and hearing Jessop's address fall on deaf ears. 'A brilliant speech; his elocution is perfect, his air high-bred and refined. I pitied him: this speech was immensely witty – not a creature smiled. He made point after point – not the slightest applause.' Once again it could be Charlotte Poole speaking.

In *Astray in Arcady,* Miss Flatt, the Rector's sister, eventually agrees to read Charlotte Poole's novel, but tells Hildred that she thinks the conduct of Poole's heroine is *'absolutely indecent'* and goes on to say, 'I should not have thought a *nice woman* could have brought herself to write of such things... Of course a book is a revelation of the person who writes it... Dreadful things must have happened to Mrs Poole or in her family. I should have thought she would shrink from making them public.' Mann herself was used to similar criticism of her own books. 'The trouble with Mrs Mann is she will write unpleasant books' said one editor at Mills and Boon, and in Mann's obituary in 1929 the *Times* wrote that she did not 'shrink from exhibiting the ugliness of life, whether in cottage or in villa.'

Poole makes friends with the Chisholms, tenants at the Grange Farm. She says, ' the place, having come down for generations from father to son, is loved almost as if it were their own, but with the present man I hear the Chisholm tenancy will come to an end.' Mr Chisholm has had the same difficulty making a living from farming as did the Manns and many others and Mrs Chisholm, after years of watching her husband's struggle, is determined that 'no child of hers should be a farmer.' The Chisholms represent the family in this book closest to Mann's own. In a letter to her nephew Mann quotes her husband Fairman saying to their son at the dinner table, 'Don't go into farming, it's a fool's game.' The Chisholm daughter, Nora, (a portrait of Mann's own daughter, Margery, who also loved rearing her own chickens) says she will never get married because she never meets young men of her class. She says 'they are all away in London, in Canada, in Africa, in India, or at college. No farmer who is of the class called gentleman-farmer is any longer bringing up his son to that business, and there is no other business or profession to be followed in the country.' Only one of Mann's three daughters found a husband.

When the Countess of Tatterbury and her niece Etta arrive unexpectedly at the Rectory Garden Fete, the Hobbleboys and others are forced to look with different eyes upon Charlotte Poole. Etta is gushingly enthusiastic about the play she has just seen in London that is based on one of Poole's novels.

'Upon the Hobbleboys, staring and flabbergasted, was laid the onus of a momentous decision which must be made on the spot. Should they renounce their annual chance of a ten minutes' conversation with the old Earl of Tatterbury's widow, or should they risk the contamination of sitting down by the side of a nobody like the tenant of The Cottage, and of an abandoned creature such as they had decided Hildred to be? With commendable promptitude they concluded to risk the contamination.'

Poole's obvious satisfaction at having a successful run of a play of hers in London's West End mirrors Mann's own experience. The play *Little Mrs Cummin* based on Mann's novel *The Eglamore Portraits* was produced at The Playhouse theatre, London in 1909.

In June 1886 Mary Mann had written to Thomas Ordish 'I have been re-reading *Vanity Fair*. Its author has a wonderful power over me. I have altered my views of other writers who influenced me in my youth, but not Thackeray.' The influence of this favourite author of hers is put to good use in *Astray in Arcady* where Mann's main theme is class distinction and village snobbery. Charlotte Poole says: 'More than I ever dreamed, in my life in town, I realize in this thinly populated place how senseless, how injurious to character, the laws of caste can be, how cruel, how fraught with danger class hatred.'

'Mary Mann excelled in depicting the life of the country village or small town, and she had humour, keen observation and a penetrating sense of character... Her work was remarkably well constructed, and no doubt partly for that reason it was appreciated by other novelists, who admired her sound craftsmanship and sense of proportion.' Mann would have been gratified by this *Times* obituary opinion of what she called her 'quill-driving trade' and I am sure no reader of *Astray in Arcady* could fail to agree with it.

Patience Tomlinson, Stanhoe, Norfolk

To Hildred

Astray in Arcady

To Hildred

I WONDER how you will like Dulditch when you come, as you have promised, to visit me here; you and your phenomenal daughter, that 'world's lily,' the incomparable Nan?

You will find yourselves, perhaps, cramped in your quarters, and must make up your minds to rough it a little. But this, spoilt and pampered favourites of fortune as you are, you will learn to regard as wholesome discipline; or if you cannot accept it as such, you will put up with it for my sake.

For myself, I am disposed to be much in love with my new domain. It might have been designed, built, and planted to gratify the tastes of a town-bred woman, weary of the noise of crowds and seized with the desire to ruralize. The house is more than big enough for myself and my modest retinue, and only apes humility by styling itself The Cottage. For the rest it is creeper-grown, lattice-windowed, even thatched – that portion of the original building on to which the modern dining-room, morning-room, and three bedrooms have been built. The garden has a Lovers' Walk (in the old days when you were a girl, Hildred, with my George, hanging about the house, this would have been an interesting acquisition. Picture a Lovers' Walk in Harley Street!) It has a broad green alley, with espalier apple-trees trained on each side – forget-me-nots and violets grow at their roots; it has wide flower-beds, bordering the quite respectable length of drive, a tiny orchard, a lawn which has been beautifully kept, and is big enough for a game of croquet when you and the delectable daughter come to knock the balls about with me.

And, above and beyond all, it has trees.

Never in my life before have I been possessor of a tree. And here, with house and stables and all the above-mentioned accessories thrown in, for the modest sum of fifty pounds a year, I have more than a dozen of my own. Think of that, Mrs. Valetta!

As I lie in bed of mornings my eyes open upon the branches of a great ash, not so very many yards from my window. Farther on, in the hedgerow, are a couple of big acacias; these my gardener tells me will be 'ablow,' later on, with 'boonches' of great white hanging blossoms. There is a giant fir-tree, from which the lower branches have been cut away, making room for a chair or two and a table, beneath whose shade, as spring advances, I mean to sit with pen and paper to 'await the spark from heaven.' There are enormous beeches –

But that ash just beyond my window! Picture to yourself, my dear girl, that I can lie there to watch the buds form on the naked branches, swell, burst into leaf. That there 'the fowls of the heaven will make their habitations, and sing among the branches'; will feed their young there; there teach the baby birds to take the first flight. That the twitter which wakes me at sunrise 'shall grow to song, and eggs to birds.' That I shall see and hear it!

To-day, at noon, I standing agaze in an idle hour, came a tiny, elfin bird – a blue-tit, afterwards I learnt it was. Busily it crept with quick, sure movement along the naked branch of a larch-tree. Above and beneath the length of the branch it went, seeking its food with ceaseless stabbings of its resolute little beak.

Last night, among the branches of my ash, sketched with Indian ink on a fair blue sky, a little new moon was set a-swing, like a golden, fairy hammock. Oh, my dear Hildred! make haste to escape from the arms of your poor husband's relatives in New York, and come to look upon my trees.

You know why I came to Dulditch? – how I came there? You remember that my dream of late years has been to escape from the shams and the shackles of town life to the sincerity and liberty, above all the simplicity, of life in the country? But Henry would not or could not leave his profession and Harley Street; and I would not or could not leave Henry. Over this I used to bemoan my fate; I am not accustomed to keep grievances to myself, and I have no doubt I bemoaned it to you.

Poor Henry's death having set me free from the necessity to live in town, for a whole year I felt that I could not leave it; that I could not live without the familiar racket; my 'dear five hundred friends' of whom I had so often been deadly weary; my club; my constant engagements; the room in which, for lucre's sake, I have written so many thousand words daily, for many years! It seemed, in the foolish feminine part of me, that to turn my back on our home too quickly was to turn my back on Henry in his grave.

Habit is a thing of which to be terrified, Hildred. Beware, my dear widow, of getting into a groove. I, who have been the most conservative creature for all my life, am now inclined to preach Change, Change, Change, at the tag end of it. 'Variety is the spice of life'; let yours be many-coloured. Fear not the unattempted. Move on. Move on.

As for me, behold me – at last cut adrift – afraid to move from the spot to which I had been securely anchored! Besides the fact that I had lost all desire to do so, all at once I found myself shrinking from the launch forth into the deep – clinging to each familiar aspect, afraid to let it go. And all the while, Henry being gone, the Familiar looked at me with unfamiliar face. The change I dreaded to seek was all about me. Of the sick perception of the difference in daily things I nearly died.

Then, my dear boy, my George, in Ceylon, perceiving through the insight of affection what I suffered, ordered me away.

'Go, for a year at least, into the country,' he said. 'Make everything as unlike as possible to the life you have been leading. Pitch your camp "in the living out-of-doors." Write a book of the country *in* the country, not as you have hitherto written, with such excellent results of satisfying the critics and the public, at your desk in Harley Street. Have done with stage effects; the virtuous peasant of the footlights, the used-up pathos, and the second-hand scenery that every one knows. Make your own observations, write of what you see and hear. At the end of the year I will perhaps come to fetch you, and we will keep house together here, in Ceylon.'

So here I am. Alone till you come, Hildred; but no longer unhappy. The big gloomy house in Harley Street, empty of me and my dear ones for ever; the big, handsome furniture all left behind. The chairs and tables reproached me terribly while I was contemplating the desertion. 'Whose place was this? for how many years? Can't you see the familiar face gazing across the glass and flowers at you? Do you remember the gay and kind looks gathered around the board?' 'Whose favourite seat by the fireside was I?' Oh, I assure you, tongues were in the very sticks and stones of the place, sermons written on its walls; and I, alas! not deaf to hear. But that's all swept behind me; I am free, even of memories – for the time.

Did you see the paragraphs in the papers to the effect that 'Charlotte Poole, in order to study the native at first-hand and to wrench some of her precious secrets from Dame Nature herself, had retired to East Anglia. From that interesting region steeped in local tradition, and imbued with the spirit of the place, she will send forth the new book for which her public eagerly awaits.'

Very kind and polite, isn't it? and instructive to Charlotte Poole. Whether she acts up to what has been promised in her name we shall see.

In the meantime I intend to make a collection of jottings, flung upon paper as the spirit moves me, and when mail-day comes put them in an envelope and dispatch to you or George. You will both keep the scribblements and bring them with you when you come. In such manner a kind of record will be made which afterwards may be of use to me. I find it a pleasant way of taking notes which may or may not develop into something more important. To you both I offer no apology for making my scrawlings answer a double purpose. I have sufficient confidence in the love of both of you to know that what I write you care to read because it is I who have written it. Although I send him rivers of ink, splashed upon acres of paper, my son grumbles for more; and you, my dear Hildred, solitary in that adoring crowd of relatives by marriage in New York, as I, 'all of my lone' in Dulditch, you –.

To Hildred

OF my neighbours I know very little at present. The Davenals appear to have written to the people at the Hall about me. I am sorry they took that trouble. I do not care to have acquaintances thrust upon me in this way. Yesterday they called. An absolutely uninteresting pair. Fat, small, commonplace woman; thin, small, abject man. Illiterate – both of them. She talkative, with a certain facile pouring forth of words; he, very nearly without the power of expression, hanging lop-lipped upon her utterances, endorsing them, now and then, by an almost inarticulate stuttering.

Why should I, my dear Hildred, be bothered with this sort of thing?

The pair evidently labour under the impression that 'our mutual friends' (their phrase) the Davenals, are the passport to my consideration. Details poured forth from the woman: where they had met them; who made them acquainted; how they were driven into each other's society; items of the Davenals' family history even to their Norfolk cousins with titles, and their Queens' Gardens second cousins with money, were given.

When I had sufficiently endured I said I knew absolutely nothing of the Davenals; which, if it was a little wide of the actual truth, had the effect of stopping the torrent. It, at the same time, caused them to open eyes of distrust and astonishment upon me.

The male Hobbleboy – (did I say their name is Hobbleboy?) – I believe to be next door to an idiot. He merely dropped his lips at me and stared; the female, with a quite obvious exhibition of tactfulness (don't you always desire to laugh in the faces of the people who are openly resourceful?) turned the subject. She asked me in what part of London I had lived, and went on to put many more leading questions, whose intimacy I thought to be bordering on impertinence.

I took the conversation into my own hand, therefore, and talked to her. It is the only way; when you cannot escape people who fatigue you, talk them down. Your own voice, you will find, never bores you.

Before they went I made a few inquiries about the inhabitants of the place. The replies were distinctly discouraging. There is no one, according to the Hobbleboys, in Dulditch but themselves.

I had noticed some fine old houses surrounded by park-like meadows, or by charming old-world gardens, I said.

The Hobbleboys' tenants.

There was a big Rectory near the Church?

The Hobbleboys' parson and his sister.

'I thought you mean people of social standing,' Mrs. Hobbleboy explained.

I told her that the people in whom I was chiefly interested were those of the labouring class. With them, if they would allow me, I intended to make friends.

She rose to go away then. I was thankful to see the ugly broad back of her, and the stooping back of the semi-idiot husband.

They have three unmarried daughters at home, I hear. After suffering the parents I have lost all hope that these, my dear Hildred, might turn out agreeable companions for you.

Well, owing to the officiousness of the Davenals (I shall know how to thank them when I see them again!) I must go to return the Hobbleboys' call; after which I shall see as little of them as possible.

Before she went she gave me a word of warning: 'Have as little as possible to do with the cottagers,' she said. 'They are, in this village, I assure you, a people to discourage: ill-mannered, disrespectful, ungrateful.'

Had they anything to be grateful for, I asked. And was told, with emphasis that seemed to protest too much: Yes; they had.

Descending to detail, she informed me that they had the privilege of living in Dulditch under a resident Squire, while in most of the villages around the landlord was absentee, the halls let as shooting-boxes, simply.

Beyond the fact that they were disinclined to give thanks for the Hobbleboys, I could not learn in what way the peasants of Dulditch exhibit ingratitude.

They were no longer poor – the Hobbleboys appeared to entertain a grudge against them for this. Not once in twelve months did man, woman, or child go to the Hall to beg.

A proof that they were proud, perhaps, I pointed out, not that they were not poor.

They were altogether too independent, the Squire here got out in his thickly smothered voice and with his stammering tongue; what with education, and other things, they no longer knew their places. Yesterday, I understood him to say, he had passed a man who had not touched his hat –!

'The children are no longer taught in school to make their reverences,' Mrs. Hobbleboy explained; 'the school children have actually the impertinence to bow instead of dropping curtsies. No one any longer knows his place. The farmers' wives go to church with gold bracelets on their wrists. 'I,' declared the outraged woman, 'am compelled to leave my jewellery at home. They drive smart horses, and have rubber tires on their wheels.' She gazed upon her own carriage and pair standing at the door. (Such a carriage, my dear; such a pair!) 'On *my* wheels are no rubber tires,' she said.

'You are the sufferer, I fear,' I told her.

She showed her teeth, which are larger than her mouth can comfortably accommodate, informed me that the line must be drawn somewhere, and went.

The carriage scrunched the gravel as it rolled away with a noise which must have been musical in the ears of the lady anxious to mark her disapproval of rubber tires. Syers, my gardener and general factotum, at work in the long beds that border the drive, raised himself stiffly to watch the retreating chariot, spat in the rut made by the wheels, stiffly resumed his work.

'I suppose your Squire and his wife are much beloved in the place?' I remarked to him.

'Ef so I never heared of it,' Syers made answer.

I waited, watching him while he turned the sod, knowing that more would come.

'*They* ain't no matters,' he said presently; straightened himself, plunged his spade single-handed into the soil, held it upright there, pausing while his eyes followed the Hobbleboys' barouche, noisily grinding its way over the freshly-mended roads. He included me coldly in the gaze he brought back to his spade. '*They* ain't no matters,' he repeated, and having italicized the cryptic sentence by an expressive spitting on his hands, resumed his spade and began to dig once more.

To Hildred

SYERS has a mean opinion of my taste, you will be sorry to hear, and we have had a serious falling out over the high box borders edging the grass and gravel walks, which delight me, and I intend to retain. He is for digging up the box and substituting large stones smartened by a dash of whitening.

'A reg'lar old sight they be, these here old bushes!' he says discontentedly, and slaps the tall box borders with a contemptuous spade.

'You'll set these here beds with a 'splay of geran'ums and calcies?' (short for calceolarias, I discovered), he inquires of me; there is an expression in his grunting guttural that gives the question the force of a command.

That is not my intention, I inform him. I have the intention to fill the beds with bits of old-world plants from the cottage gardens; pansies and pinks, violets and musk, sweet-williams, London Pride. He hears me in silence, but with the scorn I suppose the plan merits – I know at present so little about flowers and their seasons.

'Time o' t'other woman we had a "splay," he presently volunteers. 'Calcy and geran'um; geran'um and calcy.' He digs a horny finger into the ground to show me the ancient position of those plants. 'A geran'um oppo*site* a calcy; a calcy oppo*site* a geran'um; this fashion. There was a blaze of 'em, you may take my ward for it, time o' t'other woman.'

T'other woman was my predecessor at The Cottage, and is my landlady. I took on Syers from her, and the hall matting. With the superiority in all walks of life of t'other woman I find myself continually confronted.

T'other woman, it seems, give orders to have all the bud's nests i' th' bushes made off with; she give orders, too, for a shot-gun to be allus to hand wherewith to deal destruction to the feathered songsters of the garden. With difficulty I make Syers understand I prefer the company of the birds to the few handfuls of fruit they might rob me of.

'T'other woman was set on arly guseberries,' was Syers' scornful comment.

He is a short, thick, crimson-faced man, with yellow whiskers meeting in a fringe under his chin, and a moustache growing out from his lips, straight, stiff, and yellow as stubble of corn; he has small, very blue eyes, a half-inch of forehead and a stubborn, stiff mouth. His cottage, which is near at hand, is a model of neatness; never have I seen such dazzling white of hearthstone, such red of brick floor, such a brilliance on shining surfaces. His wife is as spruce as his house. The cottage homes, into which I have only peeped at present through open doors, have a dark, uncared-for, squalid look; the little gardens in front are untended. In Syers' carefully weeded patch already the crocuses and snowdrops are showing. The value of my retainer seems to be a disputable quality; his wife I can see is an admirable woman.

I am disappointed in that matter of the peasants' gardens, and spoke of it to the Rector to-day when he called.

'The men cultivate their little plots of cabbages and potatoes when they come home from their day's work – you can't expect them to bother about flowers,' he objected.

'Of course not. It is the women who might keep their front gardens neat and gay; might train a briar rose, even, or a slip of wild honeysuckle about a porch; spare a penny, now and again, for a packet of seeds.'

'The woman has the house to keep clean, the bread to bake, the children to look after.'

'Their children are at school, all day long; other people look after them; I see the baker's cart stopping at every door, and deduce the fact that the baker bakes their bread; *are* their houses kept clean?'

He shrugged his broad shoulders and smiled upon me. 'It doesn't do to interfere,' he said.

'Why?' (You know my fatal propensity for asking questions.)

'They would take offence. They would not come to church.'

'Do they come to church?'

'Not many of them.' He smiled pleasantly as he made the admission.

'Let those that do stay away, so that they do their duty to society by keeping their houses clean; let them praise God by growing flowers in their gardens.'

He made his expostulatory gesture and smiled his indulgent smile. 'It won't do to have an empty church, you know. The Bishop wouldn't like that,' he explained.

He laughed delightedly when I mentioned with approbation the spruce little garden and cheerful-looking house of my gardener and his wife.

'Fanny Syers! Do you know that every evening of her life Fanny spends at the White Hart? It is her husband who scrubs the bricks, washes the tea-things, mends his own clothes, and (they say) Fanny's. On every Saturday night disgraceful things go on at the White Hart –'

'Good gracious! Not here? In Arcady?'

'Singing, dancing, music –'

'But these things in themselves are beautiful.'

'They lead to drunkenness – and worse.'

'Haven't you any counter-attractions? Concerts? Reading-rooms? No place where the people may indulge their love of music and dancing without the temptations of drink?'

'In Dulditch? – none. At this weekly saturnalia always two or three men, and sometimes one or two women, get drunk; being turned out, they fight, and quiet people are disturbed in their beds by the noises on the road.'

'All this is illegal. Where are the police?'

'Where is Bullet? Bullet is generally in the public-house being treated by the rest.'

'Report him.'

'And make myself unpopular? Lose all my influence at one blow?'

But what, my dear Hildred, is the use of the man's influence if he dares not use it?

And so, Syers' pleasant-faced wife dances and sings! How I should love to see her doing it!

'Also gets drunk,' the Vicar warned me. 'Do not encourage her, Mrs. Poole.'

'If you give me advice in such a tone, I shall not come to your church. The Bishop will not like that,' I threatened him.

He appears to be a very much coddled person, this pleasant Rector; not bad-looking, according to some tastes – I prefer a form and a face with more bone in them, for my part – red, and well-featured, and healthy looking. A little over forty, I suppose; no wife; a sister and a housekeeper, who apparently spend their lives in spoiling him. His housekeeper is the best cook in the world, he tells me; he certainly looks as if his food were succulent.

I have condoled with him on the hopelessness of the Hobbleboys. He confesses that an agreeable couple at the head of the temporal affairs of Dulditch would make a huge difference to the place. They do nothing, help with nothing, give away nothing.

'Yet they consider themselves in a position to call me to account, to express their wishes as commands, to keep me at their beck and call.'

'And do you submit to all that? You must have the meekness of Moses himself.'

He laughed. 'I submit. One has to keep on good terms with one's Squire, you know.'

'No. I do not know it. Why?'

'It would be uncomfortable for you, socially, if you did not.'

'Do they entertain much?'

'Two dinner-parties each year.'

'Heavens! What a whirl!'

'The first for the county people – other Squires and their wives. I go the second night, to meet the neighbouring parsons.' He grins, and pulls down the corners of his mouth, as if that society were not altogether to his taste.

'And to which do you suppose they will ask me?' I inquired.

He looked a little uncomfortable, poor man. I suspect he guessed I should not trouble to go to either.

To Hildred

CONGRATULATE me. I have found an agreeable and sociable neighbour! Luckily for me, he appears to have unlimited time on his hands, and is inclined to be exceedingly attentive.

Major Barkaway. Whether 'Major' by courtesy, simply, and by reason of the stiffness of his carriage and the straightness of his back and legs, or whether, long ago, he was an officer of the volunteers or the militia, I cannot say. With things military he certainly has, at present, nothing to do. He is a man of fair intelligence; full of anecdote; has looked about him; knows all the Dulditch people, apparently to the contents of their cupboards. Well! a man with a very human interest in other men and their affairs, and in a well-bred kind of way not above showing it.

I see him daily, and we have long talks. His name, I foresee, will often appear in these scribbles I am sending you, dear Hildred. A tall, lean, well-set-up man, wearing shabby clothes with an air of their being new ones. Bald-headed, red-skinned, fair moustached. His coldly-glancing blue eyes a-glitter, now and then, with the light of curiosity and interest.

I shall draw upon his stores of local knowledge for the notes I am making, and shall find him useful, besides, in many practical ways.

He is liberal with advice, having that which every man worth knowing must have – absolute confidence in himself. He knows what sort of horse I ought to keep; carriage; hens; has even offered to procure them for me, which will take a lot of trouble off my hands. He is having a fowl-house put up for me in the kitchen-garden under his own supervision, and has ordered me a dozen coops against my chickens come. He has instructed Syers about the pruning of the roses and the gooseberry bushes. My gardener, I regret to say, receives his counsels resentfully, and with a very bad grace.

The Major will be of great assistance to me in my financial affairs, understanding all about investments, and so on. You know, I can make money, but, beyond spending it, I am unable to cope with it when it is made; since my dear Henry's death I have been much bothered in this matter. The next thousand that comes in I shall beg Major Barkaway to invest for me. To judge from the well-worn condition of his coat and the smallness of his establishment the dear man has not much of his own to experiment with.

There is one thing I so much like about my friend, and indeed about all the people I have met here; they accept me entirely on my surface merits, and have a well-bred way of seeming to ignore any of the things I have done.

You remember how, in our set, at home, the persons who carried an introduction, or had wriggled in somehow to my presence, gabbled to me about my books – especially about my first book written five-and-twenty years ago, and of which I am now heartily ashamed? 'We have so longed to know the author of *John Trench!*' or 'Is it possible I at last stand face to face with the author of that adorable masterpiece!' or 'You cannot think, *dear* Charlotte Poole, what a joy your beautiful books are to me!' and so on. You have stood by, poor Hildred, and heard the gush of the literary outsider.

Nothing of the kind here. You would think in all my life I had never held a pen in my hand, so completely is the fact put on one side as my passport to regard. A change, indeed; and I do not deny that it requires a little getting used to; but I like it, on the whole. Yes. Indeed I do.

The Palladium Club entertained me to dinner, with much kindness if with much ceremony, the night before I left town. The great ——, who was chairman – did you see it in the papers? – was pleased to make merry over what was before me. I was going into a region where lions were scarce, he said, and therefore hunted with all the greater zeal. He pictured a country-side wildly distracted by my appearance, and became very funny in predicting the furore I was destined to create in a neighbourhood hitherto unfamiliar with geniuses.

Well, the enthusiasm of the rural population has not, I rejoice to say, embarrassed me at present; people evidently wish to prove to me that they receive me as the woman first, before the writer. Which seems to me in good taste. How does it strike you? Even Major Barkaway, to whom now and then, in the course of conversation, I have had to mention my quill-driving trade, has, with great delicacy, I think, refrained from pestering me with the inevitable questions: What are my sources of inspiration? what the effect on my nervous system of the constant strain on my health from the sedentary occupation? who are the originals of my heroes? or how much is autobiographical and how much imagination in the adventures of my heroines? You know the familiar interrogations. He is careful to give no sign, even, of the interest it is only natural for him to feel.

By the way, you will be pleased to hear my last book, *A Splendid Failure*, is selling well. Three editions in three weeks, Carter & Crisp write me this morning. From America, too, accounts are good. Critics on both sides, as usual, kind. I have shoals of congratulatory letters from friends and strangers.

I appreciate the delicate reticence of Dulditch. I do indeed.

To Hildred

I AM getting to know a 'good few,' as they themselves say, of the peasants. So far, I like the old generation of them the best.

As far as I can at present judge, Education, after so long abstinence, does not agree with the rural mind. It lies in their mental anatomy an undigested lump, and all sorts of effects – none of them pleasant – arise from it. Given time for assimilation no doubt all will be well, but at present there is restlessness and discomfort; discontent, suspicion, a souring of the temper. In fact a general deterioration in the character at once sturdy and simple with which the rustic has been credited, and a lamentable alteration in his (reputed) charming manners.

With the old, and the untaught, the generation which has not arisen under the ministrations of the Board of Education, but has derived its opinions from its experience of life, and not from the only half comprehended matter of the local press, these things are different.

I went to-day to call on old Jane Moon. She is eighty-five years of age, and is slowly dying. I found her quite alone in her two-roomed cottage. The whitewashed rafters of the chamber in which she lay sloped to within a few feet of her head; almost all the little space was occupied by the great bed, once a four-poster, dismantled now; the walls, closing in upon the bed, were papered with pictures cut from the illustrated journals of long ago.

Neighbours were kind; they came in, now and again, 'to do for her,' she told me. The 'reverend' had been to pray with her; his housekeeper had sent her jelly, clear as glass. The jelly she had not, however, 'fancied' in that form, but had got her neighbours to melt for her a spoonful, now and then, which she took, steads of wine, when she felt a-sinking.

She wasn't 'no matters' in health, that day. Having arisen in the early morning to boil the kettle, a craving for a drink of tea being upon her, she had fallen downstairs. Neighbour had holp her up agin, when she come, a couple of hours later on. No bones was broke, thank the Lord; but the stairs was steep, and 'twas upsettin', at her age.

Three primroses were in a tiny drinking-glass on the window-sill. Neighbour's Margery had put 'em there. Neighbour's Margery was a handy little maid, and give an eye to her when Neighbour herself was busy. (Margery, I discovered, to be of the responsible age of nine years.) She allust kep' her with a flower to look at, when there was one i' th' garden, and before they come, the little mawther would carry her a sprig o' rosemary. She was partial to the scent of the rosemary; a bush of it had growed by the t'rushold o' the home which had been hers as a girl.

I said to her how glad I was to find that, like me, she was a lover of flowers, because the pictures pasted on the walls, being of battles, and of scenes descriptive of the life of soldiers, had led me to believe her inclined to coarser tastes.

A light came into her dim eyes. She was acquaint with all such matters, she told me proudly; and well she might be, whose father had fought at Waterloo!

She forgot her aching bones and her bruised old body, and told me of the great fight as she had heard it when a child from her father's lips. Such an odd jumble it was, in the telling of what the father had told her, and of what she had come, with the years, to think he had told her.

'A Bunch o' Roses,' Boney had called the English. And there had been a point in the battle, when, victory seeming on his side, Boney had turned to her father, standin' by, and he says, says he – here a light sprang to her old eyes and she stretched out a claw-like hand with grasping fingers to illustrate the gesture of the great Napoleon – 'The Bunch o' Roses! I hold 'em in my hand!' But, soon as the wards was out of his mouth, Blucher, wi' his Preussians, he galloped on. The fortune of the day was changed: 'I ha' lost the Bunch o' Roses!' sighed Napoleon.

She recounted, too, how her father had said that at the close of the great day the dead lay upon the plain, thick as the 'ship' (sheep) upon the Five Elms Meadow.

Which was the Five Elms Meadow? I asked her; and she told me that it was the name of a field in her father's parish; a place she had never visited, it being a matter of seven mile from Dulditch.

I thought of the young soldier of nearly a hundred years ago, looking around the scene of that carnage, with the thought in his mind of the white sheep dotting the peaceful meadow at home. I thought, too, what a deathless thing oral tradition is, and how a statement once adopted by the crude intelligence is a fact recorded there for ever; not a subject to question, or to argue about, or to generalize from. The dead at Waterloo, lay, for Jane Moon and for all who had heard that comparison, not like the sheep in the fold over the way, full in view of the lattice window, but as they lay in Five Elms Meadow, in the parish seven miles off, which had been the soldier's father's home.

A dear old woman this. I shall go to see her often, and get her to tell me the Bunch o' Roses story again.

I called in upon 'Neighbour' next door, to encourage her in her good offices towards Jane Moon. Of a younger generation, 'Neighbour,' and far less agreeable. Ugly, slatternly, wearing a man's greasy cloth cap over her scant fair hair. The remains of a meal of bread, potatoes, cheese, and dripping, were still standing on a filthy tablecloth, hung awry.

'Jane was a sight o' trouble,' she complained; 'allust a-knocking at her wall.' (It was the signal agreed on between them, Jane had told me, by which she was to call for assistance.) 'Ef so be as she went as often as she heared the knocks, she might be allust there. And when she did go 'twas mostly on a fool's arrand; nothin' wantin' but a drink o' tea, or some fancy o' that sort. Her gal Marger' had took wonnerful to th' old woman; and she herself hadn't made no objections to her passin' her time along of her; but, for her part, she had her own wark to see arter, and a husban' and t'ree child'un; dirty mucks the whole on 'em, and making a sight o' washin'.'

'I can't think what you do, all day long,' I said to her.

'What I du?' She gazed at me, with surprise and offence in her stupid stare.

'Yes. How you employ your time.'

'A husban' and t'ree child'un make a sight o' muck. Strike me, there's enough for one pair o' hands, to rid up arter 'em.'

'But you apparently don't do it,' I said. 'How do you amuse yourself?'

She turned her gaze from mine to the muddied bricks and back again. She was too astonished and too slow-witted to abuse me for my interference, which was only what I deserved, I know you are thinking. You remember too well, my dear Hildred, how discretion is my least favourite virtue, and that when I am moved I must speak with my tongue.

'"Tisn't much "amusin'" sech as me gets,' she said sullenly.

'But if you were to scrub your floor, wash and patch your tablecloth, and brush your hair, you would not perhaps feel the want of amusement,' I told her.

She replied with a look of stupefaction only; I laid a half-crown on the filthy tablecloth, and came away.

To Hildred

I HAVE been talking to Miss Flatt, the Rector's sister, about the unsatisfactoriness, as it strikes me, of the labourers' wives, the untidiness and discomfort of their cottages.

'I don't think *saying* anything does any good,' she said.

'What, then? We can't go and scrub their houses for them!'

'*I* let them alone,' said Miss Flatt. She has a smug air of superiority which arouses within me feelings quite unworthy, I am aware, of the liberal-minded Charlotte Poole.

'That is certainly the easiest thing to do,' I commented.

'Algernon found that out in his first year here. When I presently joined him, almost the first advice he gave me was: "Don't interfere." He says he has taken those words for his motto. If you want any peace or comfort in your life, in such a parish as this, you must let the people alone, Algernon says.'

She has an irritating way of quoting her brother as if the words of the fat, commonplace parson, years younger than myself, were pearls of wisdom I should be likely to prize. She is a plain, insignificant-looking person of eight-and-thirty, undistinguished in every way; badly hung together, physically and mentally; ill-dressed.

There must be a heavy monotony about life at Dulditch Rectory, and she appears never to leave it. I am sorry for her, and shall encourage her to come to The Cottage, for the sake of the little change it affords her, poor thing. I hope the brother, who has more brains, won't discover how she bores me.

She, however, necessarily knows a little about the people among whom she lives; she visits the cottages periodically, and while conscientiously refraining from criticizing their habits, cannot help to some extent becoming familiar with them.

In the matter of Jane Moon's Neighbour I drew from her by questioning that the husband lights the fire for her before going to his work in the morning, draws the water from the well, chops the sticks, cleans the children's boots. Often, when their condition has raised discord between him and his wife, scrubs the bricks.

'Then, what does the woman do?' I asked.

'Talk,' said Miss Flatt. 'She and the women in the adjacent cottages talk. Standing in each other's doorways, leaning over each other's gates, they talk the whole day long.'

'What on earth about? Nothing apparently happens here; they see no one; they don't read –'

'They talk of you,' announced Miss Flatt.

'They know that I write, I suppose?'

'They know how much grocery comes into your kitchen, and what you feed your servants on. If you object to extravagance, they abuse you for being mean; if you are extravagant, they scorn you for wasting good food while they live on bread. At the present moment they are discussing a piece of pork your servants declined to eat, which was therefore thrown into the dust-bin.'

'But, Miss Flatt, I have not had a piece of pork in the house since I came here!'

'That does not matter,' said Miss Flatt, with indifference. 'The tale has gone about. It is all the same to them as if it were true.'

I told her I did not grudge them a piece of pork in the dust-bin; they were welcome to imagine a pig there, even, if it would relieve the tedium of their days. I told her, too, that I was desirous of learning about the peasants and their ways, their habits of thought, the condition of their lives, intending one day to write a book about them.

'*I've* never written one about them,' Miss Flatt said. 'I do not think they're worth it. I should not take the trouble.'

'Have you written a book about anything, Miss Flatt?'

'No. I have no time to do it. My days are fully occupied with more important matters. Algernon says he would like to see the woman-writers tied up in a bag with the suffragettes and dropped in the middle of the sea.'

Is this ignorance unadulterated, or did she intend the rudeness, I wonder? I looked at the narrow thick-skinned face, at the flat forehead, the feeble chin, the dull, unintelligent eyes of her, and forgave her, in either case.

Yet, who, to the woman of my trade, is uninteresting? Not even the female Flatt, about whom I have many thoughts, not all unkind ones. If there is not good in Miss Flatt, there is 'copy.' It is this consideration which makes me ever tolerant of stupidity, Hildred.

Didn't you know I was tolerant of stupidity? Then, there is a piece of news for you; and you are not to poke your fun at me any more.

I must tell you what this improbable person – most of my neighbours are improbable, but you must take my word for them – said to me before she left:

'I think it better not to discuss the poor people further. They are my brother's parishioners. Perhaps I have already said more than he would wish. I think it would be more agreeable to him if for the future when we meet we choose another subject.'

The little insufferable prig!

Well, the egregious ass is always with us, and perhaps in Dulditch, where society is scarce, I may learn at last to suffer fools gladly.

To Hildred

SINCE the last scribblement I sent to you, dearest Hildred, there has been a spell of the loveliest spring weather. In my garden – my dear garden! how I long for you to walk there with me! – all sorts of delightful things are happening.

In the narrow beneath the broad lattice window at which I write the earth is pierced with lance-like leaves meeting above the yet unfolded flowers of the hyacinths, whose sweetness I enjoy in anticipation as I watch. In the borders beyond the box-edging which margins the drive to the gate, the wider leaves of tulips droop apart to show the strong green buds pushing up their perky heads among them. Here and there, in unsuspected places, violets are lurking in their cushions of green leaves; a delicious whiff of perfume, poignant as it is fleeting, comes to me through the open window. On the brown wall which runs along the south and west sides of the kitchen-garden a peach-tree is in bloom. Beneath the hedge by the road there smiles the tenderest, modest blue of the periwinkle.

> *'Tis a month before the month of May,*
> *And the Spring comes slowly up this way.'*

Do not believe, my dear, that the familiar is the delightful thing in gardens. It is, I know, the unexpectedness in mine which ravishes me. Each day, each hour I discover some unlooked-for, sweet possession.

Syers is pruning the rose-bushes. He calls it pruning, but he appears to me to be cutting them to the ground.

'You'll maybe ha' th' better blows,' he promises me, unmoved by my remonstrances. 'T'other woman took a prize, one yare, wi' six o' her blows o' rosen.'

He says it as if he considers it hopeless for me to attempt to emulate that achievement. 'She set a walley on 'em, she did,' he adds, with an air of unspoken reproach which I am not conscious of having earned.

There is friction between Syers and me of late. Here is the history of it.

For some days past, when I have walked the garden, or have sat silent by my open window, I have noticed a curious, persistent, light tapping, for which I could not account. Judge how interested I was to learn from Syers that the sound was made by a woodpecker searching for insects in the trees hard by. My own woodpecker in my own garden, Hildred! Think of it!

When he was a baby I used to sing to George of 'The woodpecker tapping at the hollow beech-tree,' and here was one actually doing it! As Syers pointed his rake in that direction I saw the bright green head and the golden wing of him as the bird flew away.

'Ah! what a pity!' I cried. 'If only we had not disturbed him! I would have loved to watch.'

'There ain't no fear he 'ont come back,' gardener reassured me, and told me he had seen the bird busy at that same tree for weeks past.

He has such a surly contempt for my want of knowledge, and such a grudging way of supplying the lack of information, that I refrained from asking him how long the woodpecker might be expected to go on tapping at the tree; if it was an occupation, for instance, he pursued in spring and relinquished in summer. But I was filled with the hope that he at least might be visible at his work when you and Nan came, by-and-by.

This morning as I came down to breakfast I was met by the message that the gardener wished to see me. He stood in the kitchen, the great orange and green and red bird dead in his hand.

'Why, what can have happened to it?' I cried in dismay.

Syers grinned with pride as he laid the body on the table before me. 'I got a feer shot at 'm this mornin',' he said. 'Says I to my old woman, "I'll take my gun along wi' me, this mornin', on the chance of a shot. The missus," I say, "is wishful for a good sight o' the bird." "Dew, bor," says she to me. Sune as I ketched sight of 'm I blazed away at 'm; and here he be!'

Because I was silent he thought me speechless with admiration of his prowess. "'Twere a feer shot,' he repeated. 'I heared 'm a tappin' for his breakfus'. "Now I ha' got yer," I say. "The missus 'll mayhap like to have you stuffed, bor."'

Stuffed! That exquisite thing that was alive and happy five minutes ago! Stuffed!

'T'other woman had a peer on 'em, under glass, facin' a peer o' white owls, in her front hall. Theer's a man hard by as 'll stuff 'em, natcheral as life, eyes and all –'

'Take it out and bury it! I wish I never had to see you again. I shall never forgive you,' I said, and turned my back on him and left him stupidly staring.

A couple of hours later, Ethel, the parlour-maid, appeared, to ask if Syers could have a pint of beer.

'Why should Syers have extra beer to-day?' I asked.

'Syers thought, as he had got up half an hour earlier to shoot the woodpecker –'

'Certainly not,' I said. 'And tell Syers I wish he had slept for ever before he had shot it.'

Ethel is a tall, engaging-looking girl, with a superior manner, and carrying herself like a queen. She gave me a disapproving look. I had thought she would have espoused my part rather than that of the unattractive Syers in such a cause.

Syers despises me more than ever, naturally, and is aggrieved into the bargain. On the same morning I went to speak to him about the croquet-lawn which Major Barkaway tells me stands in grievous need of rolling; he sulked and walked away; I followed him.

'Did you hear what I said, Syers?'

'Ah! I heared right enough.'

'But you did not reply. I am accustomed to civility from my servants.'

'Tha's as may be!' eyes gazing away from me, the back of a horny hand passed over nose and mouth.

'I was telling you to roll the croquet-lawn.'

'I'm a-thinkin' theer'll be more wark i' your sarvice than 'll git done by one peer o' hands.'

'You found time to do it for the lady who was here before me.'

'Ah!' He breathed forth the word heavy with meaning. 'Her were another matter, t'other woman war! A little extry wark, and allust a pint o' beer; and no grudgin'.'

'I shall not give the extra beer. But if you want help with your work you must have it. Is that what you want?'

'"Tis like this here: If so be as you're a-goin' to have this here place kep' up to th' mark, there's wark for t'ree such as me, if you can git hold of the like; and so I tell ye.'

'Certainly I intend to have the garden well kept. I am assured by Major Barkaway –'

('Him!' interposed Syers, with infinite contempt.)

'– that there is no more work than can easily be done by you; but since you insist on help – get it.'

So I find my modest staff increased by the addition of a rather big, rather handsome young man of twenty, who 'didn't mind coming for a time, to oblige,' I was told.

The pair seem to get in each other's way a good deal. 'Clemmy,' I am told, 'han't that knowledge o' gardenin'' that will allow Syers to 'tarn 'm forth on his own.'

'What Clemmy's place is, is to wait on me,' Syers frequently explains.

The big, slouching young man, therefore, with the curling red hair, the red cheeks and lips, treads on the heels of the other, picks up the rubbish Syers rakes in heaps, wheels the barrow at his side, looks at his watch when his superior in office chances not to be consulting that in his own pocket – and so on.

I watch the pair from my window with some amusement, while they remain in sight, but they are more frequently sheltering from the spring showers in the scullery with the kitchen-maid, or spending long hours together in the stoke-hole, attending, I am told, to the green-house fire.

To Hildred

MAJOR BARKAWAY is indignant at my prodigality in putting two men to work in my garden where one would have sufficed. What really upsets him is my having presumed to do it without asking leave of him. An extra fourteen shillings a week! You would laugh if you could see the seriousness with which such an expenditure is regarded, and the importance attached in Dulditch to the step.

The Rector has been rallying me on the subject. Of all people in the world it seems the last I should have chosen is Clement Moore.

'But Clement Moore, as it happened, was the only man out of work in Dulditch.'

'Do you know why he was out of work?'

'No.'

'Then you should have asked,' the fat parson smiles. 'But as you did not ask, you shall not now be told.'

He has rather an agreeable smile – (did I tell you?) – it enables him to say things he could not say without it. I rather like the Reverend Algernon, at first-hand. It is when his dreary little sister repeats him that I find him so tedious.

'He is out of work because we all know him too well to employ him,' at length he tells me.

'What's he done?'

'He does not come to church.'

'But, my dear man, so many people don't go to church. I don't very often go there myself.'

'So I find. Mrs. Stubbs set a better example.'

'T'other woman? That is sufficient for me. I have a positive loathing for t'other woman and all her ways.'

He grins at me. 'She missed morning-service only six times in three years.'

'Do you, in your inmost heart, believe her to have been any the better for it?'

'She set a good example.'

'Why don't you make your services attractive to men and women of a different mental calibre from that of t'other woman? Make them half as long; preach sermons, if you must preach them, such as you could preach if you allowed yourself to get off the beaten, the now barren, track; show us how to make the best of our daily life, and leave the subjects of Judgement and the Hereafter to take care of themselves. What do you know about them more than we? Get a man to play your organ properly; get some voices into your choir; train them–'

'We do our best, Mrs. Poole.'

'You don't do anything of the kind. You do what is not far from your worst, in my opinion.'

'You don't know with what difficulties one is beset in such a place as Dulditch.'

'Are you musical?'

'No.'

'Then you ought to be. No man should be ordained who is ignorant of music.'

'I leave all that to the organist.'

'Change your organist, then.'

'In Dulditch we have to take what we can get. All we can get for the organ is the schoolmistress.'

'How much would it cost to have an organist over from the nearest town to play twice on the Sunday?'

'Perhaps twenty pounds a year.'

'And how much do you pay the schoolmistress?'

'Ten.'

'Then, while I am living here, I will contribute the extra ten pounds, and we will at least have some music. What, besides, is there that a little money can do?'

(For I am saving more money than is good for me while I am living as I do now, remember, Hildred. 'Beware of too much good staying in your hand.')

Several things are wanted badly in the church, it seems. A new Altar cloth, a new curtain for the organ, new and larger lamps. The Rector seemed pleased by my offer to supply these deficiencies, and I am greatly pleased to have the chance to give them.

The little Flatt woman has been here.

She has, like her brother, a fleshy, heavy nose (did I tell you this before?) – a feaure pardonable in a man – (what do we not pardon him?) – but inexcusable in a woman; especially when in conjunction with a face that is small and white.

The Rector was busy with his sermon or he would have called on me, himself, she told me. He had deputed her to beg me let the conversation he and I had yesterday go no further.

'If it came to the ears of Miss Petley that there was any dissatisfaction with her playing, my brother fears there might be unpleasantness. Algernon is always anxious that there should be no unpleasantness.'

'Preferring that all the inharmoniousness should be reserved for the church music? Then, he refuses my offer?'

'Yes,' with a toneless finality, her pale eyes gazing coldly past me. 'Both my brother and I think it would not do at all.'

'And about the Altar cloth? The standard lamps for the Chancel?'

'Algernon was mentioning to me last night that you had offered to supply them. I pointed out to him that your doing so would be likely to give offence to the Hobbleboys.'

'In the names of Reason and Common Sense – how?'

'When the Hobbleboys succeeded to the estate and first came to live in Dulditch, they spoke of supplying an Altar cloth themselves; and several times they have commented on the want of light in the Chancel. We think they had the standard lamps also in their minds.'

'It is seven years since they came, isn't it? They have not hurried.'

'But all the same my brother and I think the Hobbleboys might feel it as a slight to them if another person – a stranger in the place – took it upon herself to do it.'

There! Hasn't Dulditch its humours?

To Hildred

I MENTIONED to Bertha Flatt yesterday, that I had been to return the call of her Squire and his wife, for I have discovered that it is the name of Hobbleboy alone which can bring a gleam of interest into this depressing young woman's face. The spark that the sacred syllables light there showed at once in her eyes.

'Really?' She hung breathless upon the words which next should proceed from my lips.

'They were not at home.' She breathed again. 'At least they said so. But a charming family group of them stood at one of the windows when I came away, and looked solidly at me as I passed.'

Miss Flatt was mute.

'It struck me as a curious proceeding on the part of your Hobbleboys.'

She regarded me with the gratified look of one who has the key to a mysterious situation.

'Had they *asked* you to return their call?' she inquired weightily; and when I admitted that I had not deemed such an invitation necessary, her prim mouth took on puckers of inmost satisfaction.

'What do you suppose they meant by it?' I asked of her; but she ignored the question, and made a hurried leave-taking. She was so anxious to get back to her brother with the story that she did not stop to find a decent excuse for running away.

Within fifteen minutes of her exit Major Barkaway was here. I watched him approach, with long strides and at the top of his speed. The suspicion crossed my mind that he had encountered Miss Flatt, and heard the pleasing story of my discomfiture at the hands of the Hobbleboys.

The subject of the chicken-run whose erection he has promised to superintend; of Syers' attitude regarding the suggestions the Major has been good enough in my interest to make; the topic of the large supply of eggs gathered from his own nests this morning – always such a satisfaction for him to compare with the scant amount gathered from mine – gained to-day only his superficial attention. Twice, thrice, the name of the Hobbleboys passed his lips. I did not rise to the bait. Had I been out lately? Driving? Walking? On which day? In which direction? I fenced with the inquiries.

At last he could stand it no longer. He gave a great sigh, settled himself more comfortably into his chair, his elbows on his arms, his hands, the tips of their fingers meeting, arched above his chest, and with a sudden outburst of unabashed, naked curiosity, put the vital question:

'And so you went to call on the Hobbleboys?'

Then, since it did not hurt me, and I saw it would give him pleasure, I told him what he wanted to hear.

He is a rather distinguished, rather fine-looking man, for his age, with no point of resemblance to Miss Flatt; but the gleam in his eyes as he gloated on the details, and the way he folded his lips as if holding back words which struggled to get forth, made him look like her for the moment.

'What induced them to do such a funny thing?' I asked him.

He screwed himself still more at his ease into his chair, snapped his forefingers with a dry sound upon the backs of his arching hands – a habit I have noticed in him when much interested – what I must now call 'the Hobbleboy gleam' in his eyes, and with evident self-restraint kept himself from replying.

'You perhaps have, here, in Dulditch, a code of manners of your own?' I proceeded. 'It is a little awkward for strangers. You should tell them what to expect.'

'You see,' he said then, mildly deprecating the wrath he believed me to be feeling, 'your predecessor, Mrs. Stubbs, *never* called at the Hall.'

'But what has that to do with it?'

He snapped the fingers, gazing at me with keenest enjoyment in his face, but offered no explanation.

I looked upon him, wondering greatly what there could be in the rudeness to me of these ill-bred people to cause to those who had shown me courtesy and friendship such evident enjoyment. Or perhaps I did not wonder. Perhaps I knew very well, and only paused to make the mental note of this one more unneeded instance of the satisfaction enjoyed in every society at the overthrow of one's friends.

Major Barkaway seized the opportunity to tell me that he himself disdains distinctions of class; that he is equally happy to be friendly with the Chisholms, the farmers at the Grange, as with the Hobbleboys at the Hall.

'I, in fact, go there a good deal,' he told me. 'There is always a place for me at their table – which, by-the-by, is an excellent one. They are people of quite as much refinement, as far as I am a judge, as the Hobbleboys. I haven't got a wife and daughters to consider, as the Squire has. As I am situated, I can go – anywhere.'

'And so you come to me? I am, really, vastly obliged to you, Major Barkaway.'

I liked my neighbour a little less than usual on that occasion.

To Hildred

MRS. CHISHOLM from the Grange Farm has been to see me to-day. It enters my mind that the Major, by his belated eulogiums of her refinement and her table, was paving the way for her visit.

That I had been longing to know her, and to see her beautiful garden, I told her; and that I had begun to be afraid she was not intending to call on me.

She was quite straightforward about it; indeed she is a rather embarrassingly straightforward person, all round, I find.

'We waited,' she said. 'We heard the Hall called on you. We don't call where the Hall calls.'

'Why not?'

'It wouldn't do,' she said; evidently thinking it explanation enough. 'However, when we heard from the Major how they had treated you we thought we should be all right in coming.'

And so, even in this lonely spot, with its mere sprinkling of civilized inhabitants, the stupid social law makes enemies of the few poor slaves who should be friends and free men!

But, oh, if you could see the lovely old garden of the Grange, Hildred! – for I walked home with her when her call was done. The Chisholms have been tenants of the place for a hundred-and-fifty years. And through all that time, and for hundreds of years, apparently, before it, the cedar has been spreading its straight branches on their lawn, the giant elms and oaks have been growing in the park-like meadow before their house; the turf of their lawn and green alleys has been rolled and cut and weeded; the tall box edgings have been trimmed, the moss and the tiny fern that loves to seed itself in old mortar have grown green upon the grey stone of the sundial before the front door; the wallflowers and foxgloves have flowered and died, and seeded themselves to flower and die again upon the eleven-foot-high buttressed wall that bounds the kitchen-garden.

The owner of the Grange is not the so-called Squire of Dulditch, a fact for which the outspoken wife of its tenant loudly thanked God. The property is in the hands of the trustees of a great London charity – liberal and not at all exacting landlords. The place, having come down for generations from father to son, is loved almost as if it were their own by the Chisholm family; but with the present man I hear the Chisholm tenancy will come to an end. The only son is at Jesus College and is to take holy orders. No child of hers should be a farmer, Mrs. Chisholm volunteered; and told me that she, who had been a doctor's daughter, had bitterly regretted marrying into that business, herself.

There is no reserve, you perceive, about this good woman. You are welcome to all that she can tell you of her own affairs or other people's, and she makes you free of her opinions as of her facts.

It grieved me to see her, the clever, capable mistress of this charming old house and heavenly garden, her pretty young daughter, her nice, decent, clean-living, clean-thinking husband by her side; in her possession, one would think, all that could constitute the well-being of any ordinary woman, yet with the fire of revolt in her eyes, the bitterness of rancour on her tongue. It grieved me to perceive in this paradise of peace in which she lives that the woman was possessed by the spirit of discontent, and filled with an abiding hatred of the social law which compels her, having chosen her place in life, to keep it.

More than ever I dreamed, in my life in town, I realize in this thinly populated place how senseless, how injurious to character, the laws of caste can be, how cruel, how fraught with danger class hatred.

A letter from Beaumont the playwright, this week, asking for leave to dramatize *A Splendid Failure*.

I have told him frankly, in giving consent, that my books don't dramatize; that the actor manager's shelves are filled with the attempts which have been made to get them on the boards. He wires to-day that the play is already made, and under consideration at the Diadem.

A very prompt person Beaumont, and consequently a successful one. You remember *Simple Sue* by him, which had a phenomenal run?

A long letter from George. He begins to talk of his home-coming, although it is nearly a year ahead of us. He asks for news of you, my dear Hildred, and for your address. The first time I think he has willingly alluded to you since your marriage. His silence, however, has never given me the impression you were forgotten.

But this is a forbidden topic. I am not likely to forget your indignant protest on an occasion when I ventured to give my opinion as that of a sane woman, on the course you and he, both *in*sane at that juncture, were allowing events to take. I said then that I would certainly leave you both to your stupidities and misunderstandings for the future. It is years ago, but I remember well.

To Hildred

THERE are no tumble-down cottages inhabited now in Dulditch. The tenements not fit for human dwelling, of which we heard so much a few years ago, are, in the country at least, things of the past. The heavily thatched, clay-walled, lattice-windowed, creeper-grown cottages of the poets, which one still gratefully recognizes here and there, are also nearly of the past. They have been for the most part replaced by ugly, substantial buildings of no features and with unhappy countenances. Two and two they stand, dotted at random about the place, without a projection from door or window or roof to break their ugly uniformity. More healthy as to sanitary arrangements, with more bedrooms; pleasanter, perhaps, to live in than the picturesque homes they have replaced, but ugly blots upon the landscape, and depressing to the artistic eye, none the less.

Instead of the single, often commodious room which formed the ground floor of the cottage, and answered the purposes of kitchen, wash-house, and living room for the family, every newly-built cottage, I find, has now its little front room, its tiny kitchen. In the former what wealth in the shape of furniture and ornament its tenant possesses is collected; the never-opened, lace-curtained window is blocked with geraniums; the floor is covered by a never-trodden-on carpet. In the latter, however tiny, the family, however large, lives.

A liberal expanse of land for vegetables at the back is generally fairly well cultivated, the husband digging and planting there when he returns from digging and planting the fields. But the little square in front of the cottage – the woman's dominion – where, in a former generation, the rosemary and lavender bushes would have flourished by the doorstep; where snowdrops, crocuses, primroses, would have bloomed in the spring, with promise of crimson phlox, and golden wallflower, and red poppy to follow – is now but a plot of mud or dust, according to the weather; battered salmon tins, scraps of paper, old rags taking the place of the flowers.

The active services of Clemmy (although he still walks faithfully beside the barrow he no longer feels the strength to trundle) have been hindered of late, I have been told, by a cold on his chest from which he suffers in common with the rest of his family. It was therefore with what I hoped might be suitable offerings that I to-day made my call on his widowed mother.

'You kin put it down,' she graciously said, when I drew her attention to my basket. Ingratitude is the independence of souls. Judged by that standard they are certainly not slaves in Dulditch.

'As your children, I hear, have bad colds, I hope the few things I have brought them may be of service,' I said.

She was sure she couldn't say. They might and they mightn't, Mrs. Moore vouchsafed.

She was standing by the square yard of table preparing a paste of flour and water in a yellow basin lined with blue. She threw quick, threatening glances from the mess in hand to the four children seated on their hard chairs pushed against the wall.

'Kep' from schule, because gov'ness don't fancy 'em there, wi' their colds,' she volunteered. 'A sight o' harm they'd du theer, poor little beggars! And me with 'em on my hands, all day!'

One of the larger children grated its heavy boots on the bricks. 'Hold yer n'ise!' the mother yelled, dragged her hands from the dough in the basin, sought for and found a handkerchief under the cushion of a chair, flung across to the child, angrily wiped its nose; while about it, performed the same not unnecessary office for the other three children.

By the fire, at the mother's back as she stood by the table, a big girl was sitting, with a baby in her arms. 'Is this also one of your children?' I asked her.

'In a fashion, 'tis, I s'pose,' grudgingly she made answer.

She tumbled the mess of dough upon the table, set down the bowl with a clatter which I felt was a protest against my questioning, and presently, in an angry, trembling voice, offered the explanation: 'I ha'n't enough o' my own, wi' my eight, I suppose; so Laura, she ha' brought me home one more!'

The big girl holding the child bent an untidy fair head above it and began miserably to cry.

'Theer ain't no good in yer a-doin' that now,' the mother cried, compunctiously chiding her tears. ''Tis far too late i' th' day.'

I asked the age of the baby, noted that it had a head of plentiful light-coloured hair, like its mother, and was clean and well-nourished. No notice was taken of the coin I put into its little grasping fist, except that the elder woman, chucking the dough about on the table, as she formed it into rounds for dumplings, addressed me in a more mollified tone.

''Tain't no fault o' the poor child's, we know right well,' she said. 'Now 'tis here, as I say to my Clemmy, we ha' got to du the best we can for it. There's them as would ha' had me send my girl to th' workhus, and have it born there; but I allus have said no flesh and blood o' mine should ever set foot in them walls. I'd choke 'em fust.'

In reply to my question she told me that 'sune as Laura was strong agin she'd go back to sarvice, to such a place as she can get without a char'cter; and the little 'un 'll have to grow up alonger mine.'

Upon my saving a word or two here which still further appeased her, Mrs. Moore was polite enough to remark she hoped as her Clemmy was a-givin' satisfaction.

'I think he is giving it to Syers,' I prevaricated. 'Syers seems to like to have Clement looking on while he is doing things.'

'There's one thing about my Clemmy,' the gratified parent said, 'he ain't afeared o' wark. I ain't a-sayin' as how he ha' allust had it to du. For why? He ha' been unfort'nate, and folks is agin 'm. But give my Clemmy work to du, and he'll tackle it.'

I ventured to ask, for my own anxious enlightenment, how it happened that Clemmy had enemies in the place. 'Your other sons keep their places, I hear, Mrs. Moore?'

'They ha' met wi' more luck,' she explained. 'Theer ain't one of 'em such a oner to wark, when he ha' got it to du, as the boy Clemmy.'

I rather liked the ill-tempered, unpleasant, unlovely woman for the way in which she stood up for her lazy lout of a son; so to please her, I said the only word which could be said in his favour – that he was a nice, respectable-looking young man, and very quiet.

'He's that!' she agreed, brightening. 'Like a lamb he is for quiteness. Treat 'm bad as you like, he don't never as much as tarn 's tongue in 's cheek agin you.' Here she paused to make a dash at one of the children on the chair. 'Di'n't I tell ye to lave off that grittin' wi' yer feet!' she screamed to him, seized him by the shoulder, shook him, thumped him hard upon the hard chair. 'D'ye want yer hids smacked?' she inquired of the other three, sitting empty-handed, apparently empty-minded, in their places against the wall.

'Take keer of his clo'es, too, my Clemmy du,' she continued with the list of her son's virtues; 'and so he du of his money. Theer ain't often a time yer'll ketch 'm without a shillun' in 's pocket.'

'But if he does not have work, how does he get the shilling?' I naturally inquired, and I noticed that the girl with the baby turned round and looked upon her mother as if she too, silently, asked the question.

'Kape it when he ha' got it; tha's Clemmy's plan,' Clemmy's admiring mother said.

To Hildred

I LOOKED in, this morning, upon Mrs. Bain, who lives at a little farm close by, and supplies me with dairy produce. When she had promised to accede to my request that a less liberal supply of salt should be put in my butter, for the future, she asked me if it was true I had taken Clemmy Moore into my employ.

'You might ha' knocked me down with a feather when I heared it,' she exclaimed. 'You was wholly wrong to do it, ma'am, I'm much afeared.'

I told her I had just been hearing what a fine fellow he was, and how, in spite of his seldom earning anything, his pockets were never empty of money – a detail which I confess had caused me some uneasiness.

'More shame to 'm!' Mrs. Bain commented. 'And to that silly mawther, his mother, that shut her eyes to it.'

Being pressed for an explanation, Mrs. Bain unbosomed herself of the fact that Clemmy had always been a thief. He had stolen ha'pence from the children at school, he had 'tuk a shillun' from the sum laid up for rent in the teapot on the mantelpiece, he had even robbed his sister of the pound she had saved up for expenses when her baby was to be born.

The sovereign had been wrop' in a bit of paper and kep' in the pocket of her best frock. And when Laura and her mother had dressed themselves and were starting forth to buy the things so badly needed, the poor mawther felt in her pocket, and theer was the paper wrop' up, safe enough, but the golden sovereign was gone. No one knowed better than Mrs. Moore – where. And the same week the eldest son appeared with a new bicycle, which – where'd he got it?

'Them poor child'un o' hers, she dash 'em about, right cruel; till they ain't playful like child'un should be, but kind o' dazed, like. Yet this here young varmint, Clemmy – it fare as if he *can't* du nothin' wrong.'

Altogether I think I had better keep a sharp eye on my under-gardener.

Mrs. Bain and her husband keep a ten-acre little farm at the back of my house. Although more picturesque, the farm-house is little better than the labourers' cottages, either in size, comfort, or furniture. The man and his wife work harder than any other pair in Dulditch. I like the woman because, in spite of this, she finds time to weed the flower-garden before her door, because a rose and a honeysuckle grow upon the yellow plaster of the walls, because the uneven brick floors of her dairy and living-room are always scrubbed, and the chairs are fit to sit down on without that preliminary dusting those in the labourers' cottages must undergo before you can be invited to 'take a seat.'

The man has a heavy and troubled look.

'We're worse off than any o' th' labourers,' the wife assures me. 'Arly and late we're at it, and never spend a penny a-waste; yet work as we can, 'tis unpossible to make inds meet. My husban' he ha' tried. We ha' both tried. His heart's broke, an' tha's the fac'.'

'You don't believe in small holdings, then? You don't sympathize with this "land hunger" from which people are said to suffer?'

'Look here, ma'am; howiver gentlefolk can talk as they du, and mislead poor folk i' that manner, passes me,' she said. 'Why, don't it stand to reason, if them wi' money at their backs can't make farming pay, we can't? With iverything to be bought at the dearest – because why? we ha' to ask for trust. – Wi' no horses, no machinery, no market that such as us can git at to sell what we want to sell. My old man he was shepherd at Chisholm's; arning his sixteen shilling a week, he were, and we was well off. He arned, and I seft. And what we seft we put in here. Wheer is it? Theer's Sam, poor old chap; his heart's broke. Ask him.'

From Sam, poor man, I got no intelligible answer when, being thus encouraged, I asked his opinion of small holdings. His feelings, I know, are acute; his face is full of sorrow; his head, bowed with anxious care, I am sure teems with reasons why such an occupation as this he holds is hopeless and ruinous; but he has no power at all of expression; can only shake a hanging grey head and murmur, 'A bad job, bor; a bad job 'tis, I fare.'

I suppose he sometimes is more expansive: the emergencies of business, the exigencies of daily life must compel his slow tongue to wag to other words; but with me, so far, he confines himself to the phrase so sadly appropriate to his affairs.

He still wears the smock which was his ancient badge of service, and his wife tells me sorrowfully he sadly misses the sheep he used to tend.

'He ha' lived with a flock since he was right a boy,' she says. 'Arly and late he ha' looked arter 'em, and had 'em on's mind. If so be as they done well, and theer was a good fall o' lambs, and fine hoggets for the selling, 'twas a good year, Chisholm say – and no credit to Sam. But bein' as how they done bad, 'twas shepherd's fault! and not a ward o' th' frozen turmits, or th' middow under water. Here be Sam. Ask hiu celf if that bain't so.'

'Ah!' Sam ejaculated. He looked with admiration at the wife, so miraculously capable of giving tongue to that which with him was unutterable, then turned the eyes so brightly blue still in his weather-tanned, simple old face upon me for sympathy. 'Ah!' he sighed again.

'So Sam, as you may say, he ha' carried his sheep on 's heart; and stan' to reason, when he's parted from 'em he feel it.'

Sam's mouth was wrung a little, he wiped his peaked, sorrowful nose on the back of his hand. ''Tis a bad job!' he said, slowly shaking his head; 'a bad job, bor.'

'Still, you are your own master, now,' I pointed out to him. 'You have a couple of cows in place of your sheep. All that you have is your own. How came you to leave Mr. Chisholm?'

'My old man he had the rheumatics bad, the last lambing he done. 'Twas a snowy March, and him boxed up in his hut without a mite of air in it, then tarnin' out into the bitter nights; his sufferin's was somethin' crule. The master he seed how 'twere wi' 'm, and he fancied as how he'd du hisself more justice with a younger shepherd. He behaved well to Sam, Chisholm did, I ain't a-sayin' as how he didn't, but 'taint likelies as such as him'd give a thought to how my old man 'ud pine for th' sheep.'

To Hildred

AT the request of the Flatts I have been to a meeting at the Rectory this afternoon to discuss what they are pleased, somewhat pretentiously, I fear, to call a Garden Fête; an annual affair, it appears, which is held in August in the grounds either of Rectory or Hall.

The half-dozen women present talked of the matter on hand with perfervid interest. No one had a suggestion to make; everything was to be as it had always been because, as it seemed to me, all were too supine to rise to an effort at originality.

'Let it take place this year at the Grange,' I proposed. 'In those beautiful old gardens.'

Miss Flatt gazed upon me with the cold and slightly surprised disapproval of one who rebukes an impropriety.

'The Fête is always held at the Rectory or the Hall,' she said.

'So much the more reason it should now be held somewhere else,' I protested. But Mrs. Chisholm with a quelling look at me, and a very red and angry face, announced that her garden, for that purpose, was out of the question.

Then I had an inspiration. 'For this year you shall have mine, then,' I said. 'You may use my name. Advertize that the Bazaar is to be held at the house of Charlotte Poole. The Great Eastern will run trains from the places near, and from town. Friends of mine will come to act. I know some singers for your half-hour concerts. It is just the place for a pastoral play. We will give them the fairy part of the Midsummer Night's Dream on the croquet-lawn. Bottom can fall asleep beneath the branches of that giant spruce in the corner, and the fairies can come and go from the shrubberies round–'

(I see you laughing at me, Hildred. You know I always like to have a finger in the pie, you are saying. I own the stagnation around me makes me a tiny bit rampant at times; I feel the impulse to make things hum ever so little.)

Well, I can't say they refused my offer. They simply ignored it.

'It will be the turn of Mrs. Hobbleboy, this year,' Miss Flatt said, and turned with a sweet deference to the long, lean daughter representing that noble family. 'If it is quite agreeable to her and to you all we will arrange that the Fête takes place at the Hall.'

And so, having accepted as a matter of course and as only my due other people's adulation all my life, here I am in my old age learning the lesson of humility set me in Dulditch! In the trough of the wave, Hildred, instead of on the crest. When at last you come to me with that Nan I long to see, you'll find, instead of the Charlotte Poole you know, bristling with 'pride, rank pride, and haughtiness of soul,' a sat-upon, humbled little creature, arrived at a true sense of her value, and of less than no account in her place. You don't believe in such a sudden 'modest, coy submission'? Perhaps I'm a little doubtful of it still, myself.

But the truth is I begin clearly to perceive that more amusement will accrue through accepting the local valuation of me than in insisting on that set on me in, I hope, a more enlightened sphere. For the future I will bow before the majesty of the Hobbleboys; let their untired wheels bespatter me with mud, as they pass me on my way. I shall take Mr. Flatt at his sister's estimate, hanging on his words of wisdom as reported to me by her; and shall even accept Miss Flatt herself as an oracle.

As for Major Barkaway – I must make a confession about Major Barkaway, my dear Hildred. You appreciate the frankness of my nature, and know that I have no secrets (that I wish to tell) hidden from you? Then know, that the suspicion I had entertained that the above eligible, and most personable, I assure you, gentleman was about to enrol himself among the half-dozen impecunious men who, since Henry's death, have proposed to take his place with a view to securing me to make a living for them, I now perceive to be entirely unfounded. Major Barkaway holds me far too cheaply for any such sacrifice of his gentility.

It is astonishing how quickly a sensitive person comes to regulate his importance in the scale at the appraisement of other people. Major Barkaway in his secret soul sniffs at me as a nobody. For the time being – when in his society, at least – I am a nobody. Just Mrs. Poole – doctor's widow. A short, commonplace little woman, not very handsome, rather fat, who aspires to carry on a humble existence beneath the magnificent patronage of Hobbleboys, Flatts, and Barkaways.

To Hildred

THE Major was a little put out of countenance the other day, when, wishing to speak to him, I took the simple means of seeking him at his own house.

I met Miss Flatt on my way there, and acquainted her with my destination. She regarded me with shocked, pale eyes, looking out at me from above her brother's fleshy, long, tip-depressed nose.

'It isn't possible, I thought, for a lady to call upon an unmarried gentleman,' she said, rebukingly.

'I will show you that it is,' I told her, and left her gasping; looking after me with the expression of one of my sickly chickens, hatched last week, and suffering from what Syers calls 'the gapes.'

In Dulditch, where only the little things seem big and the great ones of no moment whatever, one always repeats things; I retailed to Major Barkaway, therefore, the above otherwise unnoteworthy remarks.

'You and I are too old for such nonsense as that,' I finished; and I do not think he was at all pleased with the comment. Come to think of it, he being such a visibly well-preserved man, I might have spared him the brutality.

He has discoursed with so high a tone of authority on how things should be done in my establishment, and has been so liberal of advice on all subjects, that I confess to being a little taken aback to discover what a piggery the man lives in. From the strictures he has passed on Syers' methods in garden and poultry yard, I looked for perfection at Vine Cottage. I found, I am bound to say, muddle; what looked like continued neglect; I breathe it with bated breath – dirt.

He escorted me over his grounds and premises, however, with a high unconcern or sublime unconsciousness of this condition. He gathered for me a stubbly violet or two from what looked like a rubbish heap but was called his rockery. He pointed out the superiority of his white Hamburgs over mine – pronounced too long in the leg, or too short, I forget which, too much of one thing or too little of the other. The perfect specimens of the race upon which I now gazed had the air to the uninitiated of being a miserable crew: corns on their feet, their eyes bunged up with swellings, indecently bald in places. His garden is large. No such cabbages, potatoes, roses, grow in Dulditch as on its soil, I have heard him say. I can testify to the fact that it bears a rich and flourishing crop of weeds.

Indoors, to a less extent, the same neglect is visible. But he does the honours of the little place as if he were in the kind of palace which, you gather from his conversation, was his ancestral home.

A few nice things are present to bear witness to the fact that he has known better days. Or do they? He drew my attention to some portraits on the walls. Above one, of an old man in uniform, a sword was hanging in a handsomely plated scabbard.

'My great uncle,' the Major said. 'Was a friend of Wellington; fought with him at Waterloo.'

'I wonder if he met old Jane Moon's father there!' I could not help saying.

He shot a rebuking glance at me out of his cold blue eyes, silently declined to answer a remark which of course was beneath contempt, and passed on to his other ancestors. But I could not help observing that the great uncle, the friend of Wellington, was wearing a uniform which proclaimed him rather a friend of Marlborough, while the sword hanging above him looked to be of quite modern manufacture.

Off a case of miniatures he obligingly wiped the dust for my inspection. He put names to them all, his grandfather, grandmother, aunts (he pronounces it *ants*) and uncles. But the poor man apportioned wives to husbands in different centuries and made sons and fathers reverse the order of their periods.

Either my poor Major has a careless memory, and not sufficient veneration for his forefathers to remember their histories, or he has, not for the first time in the story of aspiring humanity, bought his ancestors, and endowed himself with the great uncles and 'ants' of other people!

The immediate cause of my calling at Vine Cottage this morning was a letter I had from poor Henry's brother, John Poole. He sometimes advises me about investments, and he wrote to tell me of a report that Barrell & Co. Limited were not doing well, and to warn me if I still had shares to sell out. The Major, who was once, he tells me, on the Stock Exchange (it was there, I suspect, that he came to smash), has promised to see into it, to instruct my broker to sell out, and to manipulate a safer investment for me. It is only a matter of a few hundreds; but he is immensely kind and helpful in all such affairs, and you know how glad I am to shuffle out of them.

Before I left I told him of the meeting at the Rectory, and of the neglected offer of my garden for the Fête. He was immensely moved. He lay back in his chair beneath the portrait of the friend of Wellington, and made a tent above his chest with the meeting of his finger-tips in his favourite attitude. He was torn, I could see, between an almost irrepressible impulse to point out to me my offence against the majestic Hobbleboys and his natural desire as a gentleman to be courteous.

'The thing is, you understand, to *attract*,' he said, in a carefully temperate tone, endeavouring to put the case judicially before me. 'To the Hall the neighbourhood comes, because people are either friends of the Hobbleboys or wish to be.'

'Wish to be? Why?'

He lowered his lids upon the irreverence.

'These things in the country are always bores,' he went on. 'People won't drive half-a-dozen miles to them unless there is some attraction besides the specified object —'

'Attraction! Am I not telling you I will get —— and —— to come down, to play and sing; and —— to recite. I will! I know them; and for love of me they will come.'

And, bless their dear hearts, they would have done so, I know; but I wonder what the celebrated triumvirate would say if they heard that in Dulditch their names, even, are not known!

Major Barkaway remained unmoved.

'At the last Garden Fête held at the Hobbleboys, Lady Phipps-Creake came,' he said, carefully dispassionate.

Who this good woman may be I know not, but I saw that the mention of her was supposed to cut away the ground from beneath my feet. However, having left me, metaphorically, dangling in thin air for a moment, he mercifully changed the subject.

'I hear the telegraph messenger was at your house twice this morning,' he said. 'No ill news, I hope? I was coming up, this afternoon, to inquire.'

'It was from John Beaumont,' I said. 'I've been dramatized successfully at last. A play founded on *A Splendid Failure* goes into the bill at the Diadem Theatre at once.'

I was still excited, to an extent, to tell you the truth, Hildred, over that item of news. An artist, after all, must speak of his work, sometimes, or burst. I talked away for a little, therefore; gave him the situation at the end of the first act which John Beaumont thinks will make a hit; told him how lovely Mrs. St. Helma would look in Belinda's part, and what a fascinating creature she would make of my heroine. Told him that we had so far resisted the importunities of the actor-manager for a happy ending, and were going to stick throughout to the gentle melancholy of the book.

Poor Major Barkaway remained silent, looking at me with his small, not unintelligent, blue eyes, snapping his forefingers down with a dry sound, as if the skin were parched, upon the backs of his hands. It was a subject, I knew by this time, on which he would have very little to say; but I wanted to talk; I realized that it was because I had to tell my piece of news to some one I had come to Vine Cottage this afternoon. Not really to inquire about investments, to see his hens and roses, and the superiority of his arrangements.

So, on I went; for the moment not discouraged by his unresponsive stare. Asked him to imagine what a pleasure it would be to hear my own words put into the mouths of men and women trained to give to the feeblest phrase weight and distinction. What an interest, almost too keen for enjoyment, to see my heroine in the flesh, older than I had intended, certainly, leaner, in far smarter clothes, but sweeter, lovelier, at once more winsome and stately than I had had the art to make her.

The Major dragged his long length from his chair. 'Come and look at my pig,' he said.

His pig is a sow, Hildred. An indelicate creature, not at all agreeable to look at; her sty is of home manufacture, her odour to the unacclimatized indescribably offensive. Her proud owner picked up a crooked stick, and repeating her grunts of pleasure to himself, rubbed and scratched the scurfy, pink skin of her.

Oh well, if he is pleased with his pig, you will say; if his pig suffices him –! But I did not find myself at the moment in a philosophical mood.

'What a pity you never married,' I said to him.

There was an instant's alarm in the questioning glance he cast upon me.

'What a pity you have not done something! How deplorable it seems to me that you should be content with this.'

He stayed his ministrations to the pig to consider me, coldly surprised.

'To scratch a pig's back is pleasurable,' I explained; 'but to a man still in possession of strength, and with all his faculties, the world offers greater prizes.'

'I know the world,' he said; 'I prefer this.'

He meant simply what he said, I am sure, intending no satire.

'You do not imagine me without occupation?' he presently asked. 'With the exception of occasional help from my housekeeper and the boy who pumps the water, I do the whole work of my garden myself.'

He said it proudly, with a wave of his narrow hand over the hopeless litter of the neglected place. He is perfectly satisfied with its condition and his own.

And is there not enough discontent in the world, enough struggling for place, enough striving and strenuousness and clamour? Should I not be a fool – a wicked fool – to attempt to win Major Barkaway from his dilapidated garden and his pig?

To Hildred

THERE is, about a half-mile from my house, a ten acres or so of waste land called Dunn's Heath; a delightful region which, at present, affords me more joy than any other spot in Dulditch.

Except in cleared spaces, where the turf grows soft and fine like that of a well-kept lawn, or in the fairly frequent 'pits' – little hidden pools of water – the gorse, now bursting into bloom, is over all.

– Such a gorgeous field of cloth of gold as in another fortnight it will be! So beautiful it is, already!

Straying on the yielding turf of broad green alley or foot-wide grassy path, you come upon small, still lakes of irregular shape reflecting the sky; upon the big disused gravel-pit; or, if you do not lose yourself in the maze of furze bushes, you may reach the belt of fir-trees, the boundary in one direction of the heath, and dividing the river from the ditch which runs alongside. So tiny a stream is the river, so broad and deep the ditch, that they might almost make an interchange of names and no harm done.

Undiscovered, I believe, by the people of Dulditch, unheeded at least by them, I have appropriated for my own a charming spot in this fair region, of which I am the Columbus. Here, on the day when I had read of the successful first night of *A Splendid Failure*, I repaired. Here, on a circle of wide green banks sloping upward, amphitheatre-like, from a rugged arena of rough grass and gorse bushes, with here and there a pool of water reflecting the gold and green, I sat down. Since to none in Dulditch could I speak of what just then my mind was full, here, vain and foolish woman that I was, to Nature would I unbosom myself.

On that rough platform would I place for myself my play. On the wide banks of green should range themselves to my fancy the hundreds of excited faces of a first-night audience; as I went through the play, scene by scene, situations I had devised, dialogue I had written should move them to laughter, should thrill them to tears.

All this I resolved to do on that heavenly morning of spring, when the press – my breakfast plate had been piled with newspapers – had spoken, and spoken favourably. But, arrived on the spot, I am happy to be able to say for myself, my dear Hildred, I was not powerful prig enough to carry out my design.

For there the Heavens proclaimed the Glory of God, and the firmament showed His handiwork. The scent of the golden gorse blossoms was as that of a burnt sacrifice; the birds sang their anthems in every bush. At my approach a score of tiny rabbits, their white young tails tucked up firmly on their grey fur backs, scurried to their homes in the banks. In the pools of water beneath, a busy crowd of newts and tadpoles darted hither and thither, safe from assault. In the air a multitude of gnats were buzzing; and above, scattered upon the darling blue of the sky, a thousand little fleecy clouds lay like sheep upon a celestial meadow.

'Ere man was aware
Spring is here;
The flowers have found it out.'

Not a sound, not a sight of mankind. Not a sign that he had yet made his appearance in that flowering Garden of Eden!

To think that I had come to obtrude myself, my personal ambitions, my vulgar vanities, my selfish hopes, the rubbish which was the emanation of my little mind, upon such a scene!

So, instead of sitting to watch the manikins I had constructed with such foolish elaborate art strut through their stilted parts, I roamed about; and let the beauty of this unspoilt space, its silence, its eloquence, sink into my heart. I listened to the twitter of the reed sparrows in the dry reeds by the little pools, to the song of the lark as it dropped from the sky; I held myself breathless in order not to frighten the sweet furry people, coming happily out again to play. I lifted a heart to thank, on their behalf, the Creator who had made such a refuge for the dear timid things of nature; – and altogether, as I hope you perceive, my dear Hildred, had brought myself into accord with the scene; when its harmony was broken and its beauty destroyed by the cry of a wild thing in pain.

Cry upon cry, and the frenzied scratching of the soil, led me to a spot where a hare was caught in a steel-trap.

You know how I hate to look upon anything in pain – put it, if you like, how careful I am of my susceptibilities. Give me credit, therefore, for the fact that instead of obeying the impulse to stop my ears and run away, I stayed and did what I could.

The poor beast had dragged himself into his form; I thanked God I could not see his glazing, piteous eyes. The trap, around which the leg was horribly twisted, protruded. The only merciful course was to put the wounded thing at once out of its suffering. I had neither the nerve nor the strength to attempt to do this myself, and it took me a half hour to find any one who would show that amount of grace.

I shouted over the hedge to a man in a cart driving along the road; he stared stupidly at me, open-mouthed, when I called to him that a hare was in a trap, dreadfully hurt; that I wanted him to come at once to kill it.

'Tha's keeper's wark,' he called back, at length. 'Billy, he'll be roun' theer some time to-morrer, ef so be he ain't called t'other way. The hare she'll kape till then,' he bawled; slapped the reins on his pony's back, and drove away.

I dragged my feet across the heavy, chocolate-coloured soil of a field where a man was ploughing. He heard what I had to say with a vacant grin, never stopping his horses while he listened. Picture one sinking over my ankles in the rich earth as I struggled desperately after him.

'Tha's more'n my place is worth,' he drawled, when I had made him, repeating it many times, understand my request. 'Th' old heer ain't none o' my business.'

A grin of slow enjoyment stirred the habitual vacancy of his expression. I think the fact that any one actually cared for the pain of 'an old heer' having penetrated the obfuscation of his brain caused him a certain amusement. I had the dreadful feeling that at the struggles of the trapped creature in its torture he also would have grinned.

As I gained the road again I was so fortunate as to encounter the Rector, who came at once, and willingly, with me, and put the poor beast out of its pain. We found a piece of bone from its mangled leg lying on the spot where its first frantic struggles had taken place.

Mr. Flatt looked on, making no remonstrance, as I took the heavy iron trap and flung it into the still pool at the bottom of my amphitheatre.

'It is hideously cruel,' he said. 'The keepers are supposed to visit these traps every few hours. I have known them to be left for days. I have found a cat starved to death in one that was fastened to a tree. To kill, and to kill – no matter how lingeringly, or what harmless, beautiful things suffer – that is the gamekeeper's creed. Look there!' he said, and pointed to a branch of an elm by the gate of a plantation, where, among some dozen little skeleton forms of stoat, of rat, of weasel, a couple of freshly-slaughtered squirrels hung. The rich red brown of their glossy coats shone in the sun, their beautiful, bushy tails hung limp. 'What possible harm do these charming little beasts do? They take their toll, perhaps, in the plantation, of a few beech-nuts and acorns which nothing else wants.'

'I had one in my garden all last summer,' the Rector related. 'My sister and I hushed our breathing, and muffled our footsteps, when we saw it, hardly daring to look, lest we should frighten the timid, bright-eyed thing away. I found a score of school children gathered round the beech at my gate, one day in the autumn. They had stoned the squirrel to death.'

'"Ivery arternoon when we come from schule we ha' hulled stones at 'm," they told me. "Walter Bunn, he ha' done for 'm at last."'

'What did you do?'

'Sent them off, flying. The squirrel was dead. What should one do?'

'I would have sent Walter Bunn up into the branches of the tree and set the rest to stone him.'

'You wouldn't. It is just what all but Walter Bunn would have enjoyed. You can't do that kind of thing, Mrs. Poole.'

'Of course you can't. But you can do something. What do you do?'

He resents my habit of asking questions as an impertinence, I can see. He lifted his hat; said that he must be hurrying on; left me. Left me to ask of green earth, and blue sky, and the dead, red-brown squirrels, dangling upon the branch, of what use was he in the scheme of creation; of what use was his office, if nothing more practical could be shown for it than the wearisome Sunday ritual, whose recital he spent the rest of the week in coaxing, bribing, bullying his parishioners to attend?

To George

To George

AT last Hildred is here; and Hildred's child – a much more important personage. I never gauged the limitations of The Cottage till Hildred's daughter had to be accommodated in it.

She is nine years old. Do you remember her mother at that age? When she first came to live with us? Of course you do, my dear boy. The quiet, gentle little girl who used to stand at your elbow, and fetch books for you when you were doing your lessons at night; and who asked for nothing better than to trot at your lordship's heels, whenever you would permit her to do so.

I don't remember, although she was as a daughter to your father and me and we loved her devotedly, that we ever thought very much about her; that we treasured and repeated her sayings, anxiously superintended her distractions, struggled to acquire and to retain her approval. A blessing she was to us, undeniably; but we accepted her, I now perceive, rather as a matter of course.

Children were treated in those agreeable days as we treat the violets and primroses blooming round the roots of the trees in the garden, tending them to the necessary extent, of course, conscious of their sweetness and beauty, letting them grow. In the present age, they are the rare plants whose cultivation is a matter of never-ceasing care and speculation, whose daily history is the obtrusive topic, whose growth and training are considered of universal interest.

It is all right enough, I don't doubt. 'The child, the father of the man,' 'Heir of all the ages gain,' and so on. It is we, 'us old uns,' who were wrong. The theory is quite admirable; it is the practice which I find such a bore.

The little bedroom I thought large enough (and good enough) for Nan, looked north. Occupying it, the child would not wake in the morning sunshine which is so good for her. A tree grows rather close to the window, obstructing the air (it does not do anything of the kind, as a matter of detail). For Hildred herself the room would do perfectly, if I would permit her to make the change.

So, in that somewhat cramped (I admit) apartment, Hildred lies; while the daughter revels in the space and sunshine of my best guest-chamber.

As her own nurse refused to come into the country, and Hildred cannot trust in such an important matter as diet the pretty cottage-girl I have hired to take her place, no nursery meals are to be served, and the hours of our own must be altered. The menu is arranged with a view to Nan's tastes alone, and to that which it is good for Nan to eat.

There was nothing of this when the little Hildred was permitted, on occasions, to sit, as a treat, at our table. Now and again your father would say, 'You don't eat enough vegetable, Hildred'; or, 'Don't give the child two helps of pastry.'

But now pastry is banished from our table, because if Nan sees it she insists on having it, her mother tells me; and adds that she always endeavours to avoid friction with the child.

Fish, chicken, and mutton, boiled, are the viands good for Nan. Decent fish is unprocurable here, so chicken and boiled mutton at every meal her mother and I humbly and patiently eat.

Nan monopolizes the conversation when with us, and absent, keeps us in a ferment of wonder as to what she may be doing, alternating with a sickening certainty that what she is doing is bad for her.

You know how perfectly sweet-natured Hildred is. But already – and she has only been here three days – she and I have 'had words' on the subject of Nan.

'Dear Hildred, you make yourself a slave to your child,' I could not help saying. I pointed out to her that these things were not so when you and she were young. Children were kept in their places, then, I reminded her, and knew themselves to be of less importance than their parents.

'The world is wiser now,' she said, with a sententiousness quite new in Hildred. 'Parents, above all, are wiser. It is the children who are of more importance than their parents, Cousin Charlotte. The world is theirs.'

'And do you think your Nan, for instance, will grow up to be a better, more lovable woman than you?' I asked her.

'Than I?' You should have seen the ineffable smile! 'What am I, Cousin Charlotte? Nan's mother. I aspire to be considered as nothing more. Nan may do *great* things.'

'Nan may grow up to be a conceited, self-conscious, insufferable little prig,' I said. 'Of course I don't allude to Nan specially,' I hastened to add.

'And she may grow up (I also do not allude to Nan specially, Cousin Charlotte) to be a grand creature. A blessing to humanity. It is the infinite potentiality of Nan, you see, we have got to remember and to reverence.'

'I don't reverence her a bit, for one,' I said; for Nan had at the instant appeared upon the scene.

'I thought Reverence was a clergyman,' Nan said, and came and planted her square-toed shoes upon my corns, and leant upon my lap. 'If it was to make a clergyman of me I wouldn't have you do it to me on any account, Charlotte Poole.' (It is so, tout simple, without any title, she chooses to address me.)

'But you like *some* clergymen very much, Nan,' her mother anxiously reminded her.

And Nan was complaisant enough to admit she liked the curate at the hotel at Cannes: 'Because he went on all fours and I rode on his back.'

'And pray, Madam, what were you doing while your daughter rode the curate's back?' I inquired of Hildred; and got no other reply than her blush and her soft laugh – you remember what a pretty sound it is?

Well, it is more than probable Hildred has not spent the whole of the eighteen months she was in New York and on the Continent in mourning her husband's memory!

You are longing, I am sure, to hear what looks she is in. She is as pretty at thirty-four as she was at twenty-four when she married – prettier, perhaps. For her fair face has a more placid look, and she has now all the advantages of wealth with which to set forth her beauty. She is always charmingly dressed, and bears herself with a gentle confidence in herself and her position, which was lacking, poor girl, at the time of her marriage.

I want you to come home to see her as soon as you can, George. But in the meantime, my dearest boy, think of Hildred Valetta as more charming, more lovely and lovable in her maturity than she was in her girlhood, even.

She is much pleased, she assures me, with my little home here, and with Dulditch; while I am, for my part, curious to see what effect the presence of this attractive young person will have upon the social life of the place. I said not much about her before she came, because I wanted Hildred to take them by surprise. Living in such a small society, the few who compose it come to be of far more importance than the multitudes who make up the circle of acquaintance in larger places. I do not recall myself, in Hailey Street, as greatly interested in the impression made on our friends by a visitor to our home.

You see, I am sure, by my letters how I am now given over to the trivial. It was always the bent of my mind, I fear me, George, and the propensity has perhaps helped me to write novels that people will read. Since I have lived here, a Poet has died; there has been an appalling disaster, costing millions of money to the nation, costing hundreds of precious lives at sea; an earthquake has swallowed up a numerously inhabited town; and the papers are shrieking about an inevitable war. Never have I heard allusion made to one of these subjects. But the detail that Mr. Chisholm's riding mare has gone lame in its off fore-leg is a theme constantly in people's mouths. The fact that I keep thirty white Minorca hens and have only averaged four eggs a day from them since March is a matter which interests Major Barkaway, for instance, as the rise and fall of empires would fail to do.

Every day the good man comes down here to ask for the tale of my eggs, giving me triumphantly the tale of his. Suspecting an egg-thief at the Grange Farm, it appears, they had the inspiration to set a steel-trap in the nest placed high on a hay-rack in the horse-stable. They caught, unfortunately, the farm steward, a man of immense importance and high integrity of character. He was so valuable a man in his place, and so greatly respected in the parish, that the affair was anxiously hushed up, apologies were made to him, his wounds dressed in secret. Major Barkaway has, however, suggested the device of the steel-trap concealed in a nest to me.

But I once saw a hare in one, and have declined.

To George

TO-DAY Nan came in to dinner – we dine at one o'clock now, for Nan's digestion's sake, and sup (off rice and stewed fruit, principally) at seven, for the same all-important consideration – with the intelligence that she had found a new nest in the rockery at the back of the house with nine eggs in it. Going to inspect this treasure-trove when we had disposed of our mutton (boiled) and sago, we found but one egg in the nest.

Syers and Clement accuse the rats. I rejoice to say I have not seen one of these creatures, but according to my gardener and his henchman the place is infested with the vermin. Rats have the greatest sagacity, and develop the most surprising attributes where eggs are concerned, and a no less marvellous cunning, I have learnt.

They abstract eggs from wheresoever, above or below ground, they may be laid; they roll them in safety to their own homes. They are reported to make holes in the eggs and insert their tails which they afterwards suck dry. It is certain eggs so despoiled are frequently found around the nests.

'They're masterpieces, rets are!' Syers declares, lost in admiration of their craftiness.

'But would rats come in sufficient numbers and determination to remove eight eggs in the half hour it has taken us to eat our lunch?' we asked.

Syers smiled his contempt of our inexperience and want of faith. 'Theer's armies of 'em!' he assured us. 'You ha' seed 'em in armies, Clemmy, bor?' he appealed to his assistant.

'Times!' asserted Clemmy. He gazed heavily upon the rifled nest, unmoved to any exhibition of interest in the subject.

The sun shone on the enormous crop of his red-curled hair, on his extraordinarily crimson lips, in his dark eyes. 'Quite a good-looking rustic!' Hildred declared.

So I told her something of the household of which Clemmy is a member: of the extra, unwished-for, unlawful baby; of the four little ones with colds who sat on chairs against the wall and had their noses polished with the duster from under the cushion of the chair, in the pauses of dumpling manufacture. Finally, at her request, I took her through the kitchen-garden and across the meadow to call on the handsome Clemmy's mother.

She happened to be baking; and a huge custard of the colour of daffodils, a rice pudding of the same rich depth of tint, stood on the table, hot from the oven.

The face of Mrs. Moore was hot too; her manner, aggressive as ever, was yet somewhat flurried. She had not laid to heart the lesson of the proverb which casts suspicion on the person foolish enough to excuse himself, and hastened to tell us that, driven to the extravagance by the indisposition of her youngest child, who had a cold on his chist and wanted nouraging, she had laid in t'reepennor' o' eggs – eggs bein' chape at this season o' th' yare – and had made 'm a pudden.

'I hope that there will be enough for Clemmy also to have a share,' I could not help remarking.

Mrs. Moore did not take the speech in good part, for some reason. The colour of her face grew deeper, her manner more inimical.

She supposed there were no one wi' th' right to grudge Clemmy the mossel that fell to 'm, she said. A lad that warked arly and late, niver sparin' hisself, had a right to 's wittles, she supposed.

Here follows the elucidation of the egg mystery, and the conclusion, I hope, of the whole matter. I did not think to be able to give it so soon.

Hildred, waking at five o'clock, to-day, and going to her window, which, facing north as I have said, opens upon the back premises, to see how the apple-trees, pink with blossom, look in the mistiness of the early morning, was in time to discover Clemmy, as we affectionately call our under-gardener, going from one to the other of the half-dozen nests within range of vision, and taking eggs from them all.

Hildred, lest her eyes should be deceiving her, came for me that I also might testify to the fact. By the time of my arrival, Clement, feeling faint from his exertions, was engineering that little hole at the bottom of the shell into which the 'ret' was accused of inserting his tail.

Less tastefully equipped for the manœuvre than the rat, it was his red lips Clemmy applied to the orifice, replacing the shell when empty in the vicinity of the nest.

Those eggs he did not suck he stowed away in the pockets of his velveteen jacket.

'When he begins to work he'll smash them,' Hildred feared.

I was able to reassure her. The labours of Clement since he has been in my service are not of a nature to endanger the resisting power of an egg-shell.

I gave our Clemmy a week's notice, after breakfast, and begged him, for the remaining tenure of his office, while in pursuit of the other arduous duties for which Syers had engaged him, to desist from the self-imposed task of collecting the eggs.

He gazed at me with his shining dark eyes, saying nothing. Lest there should be any doubt in his mind of my meaning: 'I saw you stealing, and sucking my eggs, this morning, at five o'clock,' I told him.

He will ask to be forgiven, and I will give him another chance, I said to myself.

However, in this confidence I deceived myself, and traduced that spirit of glorious independence flourishing in the free soil of the agricultural labourer's mind. Clemmy listened in the silence of absolute stolidity, making no denial, no excuse, no appeal.

In the afternoon the mother appeared in a tempest of passion. Her hard, ill-featured face livid with wrath – Vengeance incarnate.

Her son was at the moment assisting Syers in the setting out of the seedling asters. The pair had for once equally divided the onus of labour. Clement with a blunt stick in his hand was making in the soil at even distances down the border three holes in a group, while Syers, following after, proceeded to drop therein three minute plants from the collection he held in his hand.

A glorious afternoon: the sun glistening on the gravel paths, and warm upon the lawn. Now and again our precious pair paused in their labour; straightened their bent backs; looked in each other's face; looked at the horizon; consulted their watches; slowly, with sighs, resumed their arduous task.

'You go home!' his mother screamed, furiously hailing her offspring. The high shrill voice reached me as I stood in the open window. 'How come you to demane yerself, Clemmy, by doing a stroke more wark i' this here garden? I'm sorrow as yer ever set fut i' th' place, to sarve them that don't know how to trate a hard-warkin' young chap when they find 'm. Wha's the vally of a few mucky eggs i' th' spring o' th' yare, I should like ter know, that a man's char'cter is to be tuk away for 'em? Come on, Clemmy, I say. Lucky you ha' got me to stan' up for ye. Them that call my boy a thief 'll ha' to prove it.'

'I can prove it quite easily,' I said, having at that moment joined the little group on the drive. 'I saw your son steal a pocketful of eggs, Mrs. Moore. I saw him suck those he would take away with him –'

'You'll have to prove what you say. Theer's them as have had to be punished for sech wards,' the woman shouted savagely. 'Them that cast sech accysations ha' ter prove 'em.'

She went away calling out vituperation; the 'honest, hard-workin' young chap,' stolid indifference to the matter in hand written on his face, slouching at her heels.

Syers was dibbling his own holes now, and dropping in the delicate little aster plants. 'I saw him steal the eggs with my own eyes,' I said to him, in the disturbance of my mind seized by the weak desire for his approval.

He dibbled the holes and inserted the plants without a word.

'Perhaps you also think it is right that I should be robbed and say nothing?' I continued to the stubborn-looking, stooping back.

He growled an unintelligible reply.

'What is it you are saying? Stand up, and answer distinctly when I address you,' I commanded him.

He went on dropping in the seedlings. 'A matter of a few eggs here and theer – what is ut?' he muttered, without lifting his head.

To George

So far the month of May has been a disappointment generally; wet and misty days, grey skies, cold temperature. Hardly the bounteous May of the poets, with her lap full of flowers. And yet a May that to me, watching her young beauty for the first time at close quarters, has been a most delicate delight.

There is grumbling on all sides. From Syers in the garden, lamenting that for the first time in his memory a score of his Crown Imperials have come up without flowers; that the blossom of which they were full has rotted on the trees, and no fruit set; that the sparrow-grass which should ha' been cut at Easter is still but a sprinkly growth. From the farmers, telling doleful tales of wheats beginning to look yellow, of scant grass for the cows, and too much wet for the welfare of the lambs. Nora Chisholm's turkeys are doing badly, she tells me. Out of her fifty, twenty-two are dead. Her mother complains that the girl might as well spend her days in the river as paddling about the meadows after the fowls. The effect on her clothes and boots would be the same.

'Nora hasn't been dry for ten days,' the mother cries. 'She will perhaps clear ten pounds at the end of the season, and will have ruined twenty pounds worth of boots and clothes.'

But Nora –
> *'Blown with all the winds that blow*
> *And wet with all the showers'* –

moves her coops in search of drier spots, mixes her endless pails of food, drags her petticoats through the grass in search of missing little turkeys, quite unmoved by such representations. She is as pretty as a picture, and in blooming health; not afraid of the rain washing the roses from her cheeks or the gold from her hair, and laughing to scorn the old women's tales of the danger of wet feet.

Major Barkaway is laid up with influenza. In spite of Miss Flatt and Decorum, I have occasionally called to see him. He looks dilapidated and old and lonely, and I think it cheers him to have a listener to his oft-told tales.

I have heard all of them many times over, now. Indeed, since he has been ill I have often heard the same tale twice at a sitting. They have not much point, and consist, as a general thing, of what this person, and what that (of high social standing, well understood,) has said to him, on occasions.

He had got forward with his garden-work, before being laid low, he rejoices. I am glad to hear it, and that he is content. To my uninstructed mind the place has as neglected and woe-begone an aspect as before. He regrets that he cannot pay his daily attentions to the pig, and is openly distressed and disappointed that the Hobbleboys have forgotten to inquire for him. On the occasion of a former illness they had been extremely civil, and had even sent him a bunch of asparagus.

His room was gay with flowers. 'From the Rectory, I know,' I said. 'They were showing me their hyacinths yesterday. At least Miss Flatt has not forgotten you!'

Before I left him the pretty Chisholm girl drove up with a hot dinner, beautifully cooked and skilfully packed. The Grange people, he carelessly let fall, send him his dinner every day now that he is ill. An attention which goes for nothing against the neglect of the Hobbleboys and the omittance of the bunch of asparagus.

To George

WE have had three wet Sabbaths in succession; a nearly empty church, I hear, at each service. This touches the Rector in his vulnerable spot. On the rare occasions when I have seen him (he is morbidly afraid of wet feet and is inclined to mope at home over his study fire) he has been depressed, and a trifle sulky. I am beginning to fear he does not very anxiously seek my society – a blow to my self-esteem, isn't it, when you reflect how very little society is at his command? I suppose my pernicious habit of asking 'Why?' is at the root of it.

But May, my dear George, May in any guise is good enough for me. The brave white blossom of the blackthorn, and the plum-tree on their still leafless stalks, the delicate greenery of the tasselled larches, the fairy foliage of the nut-bushes, are as delightsome painted against the grey sky as the blue. The song of the birds through my open bedroom window is tumultuous, though the dawn be shrouded in mist. 'The word in the minor third that only the cuckoo knows' suits best, to my thinking, the sober livery of the backward month. Its melancholy monotony is out of harmony with the gladness of a more radiant time.

The farmers here belong to a sparrow-club. Threepence a dozen is paid for the carcases of the full-grown birds, and three-ha'pence a dozen for the unfledged ones from the nest. It is not likely that the fat old woman who keeps the village shop is naturalist enough to decide whether the little naked bodies brought to her are those of sparrow, or linnet, or lark. Consequently all the nests of hedge and field and grove are being rifled, and barbarous work done. I have explained to every boy I have found bent on emptying the nests in order to fill his pockets the crime he is contemplating. But my eloquence is useless against the magnificent offer of threepence a dozen.

I have also committed to the special charge of Syers every nest on my little estate, in bush or hedge or tree.

I discovered him to-day mounted on a ladder, busy with the roof of the tool-house. T'other woman had left the roofs of the outhouses in a somewhat dilapidated condition. Syers, I at first thought, had added the profession of bricklayer to that which he so adorns, and I watched his proceedings for a few minutes with complacency.

At length becoming suspicious that things were not as they seemed, I called to him to inquire what he was doing.

He thrust his hand beneath the tiles he had loosened before turning to answer me, flung the live bodies of a half-dozen birds to the ground; thrust in his hand again.

'These here sparrers are a playin' a pretty how-d'ye-du wi' your pram'ses,' he explained. 'Tha's time some one tuk in hand to clare out yer roofs o' th' pests.'

'Leave all that to the plasterers who are coming to attend to the roofs, and come down to your gardening work,' I commanded him.

He threw down a couple of handfuls more of nestlings before he came. For an hour he muttered to himself savage criticisms on my 'goings on,' and has, indeed, sulked with me ever since. Syers knows how to make things very uncomfortable when he sulks.

Matters are made more disagreeable for me by Ethel, the parlour-maid; she, who for some extraordinary reason always takes Syers' part against mine, is sulking too.

'I told you I would have the nests carefully protected in my garden,' I explain to Syers.

'Your roof-tree ain't yer garden,' Syers wrathfully retorts. 'You never let on as ye wanted yer roofs a-falling about yer ears!'

Nan and I, walking the garden yesterday, paused holding each other in restraint, hardly daring to breathe, while we watched the parent bird dropping food into the wide open yellow mouths of a nest full of twittering thrushes safely housed in the thorn hedge which divides us from the road. Yesterday. To-day the nest is torn and empty, lying on the path, and in the air above where its place had been the frenzied little bereaved birds are fluttering with wild complainings.

To George

AT last the rain has ceased; the sun is shining on the glistening, vernal robe of the shabby old earth. The voice of God has once more awakened all things from their sleep; and every glorious creation tingling with vigorous life shouts in answer to His roll-call, 'Here I am!' The air is filled with pæans of gladness.

Hildred and I, walking this morning beneath the avenue of chestnuts just beginning to expand their green fans fully in the sunlight, met a funeral on its way. Old Jane Moon, she whose father fought at Waterloo, was buried to-day.

Because the coffin was so poor, and so few were there to follow it, Mrs. Valetta and I joined ourselves to the tiny procession; and sat with bowed heads in the empty church, to hear how the days of man being but three score years and ten, they who attain to a longer span must bear their number as a burden.

More than another decade had poor old Jane added to her reckoning, carrying the weight of her years lightly, I hear, till the shock of the fall from which she never recovered. She had kept her cottage sweet and clean; had been ever ready to 'have an eye to' a neighbour's child, to sit beside a sick-bed, to carry in a cup of tea to the friend too ill or too weary to brew one for herself.

When the mould had fallen with its unspeakably dreary sound upon the poor coffin, when the few stragglers, looking into the grave and whispering about the 'poor old dare' hidden therein, had turned away, a little girl, who had hung in the background till then, came forward, and dropped upon the nameless coffin a tiny bunch of cowslips she had held clasped in her hot, small hand.

Not a tear had been shed at poor Jane Moon's funeral. Who could mourn for the death of a lonely old woman whose kith and kin had all gone before her, who for many years had lived alone, and alone had died? But my own eyes grew moist as I saw the child's flowers fall on the deal coffin; and Hildred, who keeps, thank God, her tender heart, clasped in hers the little hand that threw them.

As we three walked from the churchyard together we bent our steps in the direction of the little two-roomed cottage in which for more than sixty years the old woman had lived; and as we went we drew from the child who walked between us that her name was Margery, that she lived next door to Mrs. Moon, and had always 'done for her' when she wasn't at school.

'Theer's suffin' for you, ma'am,' presently Margery was saying to me. 'That theer little glass what stood by Mis' Moon's bedside, and mostly held a spray o' rosema'y. She've give that to ye. An' I was to say, she drunk out of 't when she lived at home, 'long of her father, and was a little gel like me.'

The cottage was already dismantled when we reached it. The bed on which the old lady had died was in process of migration from her bedroom to that next door, it having been bequeathed, we learnt, as a legacy to Margery, who until then had shared the bed of her brothers in her parents' room. Thanks to the thoughtfulness of old Jane Moon, Margery now was to have a bed of her own, and was filled with pride and satisfaction at the thought.

The ill-favoured 'Neighbour' who was Margery's mother fetched at once for me the small thick drinking-glass, carefully wrapped in newspaper.

'She done it up herself, poor old dare,' Neighbour told me. 'More'n a wake ago, she done it up. "Ef so be as I wrop it myself," she say, "I shall know 'tis safe; and I can make shift," she say, "to du without it. The gentry," she say to me, "set a vally on sech-like, bein' 'tis ancient; and I han't got nothin' besides to offer th' lady."'

The poor little common drinking-glass, cherished possession of a faithful heart! It shall stand by my own bedside in memory of Jane Moon. And before I fall asleep I shall sometimes try to picture the little Jane playing by the cottage door by which the bush of rosemary grew when she lived at home, ''long of her father.' I shall picture the field of which the young soldier thought as he surveyed the carnage of Waterloo; the sheep-dotted Five Elms Meadow whose image was in his heart.

To George

I HAVE not yet seen the Rector of Dulditch crawling on all fours in order that Nan, mounted on his broadcloth back, may enjoy equestrian exercise, but I should not be greatly surprised if it is a spectacle to be enjoyed in the near future.

Up to the present she is satisfied with the man's pony, put largely at her service. Nan is an importunate, imperious little lady, and, accustomed to get what she asks for, does not hesitate to ask. It is imperative, I learn, that she ride *something;* it is only where horses are not forthcoming that she is compelled to ride her friends.

(By the way, Major Barkaway has not yet met with the horse he would consider suitable for me. He has kindly undertaken to supply me with one which it will be safe to drive in the victoria I brought down from London. He thought the horse-dealers would be likely to get the best of me in a bargain if I tackled them alone; and I am quite sure he is right. These bargains must, I suppose, be struck with deliberation, but the Major is, I think, over conscientious.)

(Also, by the way, I see the company in which I had my brewery shares has gone smash. I hoped the Major had got rid of them for me, but it turns out unfortunately that he failed to understand I was depending on him to do me this service. Luckily it means only a loss of six hundred pounds.)

Nan's first question to a new acquaintance is: 'How many horses do you keep?' Her next: 'Is there one which will do for a little girl to ride?'

On the answer to these inquiries hangs the result of the small person's favour, or her entire indifference.

Because he is compelled to avow himself wanting in the one thing needful, Major Barkaway has no place in her regard. The announcement, 'I have a pig,' which he expected to be received with enthusiasm, left Nan quite cold.

'I should have thought a gentleman would have had a horse,' was all she said.

She looked on with only polite attention while the scaly back of the pig was rubbed by the Major's stick in the habitual fashion, and refused the invitation with coolness when invited to join him in the sport.

After a time, however, having turned things over in silence in her own mind, she was good enough to give her entertainer the benefit of her deliberations.

'If the pig was mine, do you know what I would do with him?' she asked. 'I should change him away for a horse. Quite a small horse, you know, that could go in the sty. You can get them quite enormously small. As small as pigs. Did you know it? Then I should make the sty into a stable.'

'Would you?' the Major asked. He eyed her from the lofty eminence of his superior wisdom. He has not the faintest idea how to talk to children, and wore even a certain air of offence; his eyes were cold as he surveyed the pretty, confident little maid.

But Nan, unabashed and quite contented with herself, kindled with her theme, and went on to detail:

'Yes, I should. I should just put bricks and clean wood where all this tumbling down mess is; and not have these railings, which are dirty, but nice clean bricks built up all round, which a horse would prefer. They would, Major Barkaway, I know; because all the stables I have seen don't have railings, always, but bricks. They're so much more specially delightful for horses. Then, if you hadn't got any work for your horse to do, I could come down and ride him.'

He regarded her with a chilly aloofness: 'Would you, indeed?'

'Yes. Do it, will you?' she persisted.

When he with a cold finality refused to entertain the simple project, Nan turned away, and took no further interest in him.

But, thanks to the white pony at the Rectory stable, Hildred's daughter condescends to bestow her approval to some extent upon the Flatts.

'May I go to see Greyman?' she inquires of her mother, at least once in every waking hour. Perhaps once in every forty-eight hours she receives permission. Then, being fully harnessed herself, she gallops down the road to the Rectory, the unfortunate maid who has been hired to wait on her caprices here galloping after her, breathless, and clinging to her reins.

She goes with a message entrusted to the maid to deliver, asking that Nan may be permitted to look at the pony in the stable. After which she is to be returned at once without giving any trouble. But every one knows the futility, where this little nine-years-old tyrant is concerned, of such a request.

In a couple of hours she reappears, astride the back of Greyman, whom she is urging to his utmost speed, the poor Rector, fat and scant of breath, puffing behind her, holding on to the leading rein.

'O Mr. Flatt! Why will you do it! How good you are!' Hildred says, with her calm, coolly approving smile. And men being the fools they are, I suppose the Reverend Algernon is repaid.

'He is rather a good galloper,' Nan says, in dispassionate praise of him. 'But one day when he is very hot and puffing I hope Greyman will get away. Then I shall ride him, oh, quite an enormous number of miles away, and make him jump ditches.'

'Pray, Mr. Flatt, never let her go alone,' the mother rather commands than entreats. 'I feel quite safe about my dear little girl while you run by her side.'

I really think the exercise does him good. He looks thinner, paler, healthier, cleaner, more brushed up, since Nan has taken him and his pony into favour. We see him constantly. We have no rains now, certainly, but I believe nothing short of a deluge would keep him from his daily dropping-in upon us, on one pretext or another. The dread of getting his feet wet was an excuse invented, I begin to see, for me alone.

Ah me! such straws remind me I am more than fifty years of age, dear George. 'The wine of life is drawn, the mere lees is left.' I remember, my dear son, when these things were not so. But what do honour, riches, achievement, matter? One grows old, and threatens to grow fat; and the Mr. Flatts of one's acquaintance are afraid to get their feet wet!

Between you and me, my dear, dear as Hildred is and much as you know I love her, she is ridiculous about this child. And I sometimes think – it will wear off, of course – that, living in the society of that heavy old husband of hers, she has acquired just a little – the veriest shade – of his density.

Where this little rascal of a child is concerned, she is blind and obtuse. She firmly believes it is for love of Nan that the pretty tyrant is permitted to bestride Greyman, hitherto sacred and at idle ease in the Rectory stable; that it is because of his own anxiety for the child's neck the middle-aged Rector of Dulditch runs beside her; and for the sake of Nan's amusement alone the absurd young curate at Cannes crawled about on all fours with the little fiend upon his back.

As a reward for his exertions, while the Reverend Algernon stays with us, she tries to keep Nan at his side; and because she believes that the child's ridiculous sayings are an intellectual treat to the parson, she lets her monopolize a large share of the conversation. The poor man protests, of course, that he enjoys to have the little girl hanging on to his wristbands while he walks beside her mother, or scrunching the sides of his feet as she clings affectionately round his neck when he sits at table.

He is a pleasant, fat, lazy-bones; a rather poor sort of an apology for a man, as I have said more than once to Hildred. Still, all I have to offer her as a victim to her charms. Unless – ? There is Major Barkaway.

It pleases Hildred to laugh, and to assume a very knowing look when this alternative is put before her. 'Ah, I know better!' Hildred says. 'Man-traps and air-guns! Trespassers beware! Keep off my property!' this joker says. You see the tendency of the witticism? She thinks it will amuse me; dear Hildred!

She tells me she has received four offers of marriage in the year and a half since her husband's death. Well, I can see with tolerable clearness of vision from whence the fifth will come.

Do not fear, my dear boy, that your cousin has developed into a flirt. There is not a suspicion of vulgarity about Hildred. But you remember the old trick of sweet-smiling at every bore who is talking to her? You remember how careful she is of his feelings, and how she rarely forgets to laugh in her slow attractive way at his jokes? How she makes him show himself always in her presence in his best light, so that the poor thing becomes almost as much in love with himself as with her? She means no harm. But these methods often make me angry; and are they fair to the poor victim, I ask?

Now, if you would write, my dear George, and settle things between you! She would be happier; and so would you; and so, I admit it, would I.

I have said, more than once, that I would never approach this matter again, with either of you. For the moment I was forgetting. I will not transgress again.

Yet, it would want but a word; and you have held back too long. Be sensible, George. You let her slip from you before, for your stupid pride's sake, or for some trivial misunderstanding a look would have put right. It was your fault more than Hildred's. You should have been swifter to make amends.

She feels this, I know, and never willingly mentions your name. Yet, well I know she loves to hear it. I read her all your letters, dear; their coming is a delight to us; and mail-day red-letter day, at The Cottage. She and I are drawn closely together as in the old time. The bond between us was always you. It is you, still.

Very little Hildred says of him who is dead, Nan's father. He was, as we know, a man it was impossible any girl should have loved. Yet that gentle dignity of Hildred's goes all through her, and she bears herself as if she had loved him. She teaches Nan, who has small reverence for any living thing, to reverence her father's memory. When the child is speaking of this delightful person or that, who, having a stable full of horses, has commended himself to her respectful treatment, as 'the very nicest in the world,' she always remembers to pull herself up, and with a glance at her mother to add, 'Not so extremely nice as my own dear daddy, of course.'

To George

THE local baker rejoices in the appropriate name of Bunn. I set it forth with reluctance, having never any admiration for the form of wit expressed by the dubbing of a farmer 'Haystack' or a lawyer 'Deedes'; but 'Bunn' happening to be the good man's style and title, it would be idle to dissemble the fact.

Mr. Edgar Bunn rejoices also in the possession of a wife who is a cause of unfailing interest to the village. 'Sarah, poor sufferin' woman's, took bad agin'; or 'Bunn's wife, poor critter, was 'tackted agin, i' th' night,' are phrases with which the ear speedily becomes familiar. Blood-curdling details are given of her extraordinary symptoms. Yesterday Hildred and I went to call on the sufferer.

We found, in the small, smart, airless parlour attached to the little baker's shop, a strongly-made, well-nourished-looking young woman, with a colourless, opaque skin, and a habit of looking corner-ways at you out of her green, white-lashed eyes. In answer to our sympathetic inquiry she admitted that she was a terribly afflicted woman, and that her sufferings were 'chronic.'

'Ten year ago – since ever I married – I ha' been in th' doctors' hands,' she told me, with a proudly resigned complacency.

'It's time you tried another doctor,' I suggested.

'I ha' had four of 'em,' she announced, with the air of meekly saying, 'Get over that if you can.' 'This here one's the fif'.'

'And what did they all say to you, Mrs. Bunn?' Hildred sympathetically asks.

'They was wholly baffled. Four of 'em was. "Mr. Bunn," they say to my husban', "in our perfession," they say, "we ain't often baffled, but your good lady, she ha' done it."'

She announced the fact with an air of dignified triumph, as if, having contracted an incurable disease, she had achieved a deed of renown.

'So you gave the doctors up? Quite right!'

'"To go on wi' th' case would only be a-robbin' of you, Mr. Bunn," they say. (We owe a matter o' ten pound among 'em now.) "We ha' done our best by her," they say, "and we are wholly baffled."'

'And what does the fifth doctor say?'

'He's a more skilfuller gentleman. I have hopes of his a-gettin' at me. So have my husban'. "Never min' th' cost," Bunn, he say to me; "we ha' run up bills wi' t'others, and we'll run up one wi' this here man. Theer's hopes," he says, "of his a-gettin' at you."'

'And he really appears to understand your case?'

'You'd a'most think he'd been t'rough the affliction hisself, to hear the way he talk on't. "This here myster'ous thing," he say, "that keep a-bobbin up and down i' your chist, a'most like a great ball," he say, "a-bouncin' there; sometimes it come right up into your gullet, as if 'twas bound," he say, "to choke you." "Tha's how 'tis," I say to 'm; "and when I'm a-chokin' I can't draw no breath." "I'm a-dyin'," I say to my husban'. "Call the neighbours," I say to 'm. T'ree times last week th' neighbours was called in.'

'And what does he do to cure you?'

'He give me medicine. Perhaps you'd like to smell to it.' She produced a bottle, and handed it to me. 'Ivery bottle cost half-a-crownd; and we have to pay for it aforehand. 'Cause the doctor he ain't one o' these here reg'lar ones, and –'

'He is a quack, you mean?'

'He don't call hisself that,' Mrs. Bunn said indifferently. 'He's more skilfuller than the t'others, and more expen*sive*, 'cause he have to be paid. "He's expen*sive,*" Bunn say, "but if so be as he can get at ye-"'

'It is a great misfortune for your husband.'

'Bunn, he don't complain. "When I took a 'flicted woman for my wife I knowed what I was a-doin'," he say. "I knowed you cou'n't do a stroke o' wark, and therefore a woman mus' be kep to du it for ye," he say. "I knowed there'd be doctor's physic. But you're a 'flicted woman," Bunn he say, "and there 'tis."'

'I think, Mrs. Bunn,' I said to her, when we were leaving, "if you would exert yourself more, go out in the sun, keep your windows open, even scrub your floors, instead of paying a woman to do it, you might put out the fire, which you really do not need to-day, with the quack doctor's medicine, and would find yourself very much better.'

She gave me a glance of no good will out of her slanting green eyes, and Hildred tugged warningly at my sleeve as we stood together.

'I'm a sorely 'flicted woman –' she began.

'I have known cases like yours before,' I told her. 'Many of them.'

'Not like mine,' protested the invalid, with an air of offence. 'Four doctors I ha' had, wholly baffled, and –'

And so on.

We came out of the stuffy little parlour – it smelt of cabbages which had been cooked and eaten there for many a day – and looked in at the bake-office where the husband was kneading bread, his hairy arms, bare to the elbows, and caked with dough of an earlier date than the lump on which he was at that moment busy. He has the habit while he talks of picking off dried bits of the material which adheres to his skin and ramming them with finger and thumb into the mass of pliable stuff on the board before him.

He led us from the dry heat of the bakery to the moist heat of the little conservatory, hard by. Between the two fires he lives; his face is of a chalk white, accordingly; and we wondered if the abnormal growth of the long red hair on his arms was due to the forcing heat.

We discovered that, although with his bread his duty lay, his heart – such of it as was not in the keeping of the renowned invalid in the parlour – is with his begonias, his pelargoniums, his roses in his hot-house.

'Fare to make life worth livin',' he said, when we had looked round and praised his treasures. 'There ain't, not to say, no use in 'em all. I ain't a-denyin' as there ain't no *use;* but –' His voice trailed into a sigh. He is a dreary, anæmic-looking creature; his dull eyes strayed with a despairing affection about his shelves.

I endeavoured to hearten him by repeating Victor Hugo's dictum that 'the beautiful is as useful as the useful, perhaps, and more so.' He listened silent and distrait, coldly passing over my remark as being no concern of his, picked at the hairy arms, and stuck the morsels of hard, dried dough retrieved from them into the mould of the flower-pots as erstwhile into the bread.

'We *know* there ain't no use,' he repeated, hopelessly pursuing the debate that ever seemed to be going on in his mind. 'But there 'tis!'

He would not sell us a plant, he did not offer to give us a flower. 'If I was once to make a beginnin',' he explained, in his melancholy way, 'there'd never be no ind to it. This one a-beggin', and that one.'

We conveyed to him that he was as prudent as his flowers were beautiful; he touched the blossoms lovingly here and there, and said that they was certainly 'marvellous for beauty.'

'Theer's some as say my heart should be i' my oven,' he said, dispassionately making the barbarous statement. 'My missus – she's an afflicted woman, and should know – she's among 'em. 'Tis my oven, she say, is wheer my duty lay. I do my best, according*ly*, in my walk o' life, and few there be as kin beat me at the bread baking. But for true happiness,' he sorrowfully pleaded, as he languidly plucked at his arms, 'don't give me dough, don't give me loaves – or currant-buns, or tea-cakes – gi' me flo'rs.'

Before we left I put in a word or two about his wife. 'She is suffering from hysteria,' I said. 'Nothing else in the world ails her.'

The words evidently conveyed no meaning. 'She is an afflicted woman, poor thing,' he said. 'Her sufferin's is awful. Pounds thick we ha' spent in doctors.'

'Don't spend any more. Don't pity her.'

He looked at me with pale offence.

'Being a Christian an' her husban', you can't but pity an afflicted woman,' he said.

To George

I WISH, my dearest George, I was for the nonce as that unhappy gifted one described himself, 'A Lord of Language,' to tell you what

May is like in Dulditch now that the misty grey skies have cleared to show us her smiling face.

The gorse which was partially in bloom when I wrote of it a fortnight ago is now a blaze of beauty, shouting 'Hallelujah in the Highest.' The tall spikes of broom, – and here this plant grows in profusion, – are in golden bloom. This morning I felt inclined to take off my shoes before a great flaming clump of it that grows not far from my garden gate, as Moses did before the bush that revealed to him his God.

Do you know the delicious subtly sweet scent of the gorse in full flower? How can you describe it? It is like warm honey, perhaps, with yet a fragrance added.

The speedwells grow among it, overlooked in the grand features of the landscape, but beautiful in their detail. Their 'darling blue' must always lurk in the gorgeous embroideries of the robe of God.

On the banks, and in the plantations, the pale primroses with their jealous hue, 'sick for love,' have 'forsaken, died,' but in the water meadows the sunlit gold of the tall buttercups lies like a shimmering gilded haze above the orchises that purple all the ground.

As you walk, the pink and white petals of the apple blossom are blown soft as kisses against your cheek or drop like blessings on your head. In the hedges, on the great hundred-year-old thorns dotted about the landscape, the may is in full bloom. The great Artist puts in with a free and liberal brush that never errs great splashes of white in His grand design.

In the fields the clover, red and white, the rose-pink sainfoin, the ruddy trifolium, are growing knee-deep; for, after all the farmers' fears, the prospects are good on their light lands, and crops are looking well.

In the long grass of the meadows I have seen a foal or two beside their dams, turned off to enjoy the pleasures of motherhood for a season. Long legged, big kneed, tottering in their gambols, they scamper and gallop, and toss their heels in gamesome play around their sedate parent, till their joints apparently give way with them and they lie, legs tucked beneath them, at the maternal feet.

Sunlight and air fortunately being considered good for Nan, we have been living in the garden, even taking our meals there. A congregation of robins – apparently a whole family party of them, consisting of uncles, cousins, aunts, besides Mr. and Mrs. Robin Redbreast, and their half-dozen youngsters, bigger than themselves but without their trim shapes and red breasts – dog our footsteps as we gather the tulips in the long borders, or take up position on the backs of our chairs when we sit down to feed.

One of this colony, a particularly perfect little bird, gorged himself on crumbs from our currant-cake as we sat at tea beneath the great fir-tree on the lawn, this afternoon. When the creature – daring and importunate to the extent of flying and pecking at the cake itself, if for a minute we desisted from throwing him crumbs – had devoured about his own weight in confectionery, there arrived to him a blown-about, neglected-looking fellow with an anxious even worried expression, proclaiming him, we were sure, the father of the family.

' "You can read 'husband' in his face,"' Hildred quoted.

In his beak he carried a worm; which perceiving, his rapacious son spread wide his greedily quivering wings, squatted on the grass, opened his voracious jaws; while into them the dutiful and apparently famished father, placed the tit-bit he had procured for his offspring.

'Oh, the stupid! Why didn't he remain a bachelor?' Nan cried, laughing at poor Mr. Robin.

Nan is supposed to make herself too hot with running in the sunshine. A mandate has been issued, therefore, that for half an hour in the day she is to sit to sew, beside her mother's knee. She accomplishes perhaps five stitches in the thirty minutes, and all the time she wails and weeps, lamenting how short her time for 'playin'' is, pricking her hot little fingers, unthreading her needle, working her mother into a condition of worry and irritation which none but the beloved daughter can compass.

'Nan,' I inquired of her to-day, 'aren't you ashamed to be such a baby?'

'No,' said Nan, with distinct enunciation, fires of suddenly kindled wrath shining through the waters of grief in her golden eyes.

'Then, I am ashamed for you. Look at your dear mother; growing an old woman before her time, thanks to you and your naughty ways.'

'She isn't,' says Nan fiercely, and looks with angry alarm from her lovely mother in her white frock to dumpy me in my widow's black.

'I can see the wrinkles coming beneath her eyes, the ugly hollows in her cheeks, the grey in her hair.'

'You can't! It's what you've got, Gran' (she calls me Gran now, at my own request. An arrangement a little premature, perhaps, my dear boy, but it will spare her the awkwardness of getting used to the title in days to come). 'You've got them, yourself; because you're old –'

'Nan!' from a horrified mother.

'And – and ugly,' cries a now hysterical daughter.

When I laughed she threw her thimble in my face and stamped upon the sward. 'I won't! I won't have my dear mummy grow old! I won't! I won't!' she screamed, and flung herself face downwards upon the grass.

'You're a wicked, wicked woman,' says Hildred to me. 'You arouse the worst in her.'

'Is that your worst?' I inquired of the naughty, sobbing Nan, and she replied through her tears that it was not; but that she would kill me, if only she had a gun!

The hint of the least alteration in her mother's appearance, the suggestion that in years to come she runs the risk of becoming less youthful than now, will always provoke these demonstrations on the part of Nan. When I grow tired of seeing the poor mite plough up the skin of her pretty finger with her loathed and sticky needle it is thus I occasionally create a diversion.

She is a sweet-natured, funny little thing, and I love her to distraction. Have I told you this before? If not, you are sure to have guessed it. Having fallen out with me, and thrown things at me, she will be miserable until we are friends again.

To-day, after the above-mentioned typical fracas, she came presently, sauntering with a careful effect of carelessness, into my neighbourhood again. The words which she wished to address to me she set to an improvised chant and sang to the birds and flowers:

> *'Oh, I am very glad to be here,' she piped.*
> *'Very glad to be in this lovely place.*
> *There isn't no one here that is old or ugly,*
> *Or has wrinkles and grey hair.*
> *All is pretty, like the flowers,*
> *And I love them very much.'*

Wishing to see what would be her next move, I seemed to take no notice of the first stanza of this hymn of peace.

She had begun by making a wide circle round me as she sang, but this had gradually narrowed, until now she was kicking the legs of my chair and treading on my dress, as still she sauntered around.

I shook the dust from my skirts. 'A cat, or some disagreeable animal is trampling my dress,' I remarked.

A glance of alarm shot from the corner of her eye; she chanted still, but with now a tremble in her voice:

> '*Oh, if I said the lady was old,*
> *It is a mistake.*
> *Or ugly and with wrinkles,*
> *It is a mistake.*
> *So young and pretty she is,*
> *She is as pretty as my dear mummy herself.*'

'What is that disagreeable noise?' I asked of the air. 'I think a large gnat must be buzzing in my ears. I should be grateful to some one to remove it from my neighbourhood at once.'

Choking back a sob, she walked, crestfallen, away, and I hardened my heart to watch her go.

Her mother, who, it seems, had observed this drama from afar, came to reproach me. 'Oh, how can you be so cruel, Cousin Charlotte!' she said.

She went to peep through the window, and presently reported that the darling was writing a letter.

'Let her do it. It will be good for her, educationally,' I said. For to drive Nan Valetta to her copy-book is almost as big a task as to keep her at her needle.

Presently Ethel appeared bearing a massive-looking document on a salver. Not finding an ordinary envelope to her hand, the little rascal had seized on one of those foolscap ones I use for MSS. In one corner, in that curious calligraphy which is her laboured best, was written:

> '*Mrs. Sharlot Pol,*
> *Riter.*'

Within, almost lost in the profundity of the envelope, was a folded scrap of notepaper on which was written by a pen which had scratched, and sprayed and stuck, and performed every evil trick that pens which are not boons and blessings can effect, was the following script:

'If you do not lov me enny more, say so. I shud have thot no body who was so pritty would tese a litel gurl.'

'You have the heart of a nether mill-stone!' the tearful mother ejaculated, as I announced through laughter to the waiting handmaid that there was no answer.

But at the same moment the writer of the missive, hovering near to watch its effect, flew at me with a howl, and hung upon my neck with a 'You do love me! You know you love me! You wicked, teasing *ugly* old woman!'

To George

A HORRID thing has happened.

You remember our Clemmy? He who sucked the eggs or carried them home for custards? He is in prison.

You will say, of course, bearing the eggs in mind, it is his proper place. But then, you have not seen Clemmy, and don't know what a fine, decent-looking young animal he is; with the making in him of a good soldier, sailor – a good anything, in fact, where he could have been trained, and under discipline, and above all *kept at work*.

Alas for our broken resolutions, our good intentions which never do more than give us a false impression of our own character! What use is there now in my going to the lad's mother, and saying to her: 'I have seen your son standing about idle; I have been sorry. I knew it could not be safe for a big, strong fellow like that to be at Satan's service. I was going to take him back to watch Syers cutting the lawn again.'

This I really had intended – or thought I had intended – doing. Done, it would have saved Clement, at any rate for the time.

As it was, he has been allowed to take his chance; idle, while other sturdy, full-blooded young men were busy battling down the least desirable part of them (unknown to themselves, perhaps), digging, carrying, loading; idle, through the warmth of the day, the glare of the sun; the forces of Nature and spring-time, visible and invisible, working around him. The one thing apparently idle in creation.

I did not remember this in relation to Clemmy. Now he is in prison.

Last night when he, not having earned a crust of the bread he had eaten, had gone to bed with the rest, leaving his mother sitting up to mend the stockings which must be put on whole and clean to-morrow – for it is on the Sabbath I write these horrid things – there came a knock upon the outer door.

Opening it, Mrs. Moore found a policeman there; could dimly see in the darkness another seated in the cart beyond the garden-gate.

'Where is Clemmy?' the man at the door asked. For Bullet has drunk and laughed and sung with the boy at the public-house, and to him also he is 'Clemmy.'

'What d'ye want wi' my Clemmy?'

'Just a word with 'm, missus.'

'Yer can't have it, this time o' night, then. My Clemmy, he's a-bed.'

The policeman pushed past her, struggling to keep him back, and was presently in the second bedroom. There are only two in that cottage; in one sleep all the eight boys, I suppose; Laura and her baby and her mother in the other.

Can you picture the startled awaking; the lifting of one heavy young head after another from the pillow; the stupid, dazed stare at the policeman with his lantern?

It was only Clemmy who did not awake. The officer went to his bedside, laid a hand upon his shoulder, whispered a word or two in his ear.

Then Clemmy obediently arose, put himself into his best clothes, and, speaking not a word, making no resistance, mounted the cart and went away through the soft shades of night, seated between his acquaintance Bullet, and the policeman who was strange to him.

Clemmy, it seems, had applied for the third time for work at the Chisholms' farm, that day, and been refused. He had then betaken himself to a distant field where the last of Mr. Chisholm's barley stacks was standing and set fire to it. It was burnt to the ground.

He is to be brought before the magistrates to-morrow.

You may be sure the little virago of a mother was not so docile as her favourite son, but cursed, and raved, and fought the policemen; tried, finally, to go to prison with the boy.

While the rest were at church I went this morning to visit this miserable woman. For I have learnt that in Dulditch the poor do not desire in their grief the privacy it is our privilege to command at such time, but which they could not compass if they would. They do not mind how many strangers stand around the death-bed of their dearest, watching the progress of dissolution, making aloud comments on the well-known signs. They regard it as a slight to living and to dead, if you decline to go to look upon their corpses. To provide money, where, in time of trouble, you know it to be sorely needed, earns no gratitude from the benefited. 'She never come a-nigh me' will be remembered as a grudge against the benefactor.

The poor mother lifted to me as I entered the face of hatred she turns on all the world. She was alone in the little kitchen, freshly cleaned for the Sabbath, but for Laura's baby which lay beside her in the linen basket turned cradle. She listened in sullen silence to my few words of sorrow for her, and my poor attempt at consolation. To my remorseful offers of help, and anxious inquiries as to what I could do for her, she offered no reply, but presently burst into wild, incoherent, sobbing eulogy of the wretched boy.

'As good a lad as ever walked the arth, and as harmless. Allust keerful of his clo'es, and niver without a shillin' in 's pocket. Not one to drink away his wages as he'd arned honest as any man; at wark, arly and late, when he'd got it to du. But stan' to ra'son when 'twas took away from 'm he couldn't wark.'

I made her a present of money – I was ashamed to offer it, but what else could I offer? –

'Ye kin put it down,' she said sullenly, repeating the formula in familiar use. Her grief at least is genuine. No amount of money at this stage would console. I do not think she knew if I had given her five pounds or five pence.

'He's up to-morrer,' she said, as I was leaving her. I gathered she meant before the magistrates.

'You will not go?'

'I *sholl!* I sh'll ast them to dale with 'm at oncet. I sh'll tell 'em I can sweer he never done it; that he niver was out o' my sight all day, not till he laid his innercent hid on th' piller at night. They'll ha' to take my ward for it; and I sh'll bring my boy home wi' me to-morrer night.'

'You'll do him no good by going, and you'll put yourself to great pain,' I urged.

'I'm a-goin',' she said.

As I reached the door she flung herself round on her chair, hid her face on its hard back, and burst into noisy, choking crying. 'Oh, I can't bear it! I can't bear it!' she cried.

It all makes me miserable, George. Oh, if I only had kept Clement to look on at Syers, sticking the sweet peas, or planting the rings of asters, 'mocked' by ten-week stocks, in the long borders on either side the drive!

I do not, so far, discover in the peasant class that impulse of which I have heard, to stick chivalrously to each other in misfortune. Not a word in defence of the wretched Clemmy have I heard to-day. The idea that he will 'get the lash' has taken hold of the imagination of his friends, and appears to please them mightily.

'Him that have never had so much as a finger laid on 'm in 's life, now he'll ketch it; and sarve 'm right,' one old woman declared. Another who had heared tell his sentence would be five yare, for her part hoped they'd make it ten.

Even Syers, who had affably acquiesced in the young fellow's idle lounging through the hours at his side, and had upheld him in his stealing of my eggs, is on the side of the majority to-day.

'He allust was a ill-dispoged one, Clemmy were,' he remarked; and added, that if so be as the warmint were a-goin' to git the cat, he wished that he might be present to see 'em a layin' of it on.

'I always thought you and Clement were good friends,' I remonstrated.

Syers raised himself from his stooping position, scraped his cheek with the knife with which he was cutting the asparagus, looked slowly around.

'I niver wanted no piece o' wark – no wor-r-rds wi' one o' my pardeners,' he explained; 'I kep' all close. But I han't no opinion o' Clemmy, come to th' truth on't; and yet I never hadn't.'

He cut another head or two of asparagus. 'He were a wonnerful high-minded chap, Clemmy were,' he remarked, straightening himself and gazing past me as if, unconscious of my presence, he was indulging in soliloquy. 'Says I to him, "Clemmy," I says, "there's rough weather a-comin'. Rain and wind," I say, "for I see the double cherry i' yer mother's hidge a-blow. Never," I say, "have I knowed that theer double cherry to bring aught but the warst o' weather while 'tis a-blow." "The tree i' my mother's hidge," Clemmy he made answer, a-ketchin' of me up, nasty-like, "ain't all to thank for th' stormy weather, nayther." "Oh, ain't it?" I say. "You're wholly walcombe," I say, "to yer opinion; I'll kape mine. But ef so be as I was Squire o' th' parish I'd order that theer double cherry in yer mother's hidge to be took down on the chancest of it."'

To George

IT has been a lovely Sabbath-day, this that Clemmy has passed for his first day in prison. We have spent every hour of it beneath the cloudless blue of the sky. The lilacs, purple plumed and white, are in full bloom, for the past week; clean and unstained still; I have been thinking, as their perfume has come to me, of the lilacs that grew in the gardens of Torrens Square where we lived when you were born. Your father and I were very happy there, in those far-off days, before I had written my first book, before many patients had come to him, when we were poor and young and anxious, with our lives ahead of us, and the splendid joy of living in our hearts. They soon grew shabby and grey and smoke-stained, the poor lilacs in the square; yet their blossoming time was dear to us.

'Lottie, I caught a whiff of the lilacs this morning,' your father would say –'

Well, no lilacs will ever be quite like them again to me, but the flower has remained my favourite. And if I die in lilac-tide, my dear George, I pray you to put a wreath of the blooms upon my grave.

Above the gold and brown wallflowers the bees are humming; singing 'of summer in full-throated ease' the nightingales have been 'going it' all day long. In the avenue by the church the horse-chestnuts, Hildred tells me, are in bloom, but the oak-tree's leaves are brown still, and those of the ash scarcely green as yet. Every beech is like a gigantic plant of maidenhair; each black branch and tiny twig still showing through the airy fairy green.

Nan, as I write, has hurled herself upon me with the excited announcement that there is a rose, full-blown, upon the Gloire de Dijon which is trained by the kitchen window. May she climb on a chair to gather it?

She is so pretty to-day, in her muslin frock. The white ribbon which ties her hair back has fallen off, and the dark thick little mane is tossing wildly; her cheeks are deliciously moist and pink, the gold eyes are shining.

'Yes. Take my rose; take everything. All I've got.'

Five minutes afterwards I find my one poor rose dropped unnoticed on the garden path. I call to Major Barkaway as he walks there with Hildred, but am too late to save it from the unheeding tread of that 'dull swain' in 'his clouted shoon.'

He turns his head momentarily to me when I shout to him, but goes on chattering to Hildred without pausing to inquire into the cause of my disturbance.

The bells are ringing for evening church; but the Major, who never hitherto missed a service, still hangs around poor Mrs. Valetta, boring his victim with his oft-told, rubbishy tales. To think that such a woman must endure such a proser, in so fair a scene!

A little wind has arisen; just enough to set the pale heads of the jonquils and narcissuses (I can't possibly think of them as narcissi) nodding behind the tall box-borders Syers so despises. The low branches of the beeches sway and bow and swing with the most exquisite grace. Ah! Hildred, and Nan, and Nan's little maid, scampering with the child in and out of the Japonicas and Rhibes in the shrubbery, are in keeping with the sunshine and all the fresh, young loveliness of the time. He – the wearisome Barkaway – and I have our places too, of course; but in the shade – in the shade, my dear, dear boy.

Hear him for a moment, dear George, as they pass:

'She was a Trant, you remember: daughter of the Honourable Charles; granddaughter, of course, of Lord Soppet. I once said to her – ah, that's rather an amusing story, I will tell you that afterwards – But, as I was saying, her husband was down at Aldershot with me one day. "Look here, Barkaway," said he to me –'

'Hildred,' I called, 'come here, and listen to the nightingale. He's on that nut-bough above the laurel. He's been trying vainly, Major, to get a word in.'

'A few years ago,' the Major remembers, 'when I was staying with Algy Pelt down in Hampshire – he was member then; fine old historic mansion, and that sort of thing – "Shut your window, Barkaway," Algy said to me, "or you won't sleep for the infernal din of the nightingales." I was young then, and thought I liked 'em. Kept the window open. But, hang it all, whether 'twas the nightingales, or whether 'twas the black coffee I'd been fool enough to take, which never suited me even in those days, I never got a wink. At three in the morning, I remember, I had to get up, and close the window.'

And so on.

Hildred makes her escape; presently reappears; her white dress replaced by one of gauzy black; the long veil which proclaims her condition of widowhood depending from her hat; her prayer-book in her hand.

'Hullo! Church?' the Major cries, with a crestfallen look.

'But you have told me you are staying away. I thought it my duty to fill your place in the congregation about which the Vicar is so anxious.'

Barkaway makes for a chair beneath my tree with a dull and beaten air. 'I am writing to my son,' I say. 'Be so good, will you,

Major, as to see Mrs. Valetta through the meadow path. She is a valiant person, and not at all afraid of cows, but on such an evening as this they have the habit of regarding one at close quarters with so interested an air. It is embarrassing to the stoutest heart.'

He goes, of course, with alacrity. I laugh when I think of Hildred's reproachful glance at me. Nan and I stand at the gate to watch them cross the shadowed road and gain the path which makes, through the tall buttercups of the Chisholms' meadow, the short way to church.

Such an elegant, eloquent figure, the young woman in her mourning dress. A spacious baldness shows beneath the Major's straw hat and above the scant fringe of carefully brushed hair. He has a military carriage, as I have said; but I notice that his knees are a little inclined to knock as he walks.

'Dear Mummy!' Nan ejaculates, following the beloved parent with her eyes. 'Don't you love my Mummy better than any one in the world, Gran?'

'No. I don't.'

'Who do you love better in the world than my Mummy, Gran?'

'I'd rather see her walking through it with some one else, Nan.'

'With my own dear daddy – of course,' Nan says, under the impression she is reading my thoughts. 'That can't be, Gran, because, you see, my own dear daddy is in heaven. I tell you how I'd like extremely to see her going through the meadow, Gran. On a white prancing horse. And by her side a prancing white pony on which is seated me; and –'

'I won't be bothered about your horses; you're as big a bore with your horses as Major Barkaway with his "county people."'

'I should have thought a Gran would have liked a little girl to talk about what pleases her –'

'Tell me about your daddy.'

'He was the dearest on earth.'

'Yes. But what sort of a dear. Was he tall and handsome, for instance, like – Major Barkaway?'

Nan's chin is lifted haughtily. 'He was as different as different from Major Barkaway.'

'Like me, then?'

She gravely considers me. 'He wasn't so fat as you, Gran, of course.' (He had the figure of a tub when I saw him last.) 'Nor yet he wasn't old like you.' (He was, it happens, exactly ten years older, but

I don't grudge poor Nan her illusions.) 'And he was much more extremely politer in his conversations.'

To George

NAN has gone off to 'sleepin'-by'; the setting sun is sending streamers of red across the pale green and opal tints of the evening sky. A great lull that breathes of the Sabbath-day has fallen on all; even the nightingale in the nut-bush for the moment is still. I have wrapped myself in a shawl and gone back to my table beneath the wide branches of the pine-tree, and am going, my dear boy, to finish this budget of scribbling about nothing to you.

Those valuable notes which my letters to you were to contain – where are they? For that book you wished me to write I find the material does not grow under my hand. The daily life is not devoid of interest – ever I find myself becoming unduly interested in its small events – but is it worth recording? The country and the country people have the reverse of a stimulating effect on me. Even my powers of observation seem to slumber. One day is so like another; the people, growing from generation to generation together, as trees grow, are so alike – what after all is there to chronicle. What – ?

Hark! I hear the click of the gate. I recognize the martial tread. Here he comes; past the rockery by the gate, where the aubretias, the arabis, the alyssums make great patches of purple, of white, of yellow, among the stones; between the wide beds bordering the little drive; my ruse to be rid of him at the expense of poor Hildred was after all but of short avail. Ah, George, my dear, who is that who has well counselled, 'Love your neighbours, but pull not down your hedge'? Good-bye for to-night. He is here; Barkaway.

'The Philistines be upon thee,' I say aloud, safe in the certainty he will not apply the quotation –

To George

MAJOR BARKAWAY did not long leave me in doubt as to the reason of his return. He has not had the opportunity for any prolonged conversation on the subject of Hildred, she being continually present. Having seen her safely into church, he has seized the opportunity, therefore, and scurried back to question me unblushingly about her.

He began with almost indecent haste as he took the wicker chair beyond my writing-table.

'I forget how long you said Mrs. Valetta had been a widow?'

'Did I mention any period? I think not. I do not burden my memory unnecessarily, Major.'

'Her husband was an American who settled in Hampshire, I think I understood?'

'She and her husband lived in Hampshire, certainly. When they weren't in New York or Italy.'

He crossed his legs, joined his fingers above his chest, his small blue eyes looking into space across their tips. The subject was one, easy to see, in which he was keenly interested.

'The Valettas, of course, are people of wealth and repute. Every one has heard of the Valettas of Hampshire.'

'Perhaps. As for me, until Hildred announced that she was going to marry one of them, I confess I did not know they existed. Not that I mean for a moment to impeach their respectability. There are some thousands of respectable people in Hampshire of whom I have never heard. Nor you either, probably, Major?'

He demurred to that. 'When you are in touch with people of a certain set you get to know other people of – a certain set. In a London Club of any standing, for instance, you are bound to come across the people of people who – *are* people.'

'And at your Club you came across people who knew the Valettas?'

He would not commit himself. 'I may have done. The old man – John Valetta – was of course a man of some importance. The son – ? The son – ?'

'Also John. What of the son, Major?'

He did not directly reply. 'It is the Hobbleboys who have been asking questions,' he said. He separated and joined, joined and separated the tips of his fingers and thumbs as they arched across his shirt front. 'It seems that several years ago they met the Valettas at Geneva. They, in fact, were staying at the same hotel with them.'

'How funny! I can't picture the Hobbleboys anywhere but in Dulditch. Sad awakenings must await them when they stir out of it. I suppose at Geneva, when they announced that they were the Hobbleboys of Dulditch, no one was startled?'

He ignored my remark as beneath notice. 'As a matter of simple fact the Hobbleboys' social status would carry them pretty well anywhere, if their fortune was equal to their position,' he said drily.

He meditated with an abstracted gaze for a few seconds and presently asked me if I knew anything of the French language. I having owned the soft impeachment, he proceeded to explain to me, in a voice grave and hushed as became the solemnity of the subject, that the Hobbleboys were of Norman descent, had come over with William the Conqueror, in fact, their name being simply a corruption of Haut-du-bois.

His blue gaze held mine for a moment in a cold triumph. 'Top of the tree. Tip-top,' I murmured, translating freely. Having produced in me a sufficiently reverent frame, presently he went on to state that he was acting to-night as a kind of emissary of the noble family.

'If your friend – you tell me she is your cousin only by adoption – is the lady the Hobbleboys met in Geneva ten years ago, they would wish to renew acquaintance.'

'But Mrs. Valetta, we must remember, may not wish anything of the kind.'

He condemned me coldly with a falling eyelid. 'She is a woman of the world,' he said. 'Being at Dulditch, she could not be blind to the advantages of a friendship with the Hobbleboys.'

To George

IT was the Rector who was good enough to pilot Mrs. Valetta home by the short cut through the buttercups. The Major and I had talked ourselves into a state of ravening hunger, and a very pleasant meal we had, in my low-ceilinged long dining-room, its three windows wide open to the night and the stars. Cook had made an excellent salad for the cold lamb; there was gooseberry tart and custard, and of course a syllabub; a sweet I insist on, in its native county, for there is an old-world savour in the sound of it, and its name brings back to me all sorts of frolic scenes and rural romances.

The Rector was pale – the Sunday 'takes it out of him,' he says; he gets better-looking; his face was almost Napoleonic last night. He loves the good things of the table, and he loves a joke too, if it is sufficiently apparent; and he is not above laughing at other members of the cloth, if he treats himself as a serious matter. He is, in short, an agreeable man enough, if his sister is not there to exploit him; and I begin to think Hildred finds him so.

Hildred was very adorable in that gauzy black of hers. Sufficiently gauzy, be it understood, for gleams of white shoulders and white arms to show through. Black, let me tell you, my very dear boy, is most becoming to black-haired women; and never have Mrs. Valetta's smooth, white-skinned face, and blue, black-lashed eyes looked fairer than now in her mourning garb.

I think she is so attractive by the reason of the fact that she makes no apparent effort to attract. She ate her supper last night with excellent appetite, smiled at the efforts of the Rector to amuse her, even laughed now and again when it was humanity to do so. But she is by no means what one would call an 'agreeable rattle'; she is prodigal of no glances from those beautiful orbs of hers, and makes no effort to 'take men by her eyelids,' however that deed may be accomplished. It was, I am sure, with the like cool abstraction, the same gentle air of aloofness that she regarded the poor curate at Cannes, travelling about on all fours, the scaramouch Nan on his back.

But woe to him who thinks, because of that calm demeanour of gentle dignity, that unmoved exterior, that Hildred Valetta is apathetic, or shallow of brain and heart. She was quicker to say what she felt and thought in the old days. Now, like a wise woman, she acts on the lesson life has taught her.

'Hildred,' I said to her, 'do not, I beg, let the communication I am about to make unhinge you, or affect your appetite. On the authority of Major Barkaway I have it that the Hobbleboys wish to renew acquaintance with you.'

'And who are the Hobbleboys, pray?' asks Hildred, who had stayed in their parish for three weeks.

The Major stared, incredulous. The Rector laughed to himself, his shoulders hunched, his head bent over his plate.

'It seems you met them once at Geneva; stayed in the same hotel with them,' I explained.

'But there were probably a good many people in the hotel at Geneva.'

'You would have been nearly sure to remember the Hobbleboys,' the Major said.

'Why?' Hildred is not quite so ignorant of the pretensions of these distinguished people as it pleased her to appear to be. 'Tell me in what they are remarkable,' she requested.

It was laughable to hear the efforts of the two men who see them every day to describe the pair. Have you noticed that men and women, generally, have not the least idea what their nearest and dearest are (physically) like? Call upon them for a description, and you will find them quite unable to furnish one detail that is recognizable.

'They "carry a high colour" as the poor people say, and – and are rather like other people, I suppose,' the Rector admitted at last, with a little evident surprise it should be so.

'They have the air of people of breeding,' Major Barkaway contributed, with the tone of one who knows.

'Yes. But of what sex are they?' Hildred asked. 'If they are two men, I'd rather like to see them here; for Cousin Charlotte's sake. She is used to having a score or so of men at her feet, and misses them. If they're two women, I'd rather not be bothered with them. If they're man and wife, I'm indifferent. They can come or stay away.'

'Do I understand,' the Major solemnly asked, 'that I have your permission to say to Mr. and Mrs. Hobbleboy that you remember them in Geneva, and would be happy to have the pleasure of meeting them again?'

'Say nothing,' Hildred supplied. 'You see, in that hotel in Geneva – I forget its name – were probably a few nice people and a large quantity of people who weren't nice. I cannot possibly tell among which class these people you speak of might have been.'

Her attitude in this important matter impressed the Rector, I think. To afford to be indifferent to the favour of the Squire of Dulditch and his wife, how sure she must be of herself, how secure in her position! The Major was disappointed in her, I am sure. She had shown, in her slighting of this chance of an acquaintanceship which should have been the means of socially placing her, that ignorance of the essential in the scheme of Society which he had found to characterize me.

'But I never remember your staying in Geneva with your husband?' I said to Hildred, when the men were gone.

'I never did,' admitted that wicked person. 'He used to go there with his first wife, and never wanted to go again, he said.'

'Then it was the poor first those people met?'

'Undoubtedly. And if they have never heard she died, and my poor John married again, and married me, what a pleasing mystification for your Hobbleboys, Charlotte Poole!'

I would not be balked of finishing my scribblings to you to-night, my dear boy, so here I am in the 'still hour of thinking,' the lamp on my table, beneath the wide-spreading branches of my great tree, pen in hand.

A few stars are out in the sapphire of the sky; the melancholy bleat of a lamb comes now and then from the Church meadow, near at hand. The nightingale on the nut-bush has wakened to song again, and is answered by another in the long plantation at the back of the Chisholms' house. I can hardly distinguish, in the delicious combination, separate scents which fill the air. The most sweetly penetrating perhaps is that of the white clover just bursting into bloom in a field beyond my little orchard; but with this a scent of May in the hedge mingles, a scent of wallflowers and narcissus in the flower-beds.

What a month May is! The darling of the twelve! The pet child of creation, sumptuously endowed. And for another year it is gone! Who shall say where that of next year may find me? Not here, I begin to be afraid. For, to be candid with you, George, although I delight in the novelty (to me) of life in this rural centre, although, filled with the beauty of flower and stream and tree, I could gladly fall asleep in the bosom of opulent Nature, I have a feeling it is more profitable that I keep myself awake. My mind, you recognize, isn't of the grand order. Not a jewel to shine in a dark place. It is of a metal which requires friction in order to do itself justice; contact with other minds, the daily rub and fret of everyday, bustling life. The Hobbleboys – the Haut-du-bois – I find them beginning to fill my mind as they do my letters –

Meanwhile, here is a perfect night – the last of May. It brings back to me the remembrance of another night in the same dear month when I was a girl of one-and-twenty, and you, my fine, formidable George, were a baby of *one*.

It had been very hot and dusty all the day, and the night was close, and your father was away, and you could not sleep. And I, who had been one of a large and lively home family, was tired of my own company. So, when bed-time came, and I found you crying and tossing in your crib, I told myself that your father forgot me for his patients, and your nurse forgot you for her supper. I took you up and dressed you, rejoicing in the fact that I could do it myself, alone, for I was jealous at that time of nurse, for whom you cruelly showed a decided partiality. Then I carried you out; and in the darkness and the cool air you were very still and very loving, clinging close to me, and looking at the stars with wide eyes.

I had had a great longing for the shade and the scents of the country, all that day, so I carried you to the garden in the Square, thinking that I would sit with you there beneath the trees, pretending (I was so young that I had not quite outgrown the child's favourite game of 'pretending') that London with its dusty streets, its monotonous crowds, its dismal, endless houses, was far away, and you and I in the heart of a wood in that 'country' of which I knew nothing, or how could I have hoped to find a semblance of it in a dreary London square? We were – you and I – to belong to no busy, forgetful husband and tyrant nurse. Only to each other.

But I had forgotten that the gates of the garden were kept locked, and that I had brought no key; so that when I had carried you so far I had to carry you back as I came, and to endure a scolding from your father who had returned and missed us, and a sulking from your nurse into the bargain.

As if you wanted to hear the silly tale! But the futile doings of that May night have, for some no-reason, always dwelt in my memory; and so at last I have written them down.

I wish you could know how dear you were when you clung, with an arm tight round my neck, and now and then an anxious, questioning 'Mummy?' – the only word you could speak – to satisfy yourself it was indeed your parent who was bearing you on that foolish escapade.

But being a man only, you naturally can never know these things.

Good-night, my dear thirty-four years old baby. Assure thyself I love thee dearly, and in every corner of my heart.

Fair – fair be the night to thee and sweet the morrow.

To George

THE first of June. Morning.

Hildred and Nan late to breakfast, which gives me time for one more word with you. I have been strolling, between my 'double ringes' of wallflowers, backwards and forwards from house to gate, waiting for them. They tell me, although we were complaining of rain such a little time ago, we want it badly now. But a heavy dew is upon the grass and flowers. The 'moist eyelids of the morn' seem scarcely lifted yet, and the sun bears little power. Mr. Chisholm was complaining yesterday that his young hay-seeds – those planted for next year's crop – are withering; I rejoice to see that they must this morning be drenched with dew.

The mother of the unfortunate lad Clemmy passed me as I stood by the gate. She was on her way to the magistrates' meeting, six miles off. Such a tragic, lonely figure, with its face of hatred and love. What an errand for a mother's feet to be set upon!

'I'm a-goin' to bring my Clemmy home ter-night,' she called out fiercely to me as she passed. 'Let 'em try to stop me if they kin; and let them as is my poor boy's enemies look out for theirselves.'

So she went on her way; with a face to blight the very flowers by the wayside, but with a mother's heart in her miserable breast, urging her to swear away man's or woman's honour or life, if that would get her back her son.

'I'll bring 'm back; don't, I'll let 'em ter know,' she muttered as she trudged along.

The first of June. Evening.

She did not bring him back. Starting for our drive this afternoon (the Major has been so slow in meeting with the horse which he undertook to procure for me, and the suitable coachman, that I have on my own responsibility and while I wait for the horse and man, hired a little pony and tub-car which sometimes I, and oftener Nan, drives) we overtook her, going back as she had gone forth, alone, having fought her hopeless fight, and perjured her poor soul in vain.

We thought it best not to stop to speak to her, and she did not turn her face to us, but walked with it set towards her unhappy home, her heart with her wretched offspring on his way to the County Gaol.

I hear she made a fearful scene in the magistrates' room, appealing, denouncing, blaspheming; while Clemmy, in his Sunday suit and red neck-tie, looked on, his silly smile upon his handsome face. He is committed for trial. They say he will get a five years' sentence.

To George

DAILY we are waited on by our two attendant knights.

Major Barkaway is supposed to be mine; and to humour Hildred, who enjoys poking her fun at me, I pretend to regard him in that light. That would be a curious kind of male animal who would admire old Charlotte Poole when Hildred Valetta was by! The Rector has given up making excuses for dropping in on us at all hours, and the Major, not dreaming, I suppose, that his company could be otherwise than acceptable, has never troubled to make an apology for his appearance. In the shelter of Hildred's gracious presence Bertha Flatt's cautious hostility has begun to put forth a friendlier growth.

For my part I am sorry to say I do not find Bertha to improve in interest on acquaintance. In the beginning there was always the hope that *something*, good or bad, was beyond the tightly pursed lips and the precise demeanour. Now that I am sure that nothing is there, I do not feel disposed to take any further trouble about her. She is not favourably affected by me, I fear; finds me frivolous, because I laugh at some of her falsities, and false because sometimes, to arouse her, I speak in the language of hyperbole. She is as meek-looking as a rabbit, but has the unbounded cheek of self-sufficiency and ignorance. I can never quite help the feeling that I am showing amazing condescension in talking to her, and she calmly reproves me for my errors with a sang-froid and a sententiousness that should be only ridiculous, but is, in spite of me, irritating.

The Rector preached a foolish sermon on the fifty-first psalm the other day, trying, in a blundering, half-frightened way, to excuse or to palliate the wrongdoing of the splendid singer. 'In every family,' I said to Hildred, as we came away, 'there is one favourite child who can do no wrong. David was the spoilt-darling of God.'

Bertha Flatt, who had joined us without my noticing, turned upon me from the other side of Mrs. Valetta a face of shocked offence.

'That is an extraordinary speech,' she said; 'and I do not consider it in very good taste.'

Why should I suffer this sort of impertinence, I ask you?

Should I remark, 'It rained a deluge yesterday,' she reproves me with a solemn 'Hardly a *deluge*, I think.' If I say, 'A dozen people told me,' she pulls me up with, 'Could you possibly, Mrs. Poole, have spoken to a dozen people on the subject?'

'Well, Cousin Charlotte, you show the poor thing you despise her; you can't wonder if she turns upon you,' Hildred says.

'The fact of it is,' I retort, 'you can endure the Flatt woman no more than I, and are only civil to her because – Oh, I know very well why you are civil to Bertha Flatt!'

'Then, perhaps you will be good enough to say,' Hildred demands with dignity. 'I beseech you do not spare me.'

'Because you want to make of her brother a bigger fool than he is at present,' I throw at her.

I meant that to rouse her, and it did.

'You are leading an agreeable life in this pleasant "land of drowsyhed," Charlotte Poole,' she said; 'amid charming sights and sounds; one might have hoped that the venom of your nature would have been lulled to rest, that the better part of it would unfold and expand. But with you the world still prevails. Give up The Cottage to Nan and me; go back to your quill-driving, your club, your literary coteries, your everlasting Shop, in town; for here you are becoming, I declare, as small and vindictive as Bertha Flatt herself.'

'Anything else? Finish with me, while you are about it.'

'As for this poor Rector: why need you harp on the fact to me that you find him fat, unenlightened, servile? He is really none of these things, conspicuously. He is, on the contrary, a pleasant companion. You have given him the entrée to your house; he wisely avails himself of the privilege, pretty often; and I, for my part, am very glad to see him there.'

'Yes. And if it were not for fear of me – you know you've a wholesome fear of me, Mrs. Valetta – you'd encourage him to the laying of his adipose tissue, his lack of learning, and his cure of souls, at your feet. I declare I positively am not quite certain you would disdain the offer.'

'At any rate, I shall not refuse the man till he asks me,' Hildred asserts, and puts an end to the matter.

But what, after all, is this tolerant spirit whose possession we are bidden to strive for? Its action is to compel us to put up with things and people which are a nuisance, a hindrance and a pest, when it is much healthier to hate them with all one's power, and to say so. Arrived at the end of life, we pride ourselves on having acquired something of this habit of mind, and we find, going to the bottom of it, that it is not tolerance so much as indifference which possesses us. No healthy, youthful, vigorous mind is tolerant. Tolerance is another name for Torpor.

This country parson, for whom I am supposed to exhibit a want of charity, for ever makes moan about the dullness of his life, its want of scope, of interest. This, if he took his calling seriously, I tell him, he should be ashamed to do. He answers me he takes it as seriously as the rest, with the exception, perhaps, of So-and-so and So-and-so, of such and such places (whose names and parishes I have forgotten), who are, he assures me, impossible fellows. When I could not accept that as a definition he could give no other. I take it, therefore, that in all probability they are the only men who should be 'possible' in this vocation.

I asked him the other day, when he was idling over my tea-table, why he had never married.

He was such a modest man, he said, that he had never dared to ask any woman to have him.

'And won't you never dare, then?' Nan inquired of him, who was standing as usual between his knees. She takes it for granted that it is her society which brings him daily to The Cottage, and believes it to be an intellectual feast for him to answer all her impertinent questions, ranging from such an one as the above to the fashion of his collar and waistcoat fastening, and to whether he cleans his teeth twice a day, as Mother insists on her doing.

'I never shall, till I'm pretty sure of being accepted,' he told her.

'But under those circumstances your proposal would be as good as an insult,' I pointed out.

'Why should a self-respecting man put himself in the absurd position of a rejected lover?' he inquired. 'Men are too servile. For my part, I should sink in my own estimation for ever, if, after flattering myself that a woman would marry me, I found she would not.'

'But that would be so good for you, Mr. Flatt.'

'What? To sink in my estimation of myself?'

'What an extraordinary remark!' said the sister, who also happened to be present, and glared at me.

The Rector laughed. 'You think I have a too good opinion of myself, Mrs. Poole? But that's very startling. Interesting, too. Now, I wonder if I have!'

'Of course you have not, Algernon,' Miss Flatt hastened to assure him. 'If it is possible in this world to be too modest I should say it is your failing.'

'But what does Nan say?' he inquired of that young person, who, never feeling called upon to adhere closely to the subject under discussion, replied that if he were to curl his hair a little at the front it would not look so thin, she thought.

Reporting the substance of this conversation to Hildred, I was able to assure her that her latest victim was waiting for encouragement; that before she had him at her feet she would have to show him that she wished him there.

'Then your anxious mind is set at rest, Cousin Charlotte!' was all she said. But I really think she was relieved. She has been keeping out of his way a little, lately.

Why don't you write and ask her, my dear George? That is, if you can't come and ask her. I am always urging this upon you, and you say nothing. I am not really afraid of the Flatt man; but she won't be in Dulditch for always, and in other places are men and men and men – all anxious, remember, to marry a pretty woman with a fortune.

She will have you, my dear boy, if you write to her. Write.

I know she expects it. She does not say so, of course; yet I know she does. For what are you waiting?

She has been telling me about a friend of hers who last year went out to New South Wales to marry the man to whom she was engaged. She had known him in England for a couple of months, had not seen him for three years, and went, quite happily, all those thousands of miles across the sea, to tie herself to him for life! Well, when she saw him she hated the sight of him; had the sense and the courage to tell him so; came back to England again; and married the man whom she met on the homeward voyage. If she had had a three years' probation in the second case, she would probably have found she hated the sight of that man too.

But does not this show that a woman should not be expected to cherish an affection, in absence, for long?

I told her that I did not blame her friend.

'Blame her!' she turned upon me. 'Her conduct was admirable. In her place I should probably have hated him as Edith did, but should have married him, all the same, rather than hurt his feelings.'

Hildred has a faithful heart, I know, and is a far nobler woman than she thinks herself; but a word to the wise. Love, above all the businesses of life, is one in which you must be bold – be bold – and evermore be bold: delay is nearly always fatal.

To George

AN old man is trimming the roadside grass outside my domain, to-day. I have been leaning on the gate, beneath the shade of the laburnum which overhangs it, to watch.

He is, I discover, the village politician. He tells me that in the alehouse, o' nights, he is called on, being the man of the company with book-larnin', to expound what he reads in the weekly local paper, and to set it forth in langwidge such as they, poor critters, can onderstand. He had made clear, he said, to his neighbours, marvelling at the doings of Parlyment, and a-wonderin' what Providence could have up His sleeve next, the workings of the Agricultural Small Holdings Act.

'Says I to my mates, "Hold on," I says. "We ain't a-goin' to stop here; 'taint i' th' nater o' things we should. Theer's land for us, I say, for them as want it. We ha'n't only to ask, and we kin have. But who du want it? Du yu, Ben Warren? Du yu, Willum Bain? Du I? Wha's the good," I says, "o' land to us, that hain't got a horse to plough it with, or seed to sow it with, and no money to get 'em. But hold on," I says agin. "We ain't a-goin' ter stop at land. That ain't what Parlyment ha' got in 's hid. We're a-goin' on to have our share of other things, 'sides land. What yu set yur heart on, arst for, I say, bold enough; and gold, or honours, or prop'ty of any sort – you'll ha't."

' "Yer don't say so, Joe Stark!" says they to me, lookin' dazed like. "'Tha's what Parlyment ha' got in 's hid consarnin' us, I say; leastways 'tis how I read th' matter."'

Joe Stark is a loquacious old man; he makes onslaught on the nettles with a couple of swishes of his scythe, which, judging by the absence of effect on the nettles, appears to be of phenomenal bluntness; then holding it poised for a third attack, and staring under overhanging hairy brows, not at me but at the hedge, goes on:

Had I heared the piece o' wark Parlyment had made 'twixt old Winch at th' Low Farm and his wife's sister?

I had not, and with a scornful chuckle at the hedge he proceeds to enlighten me.

'Soon's the man's wife were dead, he fixed up that one o' th' t'other gals, the woman's sister as hadn't got no husban' of 'er own, should take up her abode with 'm, nateral like, to look arter 'm, and give 'm his wittles. Wholly content she were, and give up her sitivation i' th' shares, an' was agog to make th' journey. Then come this here new law. "No," says Winch, "stop wheer y' are," he say. "I ain't a-goin' to put no temptation i' my way," he say. "I'm wake," he say, "wheer women is, and the law bein' as 'tis, the risks is as great with a sister-in-law as wi' th' rest of 'em, as I see the matter."'

He spat upon each hand, grasped the scythe more firmly, and bending to the task, made another ineffectual sweep with the implement.

'Parlyment,' he summed up the matter to himself, 'kin make laws we 'ont deny; but 'taint to be looked for as Parlyment have eyes all round ter see th' workin' of 'em. They never give a thought, when they was a-tarnin' out that ac', to Dan'l Winch's sister-in-law.'

I asked Joe Stark his age, and hearing that he was seventy-three, inquired if he was not thankful for the Old Age Pension.

He gave a vindictive sidelong glance at me from his small, bright eyes, and pausing in his work, addressed the hedge again. 'I don't git it,' he said. 'Come th' winter I kin only du odd jobs, here and theer, and ha' ter go on th' parush. Summers, I kin contrive ter keep at wark, but come th' winter I'm hard put to't. This here pension – I'll tell ye how 'tis wi't – them that want it can't ha't, and them that ha't don't want it. This here pension,' he continued, and swished irritably at the tall tops of the nettles – 'theer's things to be seen wi' this here pension as we aren't yet aweer of. Folks was allust liars, but t'rough theer a-settin' their hearts on th' five shillun a week, blowed if they ain't fit to lie theirselves into hell.

'Look at Dulditch,' he continued. 'Theer's seven of 'em git it. Two ha' got a right, I ain't a-denyin'. T'others have it t'rough lies. "All I arn is so much a week," old Carter he say, what's warrener along o' Chisholm's. Du he say his house is rent free? du he spake of his harvest? of what's give him? of what he pick up, lawful like? of what he take wheer he can? "Wheer's yer Post-Office bank-book?" the man what come round he say. "I han't got no book, nor yet nothin' i' th' bank," old Carter he say. "Han't ye seft nothin'?" says they to him. "Not a penny," says he to them. Lerrem look onder th' old beggar's bed! Hundreds theer! Drawed out o' th' bank afore th' man come round.'

Joe Stark moistened once more, after his simple, effectual fashion, his horny palms, made another slow swoop upon the nettles still defying him. 'This here pension is a-goin' to be the ruin o' th' banks as I look at th' matter,' he concluded. 'Them as ha' made shift ter save 'll hide th' matter. 'Taint ter be looked for they'll hamper theirselves wi' bank-books ter tell th' tale.'

To George

THE Major sought me in an hour when he knew Hildred and Nan were taking their morning walk. He was solemn and confidential.

Did I not think it a pity that Mrs. Valetta should reject the Hobbleboys' offer – it was really as good as an offer – to call and make her acquaintance? 'You see, Mrs. Poole, she comes without an introduction to any one, and is unknown, and therefore at a disadvantage.'

'She comes to stay at my house.'

He tapped the dry tips of his fingers together in an eloquent silence.

'Being under the wing of the Hobbleboys would offer to her social possibilities.'

'As far as I have seen of your neighbourhood your social possibilities do not exist.'

On the contrary, the neighbourhood was rich in social advantages – *to the elect*, he intimated, with his air of being specially in a position to speak, but refraining out of consideration for me.

He thought of saying to the Hobbleboys, to whom he had not as yet communicated Mrs. Valetta's discouraging reception of their advances, that that lady, although not actually recalling them at Geneva, hoped to be able to do so on being confronted with them. In order to give her this desired opportunity she looked forward to the pleasure of making their acquaintance.

'Look here, Major!' I said. 'If you set your Hobbleboys to call at my house any more, I give you fair notice, Syers shall have instructions to stone them off the place.'

The poor man is absolutely devoid of a sense of humour, and has gone away, in all probability, thinking that I meant it.

'Living the life of recluses is all very well for you and me,' he said, as I saw him off the premises. 'But for a beautiful young woman of – I suppose – fortune – ?'

He paused. I said no word.

'Of even small fortune?' I gazed before me in silence.

'She is a young woman of fortune?'

'I really cannot tell you the amount of her income, Major.'

'But every one knows old John Valetta was a rich man. He had a son.'

103

'Also John Valetta. You have been refreshing your memory, Major Barkaway.'

'The son married disreputably.'

'He also is dead. De Mortuis – Major.'

'But the Hobbleboys, having met Mr. and Mrs. Valetta at Geneva, and having taken the trouble to learn these few particulars, are interested to learn more.'

'Indeed?'

'They – knowing I have knocked about a good deal and met several people – are asking me if I could tell them what had become of the widow of the son.'

'And could you? By the way, have you noticed that the Gloire de Dijon over the kitchen window is now in full bloom? Come with me to the long walk to see what a sight of beauty the Carmine Pillar is.'

He comes, but declines to admire the rose, finding fault with Syers' training of its branches. He detects flaws, as he looks into the pinky yellow hearts of the Gloire de Dijon. He promises me one of his own blooms, in order that I may gaze upon perfection.

Hildred was coming down the road, through its sunlight and shadow, as we reached the gate, a bunch of long-stalked buttercups and ragged robin in her hand; Nan, short-skirted, long-legged, behind her, the whip in her hand by which with a whack upon her mother's dress she reminds her that they are 'playing horses,' and that she must, since she will not run, at least jib, or shy, or caracole, to show she remembers the game.

She is of the order of women, whose fortune, whose antecedents even, should not value a jot in the eyes of any man worth his salt. She is so gracious to this poor old masquerader that if he, as well as the Rector, does not lose his head over her, it will not be, as I tell her, her fault. With perfect attention she listens to his again and again repeated, stupid tales; asks his advice; agrees with him that his roses when he produces them are beyond comparison better than any roses by her, hitherto, beheld; calls on him to take her side, which he speedily does, in any argument between her and me. When a rarely exercised politeness keeps him chained to my side while he longs to be by hers, his little blue eyes lose their coldness, glitter, follow her about the garden.

As for me, I am by this time sick unto death of him. By taking his advice in the matter of a small investment he has caused me to lose several hundred pounds; the commissions he has undertaken for me, nearly forcing his services upon me, still remain unfulfilled. As a man of business I have proved him to be a pretender; as a man of the world he is laughable.

'He pays me a little natural attention, and you are jealous,' Hildred says.

'He is a snob; and he is a bore.'

'But look, Charlotte Poole, at those shabby clothes, so anxiously cared for; those wristbands, clean, but pathetically frayed; that occasionally remembered, generally forgotten military air. Think of the aspirations he probably had at his starting, and to what they have come. And remember always that such as his fate is he accepts it, and never grumbles at Fortune or complains.'

'I am weary to death of him. He is a snob; and he is a bore.'

To George

I HAVE been, perhaps, so far, a little disappointed in the East Anglian peasant, of whom, relying on the poetic account I have read of him, I doubtless expected too much. Yet I do not make the mistake to imagine that, in the space of three months' limited acquaintanceship, I have formed a reliable estimate of his character; or, of a subject extraordinarily suspicious and distrustful, learned the heart's hidden secret. Because an ungracious, irresponsive sullenness baffles me in the effort to establish a better understanding, I know it may only be the mere husk, the protective armour, of the Man behind it whom I am not yet permitted to see.

I went to-day into the bedroom of a poor woman who is dying of cancer. It is not my first visit. The room is poor and squalid in the extreme. Yet now I found the broken, whitewashed walls made beautiful by some great spreading branches of the newly-leaved beech-trees hung upon them.

'I was a-sayin' to my husban' I shouldn't never see the laves a-comin' out on the trees agin,' the poor creature explained. 'An' when he come home for 's dinner to-day he'd brought me these here branches. "Nail 'em wheer I can look at 'em, Dan," I say; and he took and nailed 'em to th' wall.

'I know wheer they growed,' she went on presently. 'They're off them trees by th' roadside, 'twixt here and the village. Times, I ha' walked beneath 'em when I was a little 'un, runnin' to school, and later, when I ha' been a-goin' to th' shop. Las' time I dragged myself theer 'twas Autumn. Th' dead laves was to th' tops o' my butes. I shorn't walk theer no more.

'I lay here a-thinkin' of it: "Th' laves 'll be a-showin' green," says I to my husban'. He agreed as how they was; an' when he come home he'd brought the branches. They ha' been company.'

I thought, among the branches on the shabby wall a poem lurked, George.

To George

THE play they have on now is having an enormous run at the Diadem. They have therefore, for the second time, postponed Beaumont's version of my *Splendid Failure*. This is disappointing. I haven't the patience in such matters I possessed in my youth. Life, since your father's death, seems to me to be so uncertain – an obvious fact which, nevertheless, until then had not come home to me – that I want to grasp my good things, and have a terror of delay.

The book itself, however, is going like wild-fire. A parcel of copies of the *sixth edition* was sent to me from my publisher this morning.

When Bertha Flatt came in to my little morning room the package of books, untied, was lying there.

'You have some new books,' she said. 'How very nice! I wonder if one by Miss — is there? I have been told she writes such pretty books. Not merely nonsense, you know, like most. Everybody, I hear, reads them.'

'I'm afraid these aren't pretty,' I said; 'but I'm happy to say a few people read them.'

Hildred picked up one of the books from the heap. '*A Splendid Failure*, by Charlotte Poole,' she read out, in that tone of possessive pride she has when she speaks of me and my works. 'You've read it, of course, Miss Flatt?'

Of course she had not.

'Oh, enviable Miss Flatt! Take a copy – one of these is intended for me, and I will lend it – lock yourself in your room, or lose yourself with it among some trees where no one can find you, and read, and read, and read, from start to finish.'

'Thank you,' said Miss Flatt slowly. She eyed doubtfully the tendered volume. 'If it is a pretty book, and not simply nonsense, you know, like the rest, I shall be pleased to read it.'

For all that, she forgot it when she went away, and that absurd Hildred pursued her with it, and forced the poor book into her reluctant hand. She refuses to believe that Bertha Flatt is a Fish among women, without mind or brain or heart.

She came down this morning to tell us a wedding was to take place at two o'clock to-day; we both had expressed the wish to be present at a Dulditch wedding.

Hildred gathered all the white roses off a standard now in full bloom, which she made into a bouquet and sent to the bride. One among the many disappointments of the ceremony as we witnessed it was the fact that she did not honour us by carrying our gift, but held in her white cotton fingers, awkwardly extended, a couple of hot-house flowers backed by a leaf of maiden-hair fern; the young person who officiated as bridesmaid bearing an exactly similar arrangement with the same unnatural stiffness.

Flowers from the hedge, or the field, or the garden, are never seen at rural weddings now, I find; the bruised and half-dead blossoms supplied for a few pence by the florist at the market-town being preferred before the wealth of fragrance and beauty to be had for the gathering.

The spectacle we found disappointing by reason of the ambitious spirit of the performance. Instead of walking two and two in the rustic procession we hoped to see passing beneath the shade of the avenue of chestnuts, the bridal party arrived at, and went away from, the church door in a hired wagonette; the whip of the driver duly tied with a white ribbon; men and women 'sitting familiar,' as the old story has it – at least sixteen of them in the place of eight. Instead of the rosy-cheeked bride in her cotton dress we had set our heart on, behold a quite elegant young woman in pearl-grey draperies, with sleeves of white, and white-befeathered grey hat. Instead of village children strewing flowers, confetti were thrown.

In the bride's mother I recognized that fat and slovenly woman who had so grudgingly fulfilled her duties as 'Neighbour' to old Jane Moon, whose father had fought at Waterloo. The poor finery she wore – draggled red roses massed around a broken feather in her hat; some cheap lace stretched to cover the place where her straining bodice gaped over her too ample bosom – was a sad contrast to the elegance of the bride.

She was affable enough to stop to speak to us after the ceremony, and informed us that the heroine of the occasion, her eldest, and earning until now high wages as a parlour-maid in London, had received a sight of beautiful presents which she would be proud to show us if we would give her a look in on our way home.

In the course of the afternoon, having sought out some offerings of our own to make, we duly availed ourselves of the invitation.

The men of the party, by that time, with red faces and sheepish looks, were hanging around the door of the public-house; the bridegroom, a smart-looking youth in navy blue suit, blue tie and brown boots, a gentleman's servant, we gathered, with the rest. Within the cottage, the bride, in her grey alpaca, with the rings on her fingers, bangles on her arms, and a showy pendant at her throat, sat at her elegant ease upon the sofa, while her mother and one or two lady guests prepared the table for the meal.

The cottage had been cleaned for the occasion, I was glad to observe; a new table-cloth replaced that draggled one with which I had been familiar, and the preparations were evidently on a grand scale; the bridegroom, as is customary in Dulditch, I learnt, standing treat for all.

Our little presents were accepted with that lack of enthusiasm which is considered good form in Dulditch. The bride, not rising from her throne of state on the sofa, did not actually use the regulation phrase, 'You can put them down,' but in her demeanour of careful indifference we read that permission. The other gifts which were displayed for our benefit consisted chiefly of glass-ware: dishes of that description which is given away with a pound of tea; a glass jug in which my poor white roses withered without water; coloured ornaments, to the cost of sixpence, and very dear at that, for the chimbleypiece.

I inquired if the happy pair were returning to London by the afternoon train, and learnt that they were staying in the parent house for two nights. How they are accommodated in 'Neighbour's' already overcrowded two rooms I cannot imagine, but I am told that this is the etiquette of the occasion when the bridegroom is not a resident in Dulditch. In the case of old Mr. and Mrs. Spencer, whose cottage boasts but one sleeping-room, the same custom was followed, when, a year ago come next Michaelmas, their Jane got married to Mrs. Potter's Jarge.

To George

THIS morning comes Bertha Flatt bringing back my book.

I was sitting in my favourite seat beneath the fir-tree on the lawn when she appeared, the neat brown paper parcel into which she had tied my poor *Splendid Failure* in her hand. She laid it on my writing-table.

'Thank you,' she said, in her most precise tone, her lips very thin and straight; 'I am sorry, but I did not quite like it.'

Now don't you admire the courage of this little country parson's sister? Is there in all London a person who would dare to return to an author his book with those words?

Miss Flatt did it, however; and having delivered herself of the criticism straightway went on to announce the fact that she and her brother were going to price the things for the Jumble Sale that afternoon, and to ask us would we go to the schoolroom, and help them to do it.

Finding that this involved the pulling about and appraising of other people's dirty clothes, I declined without ceremony for Hildred and myself.

Bertha, giving me a glance of cold disapproval, did not attempt to persuade me. She turned to the subject of the Bazaar, which is now a great topic in the parish. The Hobbleboys, she told me, were giving a good deal of trouble in the matter. They had refused to allow dancing in their grounds in the evening, and no smoking was to be permitted. The men had always smoked in the evening.

'What harm does smoking do to their grounds?' I asked.

Miss Flatt said she supposed it gave a bad tone.

Before she left she asked if I had another book I could lend her. She repeated that she particularly wished for one by Miss —. There was such a high tone about them, Mrs. Hobbleboy had said.

I sent a message to the Hobbleboys to the effect that neither Mrs. Valetta nor I would go to their Bazaar, unless we were permitted to smoke in the evening.

What sort of a 'tone' do you suppose Bertha Flatt thinks there is about me?

After all, Hildred insisted on dragging me to the Jumble Sale. She said she felt peculiarly fitted to appraise the Rector's old trousers and Miss Flatt's cast-off petticoats.

Nan accompanied her, walking in an unusual silence beside Syers, sulkily wheeling a barrowful of her toys.

Nan's mother and her relatives generally, being of opinion that, although she did not care for toys, she ought to do so, are always bombarding the poor child with the newest thing from Cremer's.

'I played with toys when I was little,' Hildred says plaintively. 'I had not many, and how I loved them! What happy hours I spent playing alone with my dolls, a trouble to no one! Why should my child be such a different creature, always demanding the presence of grown-ups in her games? A shilling doll, a shilling wooden horse in a cart, were joys to me. Now look at all these beautiful and costly things uncared for!'

The box-room of The Cottage has been cleared for Nan to play in; she never spends five minutes a week in it; but there, stacked away, many of them untouched, scarcely looked at, are all her continually arriving toys.

'Here is another,' she will say, on the receipt of a gift from Aunt Hilda or Uncle John. 'Isn't it a pretty one, Gran? May I put it away in the box-room?'

She acquiesced readily in my plan to dispose of these stores at the nominal cost of a penny the article, which sum Nan was in every case to supply herself. It was only when the idea was put in practice, and she saw the contents of the box-room heaped on the barrow, that she ceased to prattle and her face became grave. She carried in her arms a certain large 'skin horse' which, its tail being pulled, neighs and turns its head, and she eyed the contents of the barrow with a portentously dubious air.

Arrived at the schoolroom, the toys tastefully and temptingly disposed upon a table at which Nan herself, a bag of pennies beside her, was to preside, I found her presently beside me. I had been told off, against my will, and in spite of spirited protestations, to dispose of an assortment of men's coats and waistcoats, heaped on the stall allotted to me. A tempting display of trousers, dangling from a line stretched behind me, afforded a becoming background for Charlotte Poole.

Nan pulled my hand, to attract attention.

'Gran,' she said, 'I wish Syers to wheel my toys home again, if you please. I wish to play with them now. I do not wish to sell them.'

'Nonsense! I won't hear of such a thing! You do not value them one bit.'

'I do. I extremely value them, Gran.'

'Well, now you will enjoy the pleasure of seeing other little girls and boys made happy with them.' She gazed reproachfully upon me, then crept back, crestfallen, to her stall.

The sale did not start till after school-hours, so all the mothers came accompanied by all their children; there was a rush of the latter to Nan's table.

I was too much engaged, for long, to bestow any attention in that quarter.

Three old women had tendered me simultaneously three eighteen-pences for a pair of black trousers belonging to a dress suit. It was a bad beginning. The clatter that they made, each enforcing her own claim; the difficulty that I had to release the garment from their grasping hands; the abuse the two rejected cast upon the one in whose favour I at length decided; their black looks of hatred at me – these things unhinged me for the struggles to follow. Over every coat and waistcoat my customers wrangled and jangled, there being at least six would-be purchasers to every garment.

Men and women crowded before the narrow bench upon which the clothes were flung; they fought to get behind it, to pull the trousers from the line at my back. They tore the coats and waistcoats from each other's hands; they tried to tear them from mine.

The excitement was furious while it lasted, but, the supply being small in comparison to demand, was, luckily for me, short-lived. After a few minutes of storm and stress I found myself left, breathless and unstrung, with a knickerbocker suit of Harris tweeds which had found no favour with the majority, a sweater adorned by the Rector's initials worked in his college colours, a bundle of starched shirt collars, marked a ha'penny each, a pair of fawn-coloured, buttonless spats, and three odd socks, to dispose of.

From the Harris tweeds, despite their repellent odour, the worn-faced mother of a family of boys seemed unable to tear herself. She stood before them pulling them about with an anxious expression of face, and awkward fumbling hands, saying nothing aloud, but evidently carrying on endless arguments for and against their purchase in her own poor mind. The sweater, after much expenditure of eloquence, I disposed of to an old woman of seventy, who told me she intended to cut off the sleeves, 'foot 'em, and make 'em into stockings for her old man,' and to let him wear the rest of the garment next his skin for his rheumatiz.

Finding breathing space at length to look across to Nan, I, to my dismay, perceived her struggling furiously with a big boy of fourteen or so, for possession of the neighing horse; kicking him, hitting out at him. I regret to tell it of Nan.

Hildred, her attention being called, abandoned her own customers, swept over to her daughter, separated her from the loutish antagonist, whispered a few reproaching words in her ear.

'I know I have to sell it, mummy,' the child said, her voice high and thin in her effort not to cry. 'But, you see, I wish a little girl like me to have it; not a large, rough boy. I don't think he'd like to belong to a boy when he had belonged to a little girl.'

Hildred took the toy and addressed the would-be purchaser.

'A great fellow like you does not want a toy, surely!'

'Yes, and du, miss. Yes, and du.'

Thoughtfully regarding him, Hildred pulled the animal's tail. There was a shout of delight from the children as the horse turned its arching neck and neighed. A score of hands, little and big, were eagerly thrust out.

'Please, miss, me! Please, miss, me!' was called in excited chorus.

'Jack Brown, he's fefteen, come Chris'mas. I'm on'y twelve, las' June, miss.'

'Please, miss, Uthel and Beetress, they got wood hosses at th' school-trate, las' yare. I ha'n't never had a hoss.'

'Please, miss, me! Please, miss, me!' Greedy fingers working convulsively, opening and shutting on empty air.

'To which of them shall we give it, Nan?'

'Not to a boy. To a little girl like me,' Nan decided, with a trembling lip.

The coveted animal was finally bestowed upon a tot of five, who received it to her arms, trembling with joy, speechless, crimson of face.

'It was my favourite of all my toys,' Nan said; and in spite of a valiant struggle for calmness her trembling mouth turned down at the corners, her tears fell.

Hildred hardened her heart. 'Take the little girl and teach her how to play with it,' she counselled; and presently the tot and the horse and Nan retreated behind the toy-stall and were lost to view.

Miss Flatt at her boot and hat table met with but lukewarm support. The fashion in hats, for those labourers' wives and daughters who can afford to buy, is their own, and set by themselves; they are not even interested in that adopted by the class above them. Of the cast-off foot-gear too, they are shy.

'I give t'reppence for a peer o' butes, last yare, at th' sale, and theer they stan', still!' Mrs. Moore complained to me with rancour. 'Theer ain't one o' mine, man nor boys, can't git into 'em.'

She haggled for a long time over a tarnished frame with a broken glass which she discovered among a collection of old jam jars, cracked jugs, leaking saucepans, damaged lamps, presided over by Nora Chisholm. The frame had been marked three-ha'pence; she finally, having left it a dozen times and returned, carried it off for a penny, carefully tied up in her pocket-handkerchief.

'I ha' got a portygraph,' she explained, as she paid for it. 'I don't know as how I can fix it in.'

A portygraph of the shameful Clemmy, I am certain.

Hildred at the blouse and dress table was always the centre of a crowd of women eager to pull about her wares if they could not purchase. She had the Rector and Major Barkaway to support her, and the former appeared to be in high spirits and a jovial strain. Now and again the rich tones of his voice, raised above the hum of the crowd, called the attention of a passing parishioner to some of Mrs. Valetta's stock.

'Mrs. Cantley – a moment, please; I am assured on excellent authority that this is a very charming skirt, newest fashion, hardly a tear; not a speck of dirt on it, only dirt-cheap. One-and-three. May I tempt you, Mrs. Cantley?'

'I bound ter say I ain't the first o' my sect you ha' tempted, nayther,' Mrs. Cantley, who had evidently a pretty wit, responded, broadly grinning, pushing her way through the throng.

'Jim Nockills, you want a present to take home to your young lady. This charming fur tippet would be acceptable, I am sure.'

'Jim, he know a better way'n that, sir, to kape his girl's neck warm,' Jim's friend called in reply; Jim himself, with a horse laugh and a ducked head, escaping from the spot.

When I had finished making my observations on my neighbour's business and returned to my own, I found that the knickerbocker suit of Harris tweed had disappeared, and likewise the worn-faced woman who had for so long held silent debate over it. Unable to pay for it, unable to leave it, she had in my temporary absence from duty adopted the only course. I put the four shillings and ninepence, the ticketed price, into the general proceeds, saying nothing, but rejoicing that I had no longer the suit under my nose, that she who had desired its possession owned it, and that, having annexed it, she was not, after all, a Dulditch woman.

We had nearly reached home before it was noticed that Nan, her little maid beside her, lagged behind in a manner unusual with a small person who generally capers on before. Turning to encourage her to join us, it was observed that beneath the little white muslin coat she wore, a strange protuberance showed. After anxious investigation the cause proved to be the hidden form of the horse which turned its head and neighed.

Being as Hildred frequently assures me, entirely without principle, I besought her mother to let Nan keep her recovered treasure.

Mrs. Valetta rose superior to temptation. 'You may know how to write books, Charlotte Poole,' she sternly chided, 'but you have not the least idea how to bring up children.'

She added, as we retraced our steps in search of the child whom Nan had defrauded, that she wondered you, my dearest George, had not turned out an assassin or a robber.

You haven't so far, have you, my dear boy?

The poor victim was quickly found. At a short distance, weeping bitterly as she walked, she had followed our footsteps to see what became of her beloved property.

When the toy was once more put into her hands by the now loudly bellowing Nan, she clutched it without a word, and before the apology which Hildred insisted on could be wrung from the older child was almost out of sight.

To George

MAJOR BARKAWAY intimated to me the other day that the Hobbleboys wished to read my last book. How could they get hold of it?

From all the libraries they might obtain it, he was assured; or, in view of the fact that they probably did not contribute to a library, they could purchase a copy from any bookseller in the kingdom; price four-and-sixpence, net.

The Major did not think the Hobbleboys would go to that extreme measure. Had I not a copy for giving or lending?

No.

However, to-day I am rendered proud and uplifted by the intelligence that the Hobbleboys have obtained the *Splendid Failure* from the little circulating library at Wotton, which is our nearest country town.

'It will cost them tuppence a night,' I reminded our visitor. 'Will the Hobbleboys' devotion to literature run to that?'

'Are they not charmed with it?' Hildred inquired.

The Major, with his man-of-the-world air, gave an evasive answer that boded no good I know to my literary reputation. It was not until he was with Hildred alone that he communicated the distressing fact that the Hobbleboys were more than a little hurt.

'Hurt? The Hobbleboys? By the *Splendid Failure*? Why?'

There was no doubt that the book hit them off, the Major explained; but at the same time, it was not surprising that they felt, and resented the fact. It had quite put them off calling on Hildred, which they were really making up their minds to do, he added regretfully.

Which of my unlucky characters in the story I wrote six months before I set eyes upon this miserable little Squire and his wife is supposed to 'hit them off,' I wonder?

But this is not the worst an author has to suffer in Dulditch.

Miss Flatt has unbosomed herself to Hildred of the opinion she holds that the conduct of my heroine is *absolutely indecent*.

She should not have married Roland while she loved Oliver, Miss Flatt holds. No *lady* could have acted in such a fashion.

Yet such things happen in real life, unfortunately, Hildred pointed out to her.

Or, if she had been so led away, she would – the *real* lady, that is – have smothered her feeling for Oliver, instead of giving way to it and making such a disgraceful history.

That then there would have been no story – no book – was pleaded.

'I should not have thought *a nice woman* could have brought herself to write of such things,' Miss Flatt concluded, with a rush of colour to her nose, and with tight lips.

This of me – Charlotte Poole – who am known to critics and librarians as, pre-eminently, and above my other ascribed virtues, a writer of 'pure' fiction!

'Of course a book is a revelation of the person who writes it,' the sententious young woman went on. 'Dreadful things must have happened to Mrs. Poole, or in her family. I should have thought she would shrink from making them public.'

'But, Miss Flatt, it is a work of *fiction* of which you are speaking!'

Miss Flatt ignored the reminder. 'Of course if the book were a well-written one it would be different,' she announced. 'But my brother and I do not think it is well written, at all. And Mrs. Hobbleboy has discovered two faults in grammar.'

'I should not think of reading any more books by the same author,' she finished.

And the earth does not open!

Hildred was moved out of her usual calm in recounting this conversation. 'I longed to shake the woman,' she declared; 'for nothing one can say has any effect. Bertha Flatt is deaf, not only with her ears but her brain and her heart. What one feels and says does not appear to reach her *anywhere*.'

I reminded her of how Robert Louis Stevenson had noticed that certain people live tied up in bags. 'You know they're there, sure enough, but you can't get at them, and they can never get out. Well, Bertha Flatt is one of these. Her dear brother, who is longing to kneel at your feet, only he is so safely and securely tied in, is another.'

Hildred eagerly demurred. 'No, no! He is not like Bertha. He has a sense of humour; a feeling for humanity; understanding –'

'Pooh! Rubbish! He is in a bag,' I told her.

To George

THIS morning, while Miss Valetta was being, as usual, advised, commanded, implored to eat the indispensable plate of porridge before attacking her more highly appreciated egg and bread-and-butter, a parcel was set before her.

'What is it?' she inquired languidly, being entirely accustomed to parcels.

I withdrew from its packings a large skin horse which, to the smallest dark grey spot on its white kid hide, was the counterpart of that she had lost; pulling his head on one side, I made him neigh a good-morning.

Nan looked up, her black-lashed, gold-coloured eyes – eyes that look to have taken in the sun – ashine.

'Is it the very same the little girl took away from me?'

'It is better than the same you sold to the little girl, being absolutely new.'

She pushed the toy away from her and returned with a trembling lip to her porridge. 'You see, I did not want a new horse, Gran; I wanted the very particular one the little girl took away from me,' she explained.

All day the brand-new horse has stood in the sun on my writing-table, his flowing silken tail held delicately away from his shapely haunches, his neck proudly arched, his brow bound above a fascinating forelock with a blue ribbon, a blue saddle-cloth upon his glossy sides, waiting patiently to give his neighing performance if only Nan will condescend to pull his tail. Nan, hovering in the neighbourhood, casting secret glances now and again in the animal's direction, pretends to ignore his presence.

In the end Hildred, out of consideration for the obstinate little wretch's feelings, has removed the toy.

To George

1 July.

THE year is crowned with the goodness of God, and all the roses of summer are abloom. If, in this flat region, there were any little hills, they would rejoice on every side, and the valleys standing thick with corn do laugh and sing. The blue sky bends above us. We are canopied by the darkly deep blue of the cloudless sky.

Each day that I live, and feel about me the peace and the well-ordered prettiness of my charming home and garden, there grows within me the sense of my indebtedness to t'other woman.

'Tis thanks to her the Madonna lilies, standing in a shining crowd in a corner of the kitchen garden, show to me to-day their angel faces, and pour their heavenly breath upon the air. Thanks to her the climbing roses stretched along their six feet high wires on each side the gravelled walk are a sight at which surely the 'vocal voices of singing singers vociferate in sweet vociferation.'

When I took Nan this morning to look upon the riotous blooming of the Carmine Pillar, glorious with the colour, the gladness, the opulence of the summer which it crowns, the child laughed aloud.

'I wondered what you'd say to that sight, Nan,' I told her with satisfaction, 'and you've said exactly the right thing. That insolent, lovely, turbulently joyous rose laughs at you, doesn't it? Laugh back at the rose, Nan.'

Well, for the luxurious Carmine Pillar, for the chaste Thalia, for the Crimson Rambler, and the delicate sweetness of golden-hearted Euphrosyne; for Helen Keller, that rose of love's proper hue, 'celestial, rosy red'; for the creamy gold of the Gloire de Dijon and the innocent pink of Clio; for the Delphiniums, their long spiky heads blue as the sky; for the Phloxes with their ruby and white beauty as yet held in store, I acknowledge my obligations to t'other woman; and greet her wherever she may be with my most grateful and respectful thanks.

And I think it would be well if all of us who revel in the sweetness of our old gardens would give now and then the tribute of a silent thank-offering to the shades of those forgotten ones who planned the walks, who laid the lawns; who grouped the little slips of laurel, of box, of arborvitæ, to form what is now the cool dense shrubbery; who first cast the seeds of foxglove, of honesty, of tall pink balsam, with a lavish hand about the barren places; who appointed the spot for the rose-beds; who set cuttings of lavender, rosemary, southernwood, great bushes sweetening the kitchen-garden to-day; who planted the beech, or the birch, or the cedar-tree beneath whose shade we sit.

They did it in faith, nothing doubting. Let us hold them blessed in our memory, for their reward.

I have been moved, of late, to inquire into the history of The Cottage farther back than its tenancy by t'other woman. It was, I find, originally a farm-house, having some hundred-and-fifty acres attached, absorbed now in the bigger holding of the Grange Farm. Started as a detached residence, on its own, the house was modernized, enlarged, much more garden-land enclosed, the approach to it replanned on a more imposing scale.

But this fir-tree beneath which I write, for instance – its boughs are cut away to about fifteen feet from the ground, and its high, wide-spreading branches droop gracefully, making a perfect shade and shelter. It is here that I sit to write, my feet upon the carpet of pine needles when the sun lies hot and dazzling on all around; and when the thirsty earth soaks up the rain falling in silver drops beyond the dark, protecting branches, I sit here to write beneath their shelter still – this giant spruce, for whose shade I am grateful, must have been planted in the days of the farmer's tenancy.

And the three beeches beneath whose wide boughs Nan's hammock swings at one corner of the lawn; and the lawn itself, which was one also in his day. The apple-trees in the orchard. He – or his good wife, more likely, finding time amid the cares of housekeeping, of dairy, of poultry, to give an eye to the improvement of the garden – must have laid out the broad grass walk that margins one side and the top of the kitchen-garden, must have planted the tall nut-bushes that border it.

Those were peaceful days of leisure in which the good farmer and his helpful wife made their comfortable living, and passed their days of alternate labour and ease. Then no injurious amount of game was raised to ruin crops and to make ill-blood with landlord and neighbour. Then the Hobbleboy of the period pottered with his gun among the turnips, a friend or so beside him, content with the modest bag achieved at the end of the day. No fear was there in that calm time of any casual outsider, afflicted with the then undreamed-of, mysterious complaint of 'land-hunger,' and assisted in his purloining by Act of Parliament, seizing on the best acres of the farm. For the manufacture of beer, barley was a necessity; the baker depended on English-grown wheat; the butcher on English beef and mutton. Produce was sold at a reasonable profit.

Those were not times of enlightenment, perhaps – 'from Ignorance our comfort flows' – but hearts were easy then, if heads were not overburthened; and in such homes as this, and in such prim, fragrant gardens, old Leisure safely dozed and waked, while Peace and Quiet reigned.

In the churchyard there are a couple of solid stone, coffin-shaped tombs, which mark the resting-place of the farmer and his wife who lived for close on fifty years in this place. No children are beside them. Either they had none, or they lie buried in other churchyards, perhaps in other lands. But near by are a couple of humbler stones bearing the names of a serving man and woman, who were, it is recorded, their faithful friends, living and dying in their service.

As I sit beneath my tree, I see the older portion of the house, its roof still thatched, I am glad to say, visible from the position. I like to think of the farmer-man and his wife coming in and out. He with his homely face shining beneath his broad hat, gaiters on legs, pipe in mouth, his mug of ale or cider in his hand – he and Peace of mind, and Ease of circumstance, and grand Tranquillity – companions of such livers in the elder day. His wife, fresh, homely, lovely in her simple ways; looking well to her household, clothing them, if not in scarlet, in the appropriate and becoming garb that suited those lost times; her husband, truly her lord and master; her servants, her friends, almost her children; her hand stretched out to the poor and needy, the law of kindness in her mouth.

Were they like that, I wonder – the pair who planted pleasant plants and set the place with strange slips from other gardens, who raised the beech-hedge by the gate, and gathered the first-fruits of the young apple-trees in the orchard? Or do we deceive ourselves by thinking that people bore sounder, cleaner hearts, and wore more cheerful faces in those days?

In any case, when I walk that way again, I will carry a twig from the fir-tree that was yours and is mine, old farmer-friend, to lay upon your grave; and you, dear dame, shall have, for memory, a spray of rosemary.

To George

NAN has made a discovery. She has found an old woman, who, having attained the age of seventy, has never been in a train; who, living nearly within breath of it (twenty miles as the crow flies; standing on the high lands when the strong wind blows from the East, I almost fancy I get the salt taste of it on my lips), has never seen the sea.

'I promised we'd take her to it,' Nan said. 'I promised you and me and mummy would take her there, Gran. She's old Libby, you know, who comes to pluck the chickens and ducks. I like her extremely much, because she ties her head up in an apron, and the young ones of the feathers stick in her eyebrows. She is quite a nice person, Gran.'

The plan of taking old Libby to the sea commends itself also to Hildred. She thinks it my duty, in the service of that Art of which I am a humble devotee, to gather at first hand the impressions of a septuagenarian for the only time in her life confronted with the spectacle of Mighty Ocean.

You too, my dear George, have said that sort of thing. I like you and Hildred to be in accord, and I am nothing if not obedient. Libby shall go to the sea, and we will go with her to hear what she thinks of it.

To George

I TOLD you, did I not, of that old ex-shepherd whose acquaintance I made some months ago? He who had invested his life's savings in a little ten-acre farm, and was like to break his heart for the missing of the sheep he had for all his life tended? To-day, by means of a few yards of rope, he is cured of his longing, and eased of all heartache for ever; having hanged himself in the little shed in his back-yard in which the few tools he possessed were stored.

He and his wife had lived together for forty years. I went to her when I heard of this disaster, thinking to find her distraught beyond consolation. I found her milking her cow.

But the cow had to be milked. She was not the less sensible of her loss for that.

Her old grey head, tied in the worn lilac handkerchief kept for that occupation, was tucked into the warm red side of the cow. Perhaps a tear or two splashed into the milk in the pail. She did not stay her business to speak to me, and most of what she said was smothered in the cow's side, or drowned in the rattle of milk into the white metal pail.

I told her, calling the intelligence across an intervening space of sodden, trampled straw, that I was sorry. I shouted the inquiry was there anything I could do for her?

She didn't know as there was, I understood her to say, with her face hidden. Presently she turned it sideways to me, still resting upon the cow's thin ribs, to add that now her old man was gone, there weren't no a-bringin' of 'm back, as she'd heared of.

At the top of my voice I acquiesced in this truth so sadly trite, and assured her that if there was anything I could do to make things easier for her, with pleasure I would do it.

She listened in silence, milking her cow.

Also in silence I waited. Looking round the dirty, dilapidated shed, home of the lean bedraggled cow, I recalled the figure of the poor old ex-shepherd, his whity, fair hair hanging in a fringe about bald head and face, the still, far-away look in the eyes that at seventy years of age had been innocent as a child's, and blue as the morning-sky. I pictured him, bent with labour, going about his weary, hopeless striving by dint of semi-starvation to stretch to a measure to cover their poor necessities the scant living to be wrung from the scrap of land. End and aim of all that fruitless labour, to keep life in their impoverished bodies in order to carry on the toil. I remembered his plaintive monotonous chant, hopeless as his outlook, "'Tis a bad job! I fear me 'tis a bad job.'

The milking done, I followed the newly-made widow with her pail into the house. She set it on a shelf in the little brightly scrubbed dairy, and took off the lilac cloth which had shielded her hair, wet with heat, from the cow's body.

'You'd like to see 'm?' she asked. 'He were put in 's coffin arter the Inkwitch, but he ain't screwd down yet. We couldn't get 'm up th' stairs, they're that awkward, so I had 'm put i' th' pantry, bein' handy and cool.'

They had stood the coffin on trestles among the few willow-pattern plates, yellow pie-dishes, and other poor earthenware goods belonging to the household.

'I ha' moved out all th' wittles,' the poor woman explained. 'I fared as how I couldn't ate nothin' that was kep' there, beside 'm. He couldn't harm 'em, we know, but we can't help our feelin's.'

With some difficulty I prevented the poor woman from removing the sheet from his face. 'I would so much rather remember him as I saw him last,' I pleaded.

It was with reluctance she obeyed. 'He ain't, not to say, a *pleasant* corpse,' she slowly admitted. She told me the story of his death, her labour-worn hand resting on the coffin.

'I'd growed to be afeared on 't,' she admitted. "Twasn't no new thing ter me. Ef so be as he were five minutes out of 's time a-comin' to 's meals, "God in Heaven, he ha' done it!" says I to myself. He'd got that look o' *seein' t'ro' things to an end of 'em* in his eyes. "Bor, what be you a-hatchin' of?" says I to him when I happened to see 'm a-gazin' at th' wall as if he was a-watchin' suffin' t'other side on 't.

'He allus come back then. "I ain't a forgettin' you, missus," he say. "No, no!"'

'But this here time I not used nothin'. Seems wholly as if 'twas to be. There weren't none o' that a-starin' afore 'm. Right at peace and at ease, he fared with hisself. He'd had a crack along of Chisholm's new shepherd, he told me. "His lambs don't look as they done onder me, and so I telled the new chap. A set of dwindlin' little bits o' things; and half the yows was lame," says he. "They're a missin' you, bor," I says to him. "'Tis a bad job," he say, but brisk-like, not down-hearted, as I ha' seed 'm afore.

'And my! What a dinner he put into hisself! A gooseberry dumplin' we had, and I give 'm a slice o' pork arter it. "Give us another, missus," he say. And wholly glad I am to think I done it now. At this rate, our bit o' mate 'on't last out till Sat'day night, think I. But I kep' it to myself; and the pork'll last now.

"'The smell o' th' shep ha' put you in appetite," I says, kind of jokin' along of 'm; for he ha'n't fared to keer muchly for 's wittles since he left th' flock.

"'Ah, bor!" says he to me, agreein' like. Then up he gits. "I'll put up yer linen line," he says; for I'd bought a new one at th' shop this week, and he was allust handy-like, my old man was, at little jobs like that. I give 'm th' line, and off he went without another ward. Never so much as looked round th' room, or twirled 's eyes on me.

'An hour later up drove Dan'l Hunt, th' carpenter. "Wheer be yer old man, missus," he say ter me. "He's a spuddin' his turmits i' th' field acrost th' road," I made answer. "No, and ain't," he say. "Then he's a hoistin' a couple of hurdles on to our bit of a haystack, for he think there's a goin' to be a wind to-night." "No, and ain't." "Then he's somewheers about i' th' yard." "And he bain't theer, nayther," says Dan'l Hunt, "for I ha' been to see. Yer old man telled me to look in, this arternune, for he'd mayhap have a job for me," says he, kind o' keerless like.

'Then I stared i' th' man's face, and you might ha' knocked me over with a feather, for sure's I'm a-standin' here, my hand on my old man's coffin – (what Dan'l got the order for, sure enough, and made i' th' night) – I knowed what had fell out. You may believe me, ma'am, if ye like. I could'n' kape a limb still. Down I set i' my chair. "Tie up yer horse, Mr. Hunt," I say. "Go into th' woodshed acrost th' way. Sure as God's heaven," says I, "you'll find my old man there. He's hanged hisself," I say, "with my new linen line."'

Here she took her trembling, knotted hand from the coffin, and held it over her eyes, and broke into hard sobbing. I led her from the pantry, and begged her not to tell me any more. I would have tried to stop her before, but could see that the relief of the telling had been great; and even now, amid her sobbing, she persisted in giving the details of the gruesome story.

The low rafters of the shed had not afforded sufficient height for the purpose, and to effect it the poor old man had knelt upon the floor. A violent, ghastly end for such a quiet old shepherd of the sheep.

'There weren't a more well-livin', peaceable man in Dulditch,' she told me. 'They tell me, at th' Inkwitch they brought it in "off his know." Not him. Not my old man, ma'am. He were as well aweer as you and me what he were about, and he'd wholly made up his mind, and carried it about with 'm since Chisholm tarned 'm off. Hard times, and the fear o' not bein' able to make inds meet, druv 'm to it, they're a-sayin'. Never you believe it, ma'am. Sure as we're a-standin' here, 'twas the missin' o' th' shep; the longin' of 's heart for th' shep, as killed 'm. His death, I take it, lay at Chisholm's door, a-separatin' of him from his shep. He weren't a man o' many wards. He made no complaint, but his heart was broke; and I see it.'

'He went to look at the flock, the last thing?'

'Ah!' She held herself very still, and looked with eyes sunken and bleared with weeping out of the door. '"A rash ac"'–'twas so the Reverend called it when he come in, las' night. I ain't a-goin' agin it that self-murder is a rash ac', mostly; but not in my old man's case. He'd thowt th' matter out, he had; 'tweren't a "rash ac"' wi' him.'

The fact that he had killed himself after thought and deliberation, in some strange way, gave her satisfaction.

'I know,' she went on, gazing stilly before her, 'I know as how 'tis a poor look out for them as ha' done sech deeds. But th' Lord knew well as how my old man didn't go in no outragin' sperrit about it; but calm and thoughtful like. Th' Lord on't put my old man among th' rash uns.'

She gazed beyond the neglected little garden, where the sweet-williams, tangled and held down by bindweed, blossomed rose and pink, as they lay; beyond the ragged fence across the road, beyond the little field which held the poor, poor haystack, lop-sided and steadied with a ladder and a couple of props, to where the blue, unclouded sky met the horizon line. She looked and looked, pondering her own thought or reading some message in the serenity of the familiar scene that touched her to the heart; for now the tears rained from her eyes and her voice was broken with sobbing.

'Th' Lord, He called Hisself a Shepherd,' she sobbed. 'Likelies He'll know how my old man, as used to be a shepherd, felt.'

To George

OUR scheme of personally conducting old Libby to Yarmouth has fallen through.

Nan was the first to call off. 'Mummy says you and me mayn't paddle, Gran; and if you don't paddle in the sea, there isn't anything you can do with it; and when you've got it you can't do anything without it,' she complained.

Hildred still thought it would be interesting to hear Libby's first exclamations of rapture and surprise when the ocean burst upon her sight; but cold reflection showed us that we could not sit with the old lady to gaze upon the wonder of it all day; neither could we leave her there to gaze alone. She thought, besides, that poor Libby would be too much overcome at the moment to say much, and that it would be wiser to give her time to put what she felt into words.

Finally, we have all decided that the old woman's description of the sea on her return will answer my purpose; which is, you understand, dear George, the enrichment of literature.

So, to-day, poor old Libby, greatly to her own astonishment, I admit, and a little nervous of what is before her, is sent off in charge of her middle-aged daughter, who had seen the sea, of course, but had 'no objections,' she obligingly told us, to see it again.

I give thanks that they have such a perfect day for their excursion. I have been thinking, as I sit here, of 'the blue above and the blue beneath'; of how the sun will turn to deep wine-red the brown sails of the fishing boats, and shine upon the silver crests of the little waves, and transform the yellow sands to a strand of gold; of how the light breeze will blow the scent of the sea in old Libby's brown face; of how awed she will be by its majesty, its immensity, and mystery.

I have been walking with Mrs. Chisholm this afternoon in her lovely old garden, listening to all her troubles. It is what one always listens to if one walks with this clever, energetic, but far from contented lady. A splendid wife and mother, devoted, I am sure, to husband and children, she abuses them all to you (for the sake of hearing them defended, perhaps) in the course of conversation.

Her husband is slack and old-fashioned in his ways, which are those of his father and grandfather, when agriculture was a business worth following, and the world a different place.

'Farmers of that sort can't live now,' she tells me. 'Look at the barley-crop last year; look at the price of sheep this. He stands to lose £300 on his sheep alone. Do you hear him even utter one word of complaint? No!'

'But complaining would not alter the price of sheep, Mrs. Chisholm.'

'No. But why sit down by things? The more you bow the head, the more clouts you get from Fortune, Mrs. Poole.'

As for her children, they do not take after their father, but are too much the other way, she tells you. They have everything to make them happy, and are the most dissatisfied pair under the sun. Where they get that ungrateful turn of mind from Mrs. Chisholm is at a loss to surmise.

She was filled with grievances against her servants – her 'girls' as she always calls them – this afternoon.

They come to her, knowing nothing, she complains; and only one, here and there, is willing to learn. She generally 'takes on' the village girls when they first leave school. Their mothers have not so much as taught them to light a fire or to wash a dirty plate. At school they learn to sew (and over-particular they have to be about their stitches; take one thread and leave two); but is there one of them who has the gumption to put a patch on her own night-gown, or to help to darn the stockings for the household? No.

'What is it they're good for?' Mrs. Chisholm asks, with spirit. 'What is it they learn in school that stands by them and is of use to the world they live in?

'The village school used to cost the parish a hundred a year, and now costs it two hundred. Who is the better of it? The children learn like parrots, and know no practical uses to put their knowledge to.

'Look at the letters you get from servants seeking places. Are they better expressed and better written than those of a generation ago? Ask the farm-boys, once in the fifth and sixth standards, to put down a sum in compound addition and add it up. They can't do it. It isn't the fault of their excellent teachers – conscientious, good women – and I'm not saying 'tis this way in the towns. Of that I know nothing. But in the villages, 'tis so. And what I ask you is – what are we paying for? To give to one or two quick-witted here and there a facility for reading the weekly newspaper and getting hold of a few half-comprehended ideas they'd be better and happier without; ideas which set them against the people they have to look to for employment when they're well and strong, for help and sympathy when illness or misfortune falls on them.

'To hate the class above them. That is what the labouring class has learnt, so far, from our improved educational system,' poor Mrs. Chisholm cries.

To George

THIS morning I have been to call on the old Libby who went to the sea. She lives alone in a little two-roomed cottage, very picturesque and neat and clean. She was sitting in a chair by the door which opens upon a small square of garden, gay with flowers. It is only with the women of Libby's generation that you find a well-tended flower-garden.

'Well! And how did you get on yesterday, Libby? And how did you like the train? And what did you think of the sea?'

'I got t'ro wi't,' Libby said, with a dejection of bearing I had not looked for. 'I must say as I find myself no matters, after it. 'Tain't to be expected as I should, come to my age, and wi' sech an ondertaking. An' tha's what my Annie she say: "'Tain't to be expected of ye, mother," she say.'

'But you're surely not sorry you went, Libby?'

'I don't know as I'm, so to say, sorry,' Libby admitted, with some grudging. Then her wrinkled face lit, and her eyes brightened. 'I see th' beautifullest chiney shop ever I see in my life,' she burst forth.

'But didn't you see the *sea?*'

' "You couldn't look at all the chiney in that shop," Annie she say to me, "not if you was to stan' here all day, mother. You ha' stood here, as 'tis," Annie she say to me, "till yer legs is like droppin' off."'

'Tell me what you thought of the sea, Libby.'

Libby got up stiffly from her chair and went to the mantelpiece, from which she took a trumpery small jar, ornamented with green moss and pink rosebuds, in relief.

'I buyed this wi' th' money you give me,' she said. 'Buyed it at the chiney shop. My Annie she buyed th' t'other one. There were two of 'em. There was an emanuel saucepan she could ha' had for the same price; and Annie she was tormented, a-comin' home, to think as she'd made that ch'ice. "An emanuel saucepan I ha' set my heart on," she say, "and I'm tormented, mother, I han't bought it."'

We could drag no more out of her. Disappointing for me, wasn't it? Whether she ever saw the sea – 'the wide, wide sea, with its ships, dim discovered, dropping from the clouds' – I cannot say. If she did, she held it cheaply in comparison with the chiney shop, the green moss jars with rosebuds in relief, and the emanuel saucepan.

After due consideration we have come to the conclusion that it was an 'enamelled' saucepan which Libby's daughter Annie so sincerely regretted.

To George

I CAME upon Nan, this morning, in the hour when she generally pretends to do a reading-lesson with her mother – we decided in the beginning that we could not be plagued with her governess at The Cottage – seated at the writing-table, told off to the task of inditing a letter. It was to be of her own composition and spelling, I gathered, because the friend to whom she was to write had made the particular request that so it might be.

When I looked in upon her she had paused in her literary labours to hold converse with a small china elephant to which she has lately become attached. The animal cost sixpence perhaps, and was begged from Nora Chisholm, whose bedroom mantelpiece, I am assured, is filled with a collection of some hundreds of animals of like manufacture. It was attired this morning in a shapeless garment of red flannel, tied here and there about its person with string; but its costumes are many and varied, and are kept in a little roll in Nan's pocket, and dragged out whenever her pocket-handkerchief appears.

This absurd child, who won't play with dolls as her mother and grandmother did before her, exhibits her maternal instinct in her care and her dressing-up of this three-inch high elephant!

'That ridiculous creature again!' I said to her. 'Let me hurl him through the window.'

'No, Gran!' protecting him anxiously from my attack. 'You're not to, Gran! Poor Hafiz! You see he is not very well to-day, so he's in his dressing-gown, and keeping quiet.'

'He's a frightful humbug. And so are you, Nan, sitting here pretending to write your letter.'

'I have been writing my letter, Gran. So there! And I don't think you at all a polite person not to believe.'

She held up a sheet of ruled paper for me to see. 'My darling Ernest,' the epistle began.

'And who is your darling Ernest, pray?' I asked her in some surprise, for I had never heard the mention of an 'Ernest' in her conversation.

'He wrote me a letter, you know; and he called me his darling Nan. I know, because mummy read it to me. I suppose if I'm his darling, he's mine,' Nan argued.

'And where is this precious letter, then, and how comes it I did not see it?'

'Mummy's got it. Mummy keeps care of his letters, for fear I should lose them.'

'But who is he, then?'

Nan, engaged with little ink-stained fingers in rearranging the toilette of Hafiz, could not be bothered to remember such a trifle as a surname.

'He played horses with me,' she vouchsafed, fumbling at the strings.

'Of course! they all play horses with you.'

'But not on all fours.'

'Ah! At Lucerne? Or was it at Cannes?'

I am enlightened, remembering the poor young curate of whom I had heard Nan speak when they first came.

'I am stang with Gran,' the letter, almost illegible with blots and smudges, with letters now gigantic, now minute, set forth. 'I wis you were stang with Gran to. We cud play –'

'What's that?' I am compelled to inquire, with my finger at one of Nan's animal sketches. She is believed by her mother to have a great talent for drawing.

'I should think any one could see it is a portrait of a horse,' the artist explained, with disdain. 'It is quicker to draw than to write, when you have to spell too. Hafiz stood for the portrait with his dressing-gown on.'

It is strange, with all her affection for me and our mutual confidences, how reticent Hildred is. I never guessed there had been an intimacy such as this 'darling Nan' and 'darling Ernest' points to! She has a way of telling you all she desires you to know and then leaving it, which I admire, but have never been able to emulate. My tongue to this day is an unruly member, and I find myself constantly revealing more than I wish to unfold.

'What a curious kind of namby-pamby young man this "darling Ernest" with whom Nan keeps up a correspondence must be,' I remarked, later on, to Mrs. Valetta.

She smiled. Asked, 'Did I think so?' Added that he was very good-natured and kind.

'Handsome?'

She raised supercilious brows. 'It depended on taste.'

'Clever?'

'About the average.'

'What can he find to write to Nan about? I should like to see his letter.'

Mrs. Valetta had left it upstairs, and did not offer to get it.

'What was this paragon curate doing at Lucerne?'

'You would not, I am sure, consider him a paragon, Cousin Charlotte, or anything so horrid. He was travelling with his mother, who was ill.'

'Poor as a rat, of course?'

She shook an indifferent head. 'I really did not trouble to inquire.'

'He made you an offer of marriage, I suppose?'

'Do you really suppose that, Charlotte Poole? How your thoughts run on matrimony, nowadays! It is the influence of Major Barkaway, I am sure.'

To George

THAT has happened which for some time I have foreseen was inevitable.

If you had settled with Hildred by letter as I have urged you to do, my dearest George, instead of putting off for your presence in England, which cannot be for at least another six months, it might have been prevented.

The Reverend Algernon Flatt has asked Hildred to marry him.

She will dispose of him as she has done of the rest, no doubt; and he, the sleek, comfort-loving creature, won't break his heart. If he gets time for thought and reflection in a sleepless night or two, declines in appetite, and loses a few pounds of flesh, he'll maybe be none the worse. But all the same, if with a stroke of your pen you could prevent such occurrences, and are only deterred by a lingering foolish feeling of resentment against poor Hildred for her first marriage, I think it is your duty to swallow your pride and put matters with her upon a recognized footing.

Hildred barely mentions your name now. I think she is hurt at what she doubtless considers your sluggishness. No woman, remember, can tolerate the laggard in love.

You had a grievance, my dear boy, I know. You have surely nursed it long enough. Give over standing upon your dignity and write to Hildred by the next mail.

Love matters are my stock-in-trade, the materials by which I gain my daily bread. One does not write of these affairs all one's life to mistake the signs. I read the impending proposal in the man's eyes, and warned Hildred; who pooh-poohed the idea and chose to make impertinent remarks about what she calls my own romance. Great Heavens, George!

This absurd Major, I confess, haunts the place. Morning, noon, and night he drops in on us on some excuse or other. It is to me he talks, I regret to say – pours out his stories of the aristocracy gleaned from the society papers and stored in a memory capacious for such details; repeats old scandals of local families whose names to me mean nothing; relates conversations, ingeniously made to bear upon any subject turning up, in which he has carried off the palm for wit and wisdom; but it is Hildred he watches. His small, cold eyes glitter when she appears, as they certainly do not glitter for me, or for any other old woman in the world. She knows it perfectly well, too, and is not displeased, although it diverts her to turn her humorous raillery upon me; and I, who like her to be amused, am civiller than I fear I should be to my tittle-tattling old bore, for her entertainment's sake.

A man has been spending a couple of nights at the Rectory who is a missionary from the Fiji Islands. He was a college chum of the Rector's; and, I gather, between him and Bertha Flatt there was an ancient, mild flirtation. If he should be successful in persuading her to go out with him to convert the Fijians, I can't help thinking he will have performed a self-sacrificing act for which the Rector should not cease to be grateful.

About fifty people, male and female, the former without exception in jam-pot collars, and waistcoats with no visible fastening, were gathered on the Rectory lawn to hear the Reverend Pevensey Pryngge tell of his experiences – mildly humourous for the most part – and of the success of his mission.

The temperature was 80 in the shade, of which, by the way, there was none on the lawn; the missionary, small, enthusiastic, something simious of aspect, standing by a table containing the usual glass of water and objects savage toilette, ornament, and manufacture, poured out the inevitable string of unpronounceable names, gave the accustomed statistics, made the attenuated jokes, familiar, I suppose, to most of the people sitting in a semi-circle on domestic, uncomfortable chairs beneath sunshades, to listen.

Nan, who was present, greatly bored, was entrusted by the Rector at the conclusion of the address to carry round the bag for collection. From Hildred had been extorted by her husband a promise never to contribute to foreign missions. Deducting what I gave – because I find it easier to give than to make excuse – I infer from the insignificance of the sum collected that no very ardent sympathizers with the missionary's cause were present.

But that is by the way. What is of importance to my story is that, the address being over, and his professional duties for the moment off his mind, the missionary, full of beans, as you would say, and tempted thereto by alluring looks from Nan as she delivered to him the bag, was moved to pursue and catch that young person as she danced over the sun-baked lawn; finally, to play and romp with her like a schoolboy.

A fact which brought the energetic little man favourably under the notice of Mrs. Valetta, and so incontinently put an end to her daughter's hour. For the lion of the occasion, enchanted with the graciousness of the beautiful young woman in her flowing black flimsy draperies, forgot apparently the claims upon his attention of every other person present, and squatting upon the grass at Hildred's feet, eagerly chattered and laughed and gesticulated, gazing into her face with his bright, speaking eyes.

The Rector, smiling a little awry, went over and said to his friend a word intended to recall him to a sense of his responsibilities. The little missionary, not so much as moving his eyes from the face above him, waved a hand with a gesture of dismissal. 'Go away, tiresome man,' he said. 'I am quite happy, I assure you. Disturbing, tiresome man, go away.'

Alas, poor Bertha Flatt! She had worn that day a new white flannel coat and skirt, some pink flowers had been added to the rosette of fancy straw on her black hat, and she had wound a pink scarf of chiffon about her throat. In her cheeks, also, pink had shown, and her tight little mouth had more than once been seen to smile. We can guess what long dormant hopes had been awakened in her breast by the coming of her brother's old college friend. They shone in the brighter, kinder glance of her eye, they were present in the gayer tones of her voice, and rang in her suddenly buoyant footsteps.

As she looked upon the ugly face of the missionary keeping his place at Hildred's feet she drooped again in her gait, and once more grew grey in the face.

She did her duty, however, in her usual flaccid fashion as mistress of her brother's house, going among the parsons and their wives with serious talk of nursing centres, garden-parties, mothers' guilds, tennis teas, and book clubs. But while she talked, and her bodily presence drooped and languished in the familiar atmosphere of those topics, it was too evident her thoughts were otherwise; and now and again she shot anxious, questioning, condemning glances at the simious-faced missionary at Hildred's feet.

She is, my dear boy, that much admired Hildred of yours, the most dangerous of all flirts – an unconscious one. Not for her the vulgar tricks of eye-glancing, of ankle-showing; she stoops to no cajolery, or efforts to attract or to pique. But, anxious only to be kind, she listens with a ready and serious sympathy to the poor wretch at her feet, eager, for his part, to unfold himself, to talk for an age of himself, his thoughts, his acts, his history. She does not do mischief for the sake of doing it, but for goodness and tender-heartedness, and loving sympathy's sake; and the mischief is so much the surer and the more deadly.

I took pity on poor Bertha's dashed hopes, pleaded a headache, and led the dangerous widow early away. Little was the use. In less than an hour the Reverend Pevensey Pryngge had followed.

'In making a friendship, I, here to-day and gone to-morrow, have no time to waste in preliminaries,' he excused himself. 'I must seize the moment's gift; I feel that I have known you already for ages. You will please believe that you have also known me for that period. It was delightful this afternoon. You had the heart to run away and leave me. Let us begin where we broke off.'

The Rector, more or less protesting, had been dragged in tow. Bertha, bent on pressing the thorn into her bosom, was there. Picture to yourself, my dear George, what a charming couple of hours I passed in trying to lessen the agony of this love-lorn pair!

If Hildred had been charming in the afternoon in her demure black raiment, imagine what she was, robed all soft, clinging white; white shoulders but half-veiled, throat and fore-arms bare, in the evening. Poor Bertha, in her useful new white flannel coat and skirt, bought with a view to fine Sabbaths, to tennis (which she plays just well enough to spoil the game of other people); destined also, worn with a white silk blouse made dressy for such occasions, for 'quiet evenings' at neighbouring Rectories, cut but a poor, dowdy figure beside her. Not that it mattered. Not for a moment was either man conscious of looking at her, shrunk and aged and withered since our eyes had first fallen on her this afternoon, smiling in her new costume beside her little monkey-faced missionary, Pryngge.

For a moment my heart was filled with a sense of the bitterness of things, the injustice of them. I was half angry with Hildred for having been born so fair, framed to make men false. I forgave to Bertha all her heavy inaccessibility to ideas, her selfassertiveness, her snobbishness, as I watched her eating her supper in silence, knowing that 'bitter as coloquintida' was the taste of food in her mouth.

It was cruel that Hildred, who had everything, should wrest from her – even Pryngge.

He stayed with us, that night, until I had to turn him from my door, and he left Dulditch the next morning, having engaged to speak upon a score Rectory lawns before he sailed again for Fiji. But he wrote by the next post and asked Hildred to accompany him.

She showed me the letter, and we both laughed over it.

He deserves that; for whereas he had been a quite human, rather humorous, chattering, laughing, enthusiastic little monkey in our intercourse with him, taking pen in hand he fatally remembered 'shop'; said that he had asked the blessing of God on what he was proposing; asserted that Hildred, with her charm of manner, and personal gifts bestowed on her as a sacred charge to be used for the glory of God, should employ their almost irresistible influence in the precious work of saving souls.

It was all more than a little sickening; and Hildred wrote the inevitable reply without a pang of compunction.

I have set down this incident, not for its intrinsic importance, but for the influence it had on what follows.

Immediately on the receipt of Hildred's answer to his proposal, our impetuous missionary wrote to offer the same opportunity for the saving of souls to Bertha Flatt. Needless to say with a different result. In two months she has to be ready to accompany the monkey-man to the scene of his labours, and the Rector will be left housekeeperless.

Now do you see the drift of my story?

Moved by the sight of the other man's open and unstinted admiration of Mrs. Valetta, and horrified at the prospect of loneliness opening before him, he has been stirred out of his torpor, and shaken from his habitual caution, to take a decided step.

He has made Hildred the second offer of marriage she has received this week.

Hildred, you must know, has business with her husband's executor, and has to go up to town to see him. She has some shopping to do, and will be away for a week. The plan was mentioned in the Rector's hearing, last night. He became silent, unusually thoughtful, and left early. This morning a sealed letter from him lay on Hildred's plate.

I knew the handwriting; I think she would not have told me the purport, but that I watched her as she read, and needed no telling.

I thought of you, my dear boy, all those thousands of miles away from her, and it enraged me to see these inferior men endeavouring – futilely, I know, but the wrong seemed none the less – to wrest from you what is yours. It was stupid of me, of course, to feel momentarily more angry with Hildred than with her suitors. Being, however, moved to speak with my tongue, I said – I forget what, but more, a great deal, I am sure, than I should have done, more even, probably, than I felt. She listened in composed silence till I had done. 'I can't refuse them till they ask me,' she reminded me then.

It sounds an irrefutable argument, but we all know it is only half a truth; and so I told her.

'Nothing is easier than to refuse a man before he asks you,' I pointed out. 'And, mind you, Hildred, every *nice* woman knows it is so; and does it. How do you like that slap in the face?' I asked her; and she calmly assured me she took it from the hand that gave it, and felt none the worse.

'To-morrow, in all probability, you'll be saying something quite different, Cousin Charlotte. Telling me what weak, unprincipled folk men are where women are concerned, and begging me to make them suffer while I have it in my power.'

'Are you going to answer your letter?'

'I start by the 11.45 train. There is not time.'

'Not time to write the word "No." Nonsense. I'll get you a pen and ink, and you can write it while you eat your breakfast.'

'He knows I am going to town. He asks me to let him wait for his answer until I return.'

'I call that contemptible. Imagine a man, really in love, willing to wait a week for an answer to such a question!'

'Sometimes they have to wait longer,' Hildred says, and gazes thoughtfully across the breakfast-table into the garden. She was not thinking of Syers, an interesting back view of whom was to be had at

135

the moment, engaged in tying each carnation bud to its own slim green stick, but of you, George, and of how you have waited. I knew it well; and my anger against her died away as I saw the thought in her eyes.

'Ah, there are men and men!' I said. 'This one' – pointing to her letter—'waits, for the reason, my dear Hildred, that he is a coward. He is afraid you should refuse him, naturally, but he is equally afraid to be accepted, believe me. Afraid you might fail in all the little futilities in which a clergyman's wife is supposed to excel; afraid the Hobbleboys might object; afraid he should have made a mistake, and marriage should turn out to be one more item in the already alarming list of things he has decided it is wiser to leave alone.

'He does not express any of those fears, poor man,' Hildred said, referring to her letter. 'But as you are of opinion he has them, and as you, we know, are always right, it will not be much of a trial for him to wait for a few days to know which way his fate is decided.'

With that she went off to London.

I thought, perhaps, the Reverend Algernon would have been to see me, for the sake of getting me to talk of the lady he loves, but, so far, not a sign of him. His sister, who in the expansion caused by her probable martyrdom in the aforementioned islands, has been almost warm in her friendship for me, comes often. She talks of her outfit, talks of how much poor Algernon will miss her, tells me of all her efforts to supply him with a suitable housekeeper.

In all these new interests the theme of the Bazaar, which before the rather unexpected advent of the missionary had threatened to nauseate, has suffered some neglect. It is to be held at the Rectory on the day after Hildred's return. If she does not send her answer, but complies with the Rector's request to give the matter, in her week's absence, her earnest consideration, the situation will be amusing. I shall be curious to see how they comport themselves under the conditions. The fat Rector in his uncertainty and perturbation of spirit; the entirely calm and self-contained Hildred, holding his fate in her hands.

Seriously, and in the interests of literature, I shall write to advise Hildred to withhold her answer to his proposal until after the Garden Fête. I shall point out to her that the Rector will be otherwise too much dispirited to attend successfully to the duties the occasion will impose. She is ever the most thoughtful lady in the matter of her care for other people's convenience, and will, I am sure, comply.

To George

THE meadow hay is cut in the field beyond the road. The scent of it is floated to my nostrils as I write. It comes mingled with the scents of honeysuckle in the hedge, of syringa in the shrubbery, of a field of 'second crop' clover beyond the kitchen-garden, of the screen of sweet peas at my back. When Nan and I walk among the newly-cut hay, the horses and labourers having left the field, we watch with anxious commiseration the parent partridges who have lost their broods, running up and down the swathes in the now unrecognizable field in eager search for children and home. Poor fathers and mothers! We pray they do not know how short is their time for the enjoyment of family cares, how few weeks separate their domestic security from the terrors of the shooting season.

The air vibrates with incessant chirpings and twitterings which take now the place of the more tuneful songs of nightingale, of thrush, of blackbird. They tell me that the robin's sweet and wistful note is heard no more until the autumn. But Robin, himself, and all his numerous progeny, I rejoice to see, is with us still, bolder even than of yore, and more determined in his raids upon our tea-table. One perched upon Nan's toe, the other morning, as she sat, her legs sticking out from her short skirts, on the grass at my feet. Another made himself at home upon my shady hat, pecking with relentless little beak at the straw.

Among birds, I am inclined to call Robin Redbreast the 'perfect pearl.' No other, in the daintiness of his carriage, the bravery of his costume, the exquisiteness of his person, the dearness of his friendly, fearless nature, and the poetry of his legendary history, can approach him.

There was a child in one of the cottage-homes who plucked one alive, the other day. I wonder the wrath of God did not fall on the village that sheltered parents and teachers responsible for the ignorance which could make such a crime possible.

Beyond punishing a horse who does not know what is expected of him, but backs when he should go forward or vice versa, the men of the labouring class are not, I am assured, cruel; the team-men who are responsible for them have a pride in, and affection for the horses under their care. But, for the reason that they have learnt no better, the younger generation is of opinion the animal world has been created for the purpose of providing targets to fling stones at, and victims for ingenious methods of torment.

O God, that seest it, do not suffer it. Avenge it; not on them who know no better, but on us, in church and home and school; who have known and have refrained from teaching.

To George

THE thermometer stands at 80 in the shade, to-day. There has been no rain for a fortnight. The lawn is turning to a whity-brown, the grass crackling beneath your tread; the young plants of sunflowers and hollyhocks and phlox are drooping, even the hardy antirrhinums seem to flag. The air is filled with insects – we have made the acquaintance of three different species of genus gnat all of which are athirst for human blood. Midges creep beneath the lace of our dresses and crawl through the hair of our heads. From the small hours of morning, when he cometh forth like a bridegroom from his chamber, rejoicing like a strong man to run his course, until he sinks unwearied, in splendour of gold, of rose, of amethyst, to his regal bed, the sun shines upon all the land. Nothing is laid from the heat thereof.

Nan and I went this evening to watch pretty Nora Chisholm feed her turkeys. She has a hundred planted out with their mothers in the Grange beautiful orchard. Where it has not been cut for their convenience the grass waves high above their heads. Nan likes to watch Nora chop the nettles she mingles so freely with their food, grasping them in her resolute little hand, unafraid. She likes to trot by Nora's side, chattering, asking her endless questions; helping to carry the curd, the barley-meal; the custard, the black oats, with which clever Nora feeds her variously aged broods.

Nora is a picture, standing beneath the apple-trees in her green cotton frock, her shady rush hat trimmed with its wreath of red poppies. The little broods run screaming to her as she appears. When the vieux papa of the families comes upon the scene, his parental attentions are sternly discouraged.

'What did you hang your father with?' Nora ironically inquires of him.

'Halter, halter, halter,' unabashed replies, or is supposed to reply, the gobbler.

Nan is immensely interested in that piece of family history. 'Yes – but do tell me, did he really – *really*, you know – hang his father?' she persistently inquires.

Nora will never get married, she tells me, soberly, and with no pretence of satisfaction in the fact.

'Who is there I could marry?' she asks. 'From Monday morning to Saturday night I do not see a man above the station of the butcher, the baker, the dealer, who comes to buy the pigs.'

'But you go to other places. I see you riding off, your racquet in your hand.'

'To other farm-houses like this; to meet other girls like me.'

'And the brothers of the girls, Nora?'

'Away in London, in Canada, in Africa, in India. Or at college, like Dick. No farmer who is of the class called gentleman-farmer is any longer bringing up his son to that business, and there is no other business or profession to be followed in the country.'

So, all the young men, it appears, are away, and for ever miss the pretty picture of Nora beneath the apple-trees.

It is a pity, one feels, as one watches the girl going sensibly through her useful days; as one listens to her, and looks at her strong figure and healthy face. And Nora, who, although she looks so young, is already twenty-seven, knows also that it is a pity. You can see it in her eyes and hear it in her voice as she talks.

To George

THE most absurd thing has happened.

That ridiculous Major Barkaway has come down and made me, in cold blood, an offer of marriage.

Hildred was always threatening me with this finale; but although I let her have her joke, I paid no heed to her prophecy.

As you read, do not, my dear boy, let your anger get the better of your laughter, as, stupidly, I let my laughter get the better of my anger when I refused him. With the result that he would not look upon my answer as final.

Then the devil entered into me, and I thought it would amuse me and punish him to keep the old fortune-hunter in suspense.

How, if Hildred and I both reserve a suitor, to refuse at the 'Bazaar and Garden Fête'? It will lend a spark of interest to an otherwise deadly occasion, and at my share in it, at least, Hildred will be amused.

The Major stared at me with offence in his cold eyes when I laughed. 'It is a serious question,' he said stiffly. 'I have given much thought to it. It will be only right that you should do so, likewise. To laugh –' he said, and glared upon me; 'to laugh – !' Words failed him to express his feeling. 'We are not boy and girl,' he reminded me.

'I am – er – fifty-two,' he said. The hesitation was to his credit, proving that he does not tell a lie glibly.

'It should be a bond between us, seeing that fifty-two is also my age,' I told him, and did not divulge the fact that I have it on irrefutable authority that he was sixty-one on his last birthday.

(He mentioned inadvertently one day that he remembered the Indian Mutiny. People who grow younger rather than older with the years should be careful what they remember.)

While we were on the subject of age I went on to say to him that I thought the husband should be older than the wife. 'Let the woman take an elder than herself,' I reminded him.

'You, who admire youth and good looks, should marry a younger wife, Major.'

He waved a stiff hand with the gracious intimation that those advantages he would forgo.

'Should you expect me to live in your cottage?' I asked him.

Hildred has often amused herself by sketching me, Charlotte Poole, in the evening of my days, leaning by the Major's side over a dirty railing, to scratch the back of a disgusting pig.

He looked at me sharply. He imagined not, he said. His cottage could scarcely be considered commodious enough for two.

'You are proposing to take up your abode here, with me, then?'

The small, cold eyes appeared to kindle as he allowed them to rove over my pretty, roomy house, and sweet spacious garden. 'That could be left for future arrangement,' he said. 'We should not be tied to any one place, I presume.'

He waited for a moment. Then, 'You are not bound by any – er – *restriction*, I suppose?' he said anxiously.

I told him gently, 'No. Unless the fact that my fortune leaves me on my re-marriage might be looked on – by some mercenary people – in the light of a restriction.'

(Put in that *conditional* kind of way, it was not exactly telling a lie, was it? If it was, I do not repent.)

You should have seen his face! The poor, transparent, old dissembler! He prides himself on his stolidity, and his power of concealing his thoughts and feelings. But they were by no means inscrutable as I dealt this blow. His jaw dropped to his threadbare necktie; he put up his hand to hide that fact, and it shook. I saw that for the moment he was unable to utter, and proceeded equably to fill up the hiatus.

'Husbands have a terror of fortune-hunters,' I told him. 'They think to protect their widows against them by that mean device. But I have too good an opinion of myself to believe that a man would want to marry me simply for my money.'

He bent an angry head in assent, without a smile.

'In the event of my doing as you propose, therefore,' I went mercilessly on, 'this place would, I fear, be out of the question. It is an unassuming little home, but it costs a good deal to keep up. I have no means of judging what your own income is, Major?'

'Small. It is very small,' he snapped.

'You would not be able, for instance, to keep a carriage for me, I suppose? Nor a house in town? Mine is let, for the present, but I am looking forward to going back to it some day.'

'I have nothing to offer you but a share of my home,' he said. He snapped the dry finger-tips loudly upon the dry knuckles, and the small blue eyes, glittering with anxiety, clung to my face.

'I have always admired your little cottage,' I told him; 'and the picturesque negligence of its garden; and your pig. I am, as I am sure you have heard me say, many times, quite in love with Dulditch and its society –'

I paused there, and seemed to consider. I saw his agony. His face was drawn as long as a fiddle, his hands trembled as he quickly snapped his fingers.

'I fear you would be making too big a sacrifice?' he said slowly.

'But – to add to our little store – there would, of course, be what I might earn at my profession,' I went on.

'Your profession?'

'I write, you may have heard.'

He gave me a cold glance of disappointment and distaste, and glowered at the distance.

'Every little, in our small ménage, would help,' I reminded him softly.

He held the fingers poised above the bony knuckles, and screwed his eyes upon my face in the moment's pause.

'We might put it down at – what? Fifty?'

'Fifty what, Major Barkaway?'

'Your earnings? Do they total up to fifty pounds a year?'

I gave the subject a moment's anxious consideration.

'While I can go on with my work, I think we might say – fifty. It would find me in dress,' I told him. 'I am not, as you see, a dressy person.'

With a glance at my black muslin dress and my shady black hat he acknowledged ruefully that I was not.

I had to do all the talking. At an emergency his ridiculous old man-of-the-world pose fails him. He sat before me, aged, and shrunken, and shrivelled, unable to find words or to force smiles to hide the fact that he had got himself into a hideous mess, and knew it.

'It will be a great sacrifice for you to make,' he reminded me many times; and I as often repeated the fact that women were always ready to sacrifice themselves, and even enjoyed the opportunity.

'There is a great deal to consider,' at length he got out. 'We must not be too hasty. Perhaps you will give – you will take time. Do not give me a final answer to-day. I can – wait.'

I promised not to keep him in suspense too long.

He walked away, a dejected and broken-looking Major, yet with an angry glint in his small blue eyes. There was something like hatred of me in his glance as I smilingly gave him my hand.

After the first shock, I confess to you, George, I thoroughly enjoyed the interview, and I look forward without a grain of compunction to the amusement to be gleaned from the situation. I am determined to wring his withers for him, and to punish the old creature to the limit of my ingenuity.

How dares he, that mindless nincompoop, propose such a thing to me? Imagine my changing the name that your father gave me – *my* name that is familiar in two continents – for – Barkaway! Imagine my giving up my independence for the society of this Major of Volunteers, of Militia, of whatever it is – and his pig! What excuse has he but that of greed?

Then, I will keep him dangling in fear and torment of mind, and watch his writhings and wrigglings to escape without remorse.

To George

VOW me no vows! Alas for the vanity of resolutions. I would have loved to give a lesson to the hero of the incident recorded yesterday, but he has known how to defeat my project of vengeance.

Late last night a note was brought me from him. It won't take me long to transcribe. You know how sparing of pen and ink loquacious people are, and the difficulty they have to express themselves on paper? Short as the missive was, I sincerely hope the Major's agonies in writing it were long and cruel!

'MY DEAR MRS. POOLE' – it ran – 'On reflection I find I ought not to ask the sacrifice of you. Please regard what has passed between us as unsaid. – With every regard, yours sincerely,
'ALBERT BARKAWAY.
'Excuse haste.'

What a letter from what an old person!

Still no rain. Whiter and whiter grows the grass beyond the needle-covered shadow of my fir-tree; the leaves of the roses, scarcely blown, fall upon the lawn; the flowers of the foxglove hang limp and lifeless on the stem; the delphiniums are scorched to a lighter blue; the caterpillars have eaten the leaves on the currant bushes; the gooseberries have 'got the blight'; and Syers has given up watering the begonias because the pump is going dry.

But all these are minor misfortunes in my gardener's estimation compared with the overwhelming calamity that a ring of inyins in his own garden has 'gone off.' 'Heart-breakin'' Syers announces that this condition of things is, and repeats at intervals – his mind on the inyins, while I, naturally, would interest him in the unsatisfactory condition of my own affairs – 'heart-breakin', tha's what 'tis, I tell ye; and 'tain't no other.'

Every evening the skies give promise of rain; toads and frogs emerge from their decent hiding-places, and, fearless and unashamed, walk the garden paths; great black spiders appear indoors, obtruding their unwelcome forms on our notice on snowy window curtains, on ceilings; are sent home to us with the clean linen from the wash, hide in the folds of the bed-clothes. Earwigs drop from every flower that is gathered, make homes in our sponges, haunt our store-cupboards. All these are signs of rain, we are told. Surely, before morning rain will fall. Every morning we arise, the earth unrefreshed even by dews, to another dazzling day.

As I watch the dawn 'come up like thunder' from beyond the fields of corn thirsting for rain; see the sun blazing at noonday, pitiless, angrily destructive; the crimson flaming sunset; I realize as never before that the sun is only a furnace, destructive, not beneficent; terrifying, awful in its nature.

In church they prayed for rain on Sunday.

'I hope it won't come till after Thursday, all the same,' the Rector remarked, when service was over.

Thursday is the day of the Rectory Garden Fête and Bazaar. For, after all, the Hobbleboys 'found it would not be convenient,' and backed out of holding it at the Hall.

'The Almighty will make His plans for the refreshment of a parched and thirsty earth with due regard to the success of the Bazaar,' I assured the man of God.

'We can't possibly postpone it,' Mr. Flatt lamented, 'because the Hobbleboys are leaving for Yorkshire the next day.'

'God won't let it rain if the Hobbleboys will be inconvenienced.'

'They certainly are always very fortunate in weather,' he smugly remarks.

He does not come to visit me, or her little daughter to whom he was supposed to be devoted, now that Hildred is away. I have seen nothing of my Major. He must be sorely missing an ear into which to pour his stories of little local bigwigs. I am not sorry, for my part, for a respite.

Nan and I are each other's companion, and amuse ourselves very well. In answer to my inquiry as to whether she does not sometimes wish for other little girls to play with, she promptly assures me that she likes old ladies best.

'You have not to be so giving up with old ladies,' she explains. 'Also there is not so much of giving away.'

When I demand enlightenment she informs me, 'When I go to parties, you see, Gran, other children has the toys as much as me. They nearly always has what I want. And when they want mine I has to give up to them, mummy says, because I'm her dear little girl; and when Ina and Doris come to my house to play, "You must give way to them because you're a lady," Nurse says. So, because I'm a lady and mother's dear little girl, I don't have any fun, or many toys. It's extremely annoying, Gran.'

'And old ladies do not demand such sacrifices from you?'

'You see, they never wants my toys. They don't want to play hide-and-seek when I wish to play horses. I wonder why they don't?' she reflected, looking with suddenly aroused interest at me. 'Why don't you, Gran? When I am old I will make every single little girl give up and give away.'

To George

WELL, my dear boy, the great day of the Rectory Bazaar and Garden Fête is over. Rain mercifully withheld, in spite of half-hearted prayers at church, and the needs of the parching earth.

A melancholy entertainment, the Fête. (Major Barkaway, by the way, persists in calling it a 'feet.' By a like eccentricity I note he says suffragette with the *g* hard, and Kruger with the *g* soft. I suppose the Hobbleboys are pleased so to pronounce those words. It would not do for the rest of us to indulge any private prejudices of our own against the authority of people who, as the Major often points out, '*ought* to know.')

A scorched lawn, without an inch of shade; a sweltering tent, and two or three tables heaped with pin-cushions and children's pinafores in the full blaze of the sun. The Wotton town band playing beneath a chestnut in the meadow between the garden and the church; about fifty women and fifteen men dispiritedly moving about; they collect, at random, heaps of useless articles from eager stall-holders, careless apparently of the nature of their purchases, so that the sum they have conscientiously devoted to the cause in hand, as the duty of men and women who would presently have bazaars and garden feets of their own, is expended. Tea at a shilling a head, served under the charge of Nora Chisholm, at little tables set out in the Lovers' Walk. (All the gardens in the neighbourhood have Lovers' Walks, by the by. They consist of winding paths through shrubberies beneath overshadowing trees.)

'In vain the net is spread in sight of any bird,' Nora quotes, when commenting on the fact that in spite of fully advertised accommodation for their comfort, no lovers come to walk there.

Nan, with a distrait air, and a trayful of 'button-holes' slung round her shoulders, wanders over the crackling grass of the lawn, offering a rosebud for sale, now and then when she thinks of it.

Major Barkaway, in charge of a target and an air-gun, collected during the day, at a penny a shot, the noble sum of ninepence.

Hildred, her tall figure draped in soft black transparencies over white silk, helped Bertha Flatt at her stall, which, with that presided over by the Misses Hobbleboy, was in the tent. Watching for the dramatic moment when he should receive his answer, I observed that the Rector was flustered and embarrassed in his greeting of her, that he made no pretences for lingering at her side, but with a forced liveliness of demeanour wandered from group to group, beads of perspiration on his fat face, his patient arms filled with cushions and embroideries, deposited there for sale by the Miss Hobbleboys.

Having speedily retired from the glare of the sun and the more active scene to the shade and seclusion of one of Nora's comfortable chairs in the Lovers' Walk, I was not eye-witness of the historic moment when Mrs. Hobbleboy and Hildred, supposed to have encountered years ago at a hotel in Geneva, at last came face to face: but from various accounts of that meeting, big with fate, I have gathered that something like the following took place.

The wife of the squire of Dulditch – I write him always with a little 's' because he is such a little squire – in making her semi-royal progress from stall to stall, came face to face at last with Mrs. Valetta, who was presented. With that charming, placid smile you remember, George – Hildred's mouth does not simply widen at such moments as do the mouths of less fortunate people, but retains in the most cunning fashion its beautiful form of bow – she offered her hand.

Mrs. Hobbleboy, making a stiff inclination of head, ignored the hand, and glared with a fierce accusatory glance into the fair face of my future daughter-in-law. Then, turning her gaze upon the horrified face of Bertha Flatt, who had made the introduction:

'This is not the lady I met at Geneva,' she said; and with that pregnant sentence upon her lips walked away with what dignity her five-feet-two of stout, outraged humanity can command, while Hildred, in blissful unconsciousness of the tragic nature of the episode, went on offering the night-dress bags, the pin-cushions, the handkerchief boxes, with propitiating smiles to the ladies in white muslin or the ladies in black voile who stopped to turn over the contents of her stall.

The dear girl's mind, she explained to me, had been diverted from Dulditch affairs during her week in town to such an extent that she had entirely forgotten what depended on Mrs. Hobbleboy's failure to establish her as the Mrs. Valetta she had met at the Hotel Bristol, Geneva.

But the Rector had not forgotten. He had followed the great little lady to secure her name and her sixpence for the lottery he was getting up for one of the cushions with which he was laden. He had seen the expression on her face as her eyes had fallen on that of the other lady, he had heard the words on her lips; and as his patroness moved away he moved hastily in another direction.

She pursued him with a grim determination: her accustomed short-legged strut was accelerated almost to a trot as he hurried across the lawn, taking refuge in the shrubbery's densest path. She marked his hiding-place, and caught him there, calling upon his name. His face was sea-green, and he wore a hang-dog look as he turned. And I in my chair, hard-by, in the Lovers' Walk, caught glimpses, through the syringas and the laurels, of the pair, and heard their conversation.

'That person representing herself as wife of the Mr. Valetta we knew at Geneva is not his wife,' she began at once.

The Reverend Algernon looked at her in a miserable silence.

'That was a stout and short and dark woman. This person does not even resemble her.'

'Indeed?' the Rector got out, sulkily discouraging.

'You see what it involves? I have explained to you before. If she is Mrs. John Valetta, and yet not the widow of the man at Geneva, she is the widow of his son. In which case you know her disgraceful history, Mr. Flatt? The history of that unfortunate young man, and of the low woman he disgraced himself by marrying? It is not possible you have forgotten?'

'It is possible there is some mistake, Mrs. Hobbleboy.'

'Mistake, Mr. Flatt? You mean that I am mistaken?'

'Mrs. Valetta is, quite beyond question, a lady-like person.' (In Dulditch they still talk of women being lady-like, and speak of gentlemanly men.)

'She was a woman of *bad character*. Her husband divorced her. Her name was in all the papers. I was compelled to take a certain interest through having met the young man's quite presentable father and mother at Geneva. I think you hardly realise, Mr. Flatt, that this person is here, in your grounds? That she is actually in the tent in which my two daughters are serving. You, who are responsible for bringing her here, must decide at once what must be done.'

'Nothing can be done, Mrs. Hobbleboy.' The tone of the harassed man's voice was irritable and exasperated. 'What are you expecting me to do, may I ask?'

'This woman is standing by your sister's side. In the same tent with Nesta and Malvina. You understand that she is notorious, Mr. Flatt? Can she not be removed?'

'That is absolutely impossible,' the poor parson said. He flung the cushion and table 'centre' on the ground. I saw the waving of his white handkerchief through the trees as he pulled it forth and passed it over his perspiring face. His courage rose. 'I have found Mrs. Valetta most lady-like,' he repeated. 'I do not believe the report.'

'Not believe? When I assure you it is so? I have had great suspicions all along, or I should have called, before we left for Devonshire. You cannot mean that you do not believe my word?'

'I mean no disrespect to you, Mrs. Hobbleboy. Of that I hope you are assured. But this lady – it is impossible to associate her with such a story! If you knew her as I do –'

Mrs. Hobbleboy's gaze must have struck icily to his bones, and he left the sentence unfinished. 'I am surprised at you,' was all she said.

'I think the tale should be corroborated,' he faltered. 'You would not wish me to act until we have corroboration?'

'I need only the evidence of my own eyes,' the lady said, and with dignity turned away. She looked back at him over her shoulder and delivered her ultimatum. 'I decline to allow my daughters to remain in the tent with that – person,' she said. 'You must decide if my daughters and I leave your grounds, or Mrs. Valetta.'

As she disappeared I called to the unhappy Rector, miserably stooping for his cushions and paraphernalia. His face grew sicklier as he turned and saw me. For the moment he gazed, speechless.

'Would you be so good, Mr. Flatt, as to fetch Mrs. Valetta from the tent, where she must be by now in a melting condition? Bring her here to have tea with me under these trees.'

It was helping him out of a difficulty; yet he moved away uncertainly, and in a minute was back again.

'I am afraid you must have overheard something of what that vicious woman was saying?' he asked.

I nodded in affirmation, as unmovedly as might be.

'You – forgive my asking – you have nothing to say in disproof of the horrible charge she brings?'

'Certainly not,' I told him brusquely. 'Anything you want to know you can ask of Mrs. Valetta, herself. I do not meddle in her affairs.'

He stood in silence before me. Against the orange and green hues of the cushions he carried, his face, flabby all at once rather than fat, was like the face of a dead man; every joint of him relaxed in drooping dejection; every inch of his large frame expressive of the misery of the defeat of a darling project, and of uncertainty what to do.

'I have these to dispose of,' at last he said, indicating his hideous burden. 'Would it be troubling you too much to ask if you would yourself fetch Mrs. Valetta?' He walked a step or two away, and then again returned with a sheepish, hang-dog look.

'My sister will now perhaps be able to dispense with Mrs. Valetta's assistance at her stall,' he said, without looking at me. 'As you say, it is very hot in the tent for her —'

'I understand,' I said. He looked helplessly at me, and went.

Nan, with her tray of flowers, at this moment appearing, dragging her feet and humming to herself, was sent to fetch her mother.

'Bring her, if you have to pull her by the hair of her head,' were her instructions.

I was dying to tell her of what had taken place. But even my reproduction for her of the scene failed greatly to rouse her.

She laughed. 'Poor stupid woman! Poor stupid man!'

'Is that all you have to say?'

'It is our fault, Cousin Charlotte. We ought not to have mystified them. We should have explained.'

Hildred has come back from town, truth to tell, in a curious mood. She seems, in just that seven days of absence, to have forgotten, and to have detached herself from all our simple interests which had grown to suffice us here. She stands aloof, it seems; looks on and listens with a far-off, preoccupied air. She has had some rather important business matters to settle, she tells me, and I suppose cannot at once rid her mind of them.

'This woman has decided you are poor Johnny Valetta's – the young man's – wife.'

'I am not half so pretty, you should have told her; nor a quarter so attractive.'

'She thinks a woman with that history would contaminate the air she breathes.'

'Poor Mary! That is what all the unco' righteous think. If only they knew!'

'She will not allow her daughters and you to remain in the same tent.'

Her eyes opened a little wider at that. The blue as she grows older seems to dominate the grey and the green in her eyes. They were blue and beautiful to-day, beneath the shade of her large black hat. 'Really?' she said. 'But the tent is horribly stuffy, and I am glad to be released. It is nicer to sit here with you, in the cool, under the trees, Charlotte Poole.'

'Have you given the Rector his quietus yet, Hildred?'

She had not. 'He has not allowed me the chance to say anything. He is working energetically, poor thing, for the Bazaar.'

'No! He is afraid. He is such a vain fool that he is not sure what your answer will be, and he dares not face it. I have watched him. He runs everywhere but where you are. He is in terror lest you should dash after him and accept him, now.'

'Is that so? Poor man! I will soon put him out of his pain,' she said; and instantly rose up, smiling, tall and elegant, from her chair. In a minute I had watched her making her way through the shrubs to the lawn.

In less than five minutes she was seated by my side again.

'Does it take so short a time as that to settle a despairing suitor?' I asked her.

She gave me a reproving glance, for Nora was now placing tea and strawberries upon the little table between us, and Nan, disburthened of her tray of roses, was also seated there.

'A most enormous, big, large motor, as big as Uncle Arthur's, has just stopped at the gate,' Nan informed us.

Nora's face lit with interest. 'It must be the Countess of Tatterbury,' she said. 'Oh, how pleased the Flatts will be! Once, four years ago, when the Bazaar was held at the Hall, she came there, but never has she turned up at the Rectory. If it is she, I do hope she'll come and get tea!'

She did. In two minutes she came, accompanied by a smiling and altogether altered Mrs. Hobbleboy, leading the way to one of Nora's tables in the shady Lovers' Walk. Behind the pair walked the male Hobbleboy and the Rector, in delighted conversation with a couple of women of the old Countess's party.

In one of these latter I recognised, of all people in the world, Etta Milgay. Often I have heard her talk of coming down to her Aunt's place in Norfolk, but until my eyes fell on her I had forgotten that she and I were in the same county.

No sooner were the new-comers all seated than Etta's restless eyes, roving around in search of something of greater interest than the fat face of the Rector of Dulditch, fell on me. I laughed at the blank astonishment of her gaze, and she flew up, ran across, seized on me.

'Charlotte Poole!' she cried – you know that strident unmanageable voice of hers, and her impulsive, irrepressible manner? – the occupants of all the little tables – the people had followed the Countess's party in a flock to tea, and Nora's hands were full – looked up and around, then decorously back to their bread-and-butter again, with pricked ears to listen.

'Well, what luck!' the noisy Etta cried. 'What luck for me! I *am* glad. Is this Mrs. Valetta? I have heard enough of you to be terribly jealous. I don't want to see you a bit, but how-d'ye-do? What a sweet little girl! Well, if I were an artist I would certainly make a picture of her and her mother; call it Spring and Summer, or something. Not very original; never mind. Come along, all of you. Some one carry the table, will you? – oh, I'm so sorry to trouble you – will you be so kind! – up to Lady Tatterbury's.

'Aunt Philippa! Who do you think I have found hiding in this forgotten corner of the universe? – I beg everybody's pardon, but it *is* rather out of the swim, isn't it? – This is Charlotte Poole. *The* Charlotte Poole, you know. You said you wanted to meet her. This is Mrs. Valetta who is going to marry her son – perhaps I oughtn't to have said that just yet, but it does not matter. This angel with the long brown silk legs and the brown lumpy curls is her little daughter. We *are* in luck to meet them here; and we'll all have tea together.'

Of course she did not get out quite so much as that without interruption, although with Etta's rattle it is difficult to edge a word in.

Have you met her, my dear boy? I forget. She is really a decent enough body, and amusing, when you are in the mood for her. She is by way of being an author, herself; that is to say, she has written a score or so of stories with which she attempts, generally unsuccessfully, to storm the magazines. She is one of the few people who would rather be seen in public with a poet than a peer. The fact that several of the latter grace her family circle may, in her case, be the explanation.

The Aunt who has not the same literary proclivities as the niece hid the fact to the best of her ability, was perhaps even a little more gracious than would have been the case because she could not recall what I had done, and thought it might appeal to her when she knew. Also because it was in Dulditch, where even a very small lion is an infrequent beast. A fact in natural history which may account for the phenomenon that its inhabitants do not recognize the animal when they see it.

In any case, before we had finished tea, Lady Tatterbury wanted to take us all back, there and then, to Trench with her, to stop the night; and, we all with one voice declining, insisted on sending a motor for us next day to have lunch with her and Etta; being thrown upon each other's society, they are, I can perceive, boring one another considerably.

(I may as well set forth here that we went. That a bundle of Etta's MSS. were returned to her by the afternoon post; that she read them to us, entreating to be told, since the magazines published the rubbish they (incontestably) do, why they refused, consistently and in a body, to publish *her* rubbish. That Lady Tatterbury fell in love with Nan, and wanted to keep her indefinitely. That Nan, being impelled thereto by the attraction of the pair of Shetlands kept for the use of the grandchild of the house, insisted on being left for a week, at any rate.

Faithless small wretch! I am dull and lost without her; while her mother sits silent, thinking of her or of you or of both, gazing and gazing into space; and very poor company, as I feel impelled to tell her.

But to go back to the 'Feet' and to Nora's tea-table.)

You can imagine, perhaps, what an effect all this gush on the part of Etta (to whom it is as natural to gush as to a mountain stream), all the affability of Lady Tatterbury had on our astonished neighbours.

Upon the Hobbleboys, staring and flabbergasted, was laid the onus of a momentous decision which must be made on the spot. Should they renounce their annual chance of a ten minutes' conversation with the old Earl of Tatterbury's widow, or should they risk the contamination of sitting down by the side of a nobody like the tenant of The Cottage, and of an abandoned creature such as they had decided Hildred to be?

With commendable promptitude they concluded to risk the contamination.

What the poor Rector's feelings were I cannot say, but he made himself busy, helping Nora to put the tea on the table; wrote down the name of Lady Tatterbury, who graciously consented 'to go in for' one of his hateful cushions, on his list; pocketed her sixpence; presently posted off, hot and pale and flustered, to the house for a fresh supply of cream, Nora's having gone sour.

By the time he had returned Nan had captured the Rectory cat, deposited it in the Countess's lap, and was on her knees beside the old lady, relating incidents in its history, and pointing out the greenness in its eyes. Etta, her straight, iron-grey hair fluffed out like ruffled untidy wings on each side of her enthusiastic, high-nosed face, was spluttering out an account of an evening at the Diadem where my play – or rather the play founded on my book – is making a success.

'The King was there,' she cried, 'and a whole crowd of great people – really great, you know.'

She ran off a list of names, having no meaning, of course, in the ears of the Hobbleboys, sitting dumbfounded with staring eyes; but not unknown to Fame, for all that.

'The curtain went up seven times, at least, after each act,' she spluttered on. 'I was so excited, so carried away, I laughed, and laughed, with the tears running down my face.'

They were running down the face of the hysterical, dear creature while she talked. She flung a hand across my lap and grasped and shook my knee. 'And to think that you wrote it all, you naughty, old retiring thing, sitting so quietly here in this lost little hole of a place; and money pouring into your coffers in hatfuls, and every one who *is* any one dying to kneel at your feet. You are a fraud. That is what you are, Charlotte Poole, with your country cottage and your shady hat –'

It was all high-flown and extravagant, of course; but I could not be sorry for the absurdity, with Mrs. Hobbleboy looking on and listening, the smile she had put on growing into a fixed and painful grimace on her common face; with the Rector, in a sickly pallor, uncomfortably shunning every one's eyes; with even the poor, ridiculous old Major, hurrying up to bow before Lady Tatterbury (who, absorbed with Nan and her kitten, took absolutely no notice of him), looking on and listening.

As all were assembled there I thought to seize the opportunity to set another matter, once and for all, to rest.

'Major Barkaway,' I said. His small blue eyes, staring at me above his tea-cup as if he saw me for the first time, were ready to drop from their sockets into his tea in his surprise at the situation. 'I think you mentioned that some friends of yours had met Mr. and Mrs. John Valetta at the Hotel Bristol in Geneva, some years ago? I wanted to tell you that I find my friend was never there.'

'It must have been my husband with his first wife,' Hildred explained, with her gentle air of indifference. 'You see, I was his second.'

But I am sure you are tired and disgusted, my poor old George, with all this silly business. I am disgusted too, with the Hobbleboys and Flatts of Dulditch; and with myself also, for being small enough to take an interest in such folastries, and for wasting my time and yours in their recapitulation.

To George

'I CAN'T think why Grans are so much kinder and nicer to little girls than their mummies are,' Nan has just remarked to me. There has been a difference of opinion between Mrs. and Miss Valetta on the subject of tree-climbing, and Nan and her mother are 'out.'

'Then I will tell you why,' I said. 'It is because mummies do not realize that they must lose their little girls very quickly; and Grans, who have had boys and girls of their own, know it only too well.'

'But mummy won't never lose me, Gran. I shall always be her little girl.'

'No, you won't. You'll be her big girl. A very different thing.'

'Mummy will have me, all the same.'

'Indeed she won't. You that are you, now, will be as lost to her in a few years as if the earth had opened and swallowed you up.'

'I think you are telling untroofs, Gran. If ever mummy wants to send me away, I won't go. I shall be *always* with her.'

'I tell you, No. A fine, big, beautiful young person, calling herself Nan, will be there; who will be kind to her mother in a condescending way, but will have to snub her sometimes; because she is not up-to-date; or because, her eyes grown a little dim perhaps, she can't see things in just the light the grown-up daughter desires her to see them; or because she is always listening to lost voices of long ago, talking of other times and other manners, and so is not quick to hear aright in the present.'

('What is "snub" Gran? It is a very ugly word.'

'It is what you will do to your mummy.'

'You are not at all a polite lady. As if I should snub my darling mummy!')

'Then your poor mummy will begin looking for you. "Where is my precious Nan?" she will say. "My precious *little* Nan?" And she will hunt for you in the old nursery, look for you under the table, listen for your voice as you play in the garden – even try to get a glimpse of you as you climb the trees, Nan –'

('My mummy *won't* let me climb the trees; it is a shame; she –'

'She'll wish she had!) And little Nan won't be there. Quite, quite gone. Lost for ever.'

('Naughty Gran! You are teasing. I don't love you at all when you tease!')

'And poor mummies don't know this. So they scold their little girls when they tear their frocks and stockings, climbing trees; and sometimes complain of the trouble of them, and weary for the time when they shall grow up and be sensible and *companions*. But Grans know; because, you see, they have experience. And so they cling to their little naughty Nans; and say to Time, "Stay! Stay! Leave her to me as she is. Don't, don't, oh, cruel, cruel years, let her grow big, or cease to be troublesome. I don't want her to be wise; I don't want a grown-up companion. Let me keep my little Nan!" That is what the Grans say.'

Nan considered the situation gravely for a minute.

'And I don't wish never to grow up, neither,' she said then. 'And I think the Grans are the wisest.'

'Well, tell your mother so.'

'That, you see, Gran, would not be at all polite,' said Nan reprovingly.

To George

I HAVE had a shock this morning. To you, my dearest son, it will be a shock also, and I hardly know how to tell you, that you may least feel it.

Among my roses in this 'pleasing land of drowsy-hed' I have been living such a peaceful, lazy life, so secure as it seemed from annoyances; with Hildred for my sole companion; only my gardener to contradict me; only Nan to tease. If my brain has been growing torpid, my wits dulled, my working powers atrophied, I have yet felt so much at ease, so sheltered from annoyances, so safe from alarms!

'You see, The Cottage is such a laughing place,' Nan says.

And certainly the spirit of Cheerfulness did seem to have laid his hand in blessing upon my little pleasant home.

But to-day a blow from the blue has fallen; and as is always the case, the grief I am called on to bear appears at the moment to be that I am least capable of bearing with fortitude.

When you were quite a tiny boy and cut your finger, you explained, I remember, that you did not cry for your own pain, but for 'mummy, who would be so sorry.' Well, I used to feel all your bruises and your baby wounds, I know, in those far-off days; and whatever harm happens to you now, George, I suffer from it still.

That warm-hearted, tête-montée, gushing Etta it is to whom was due the thunderbolt which has shattered and scattered our peace. Twice or thrice in Mrs. Valetta's hearing she spoke of the fact that Hildred was to be my daughter-in-law. Once or twice, Hildred either did not or would not hear; on the third occasion she said smilingly, but with emphasis, that Etta had been wrongly informed; and when we were alone again she expressed a certain annoyance with me for allowing a wrong impression on this matter to gain ground among my friends.

'My dear woman,' I made answer, 'you are not about to turn prude, I sincerely hope. Are you, at your age, like a silly bashful girl, afraid to acknowledge the fact that she has a lover until the man is her husband, almost? You know very well that George is devoted to you; *is* your lover; only waits the moment to put into words that which no words are required to express. Perhaps I have said as much to Etta Milgay – what harm is done?'

Then the blow fell.

'I have been waiting to speak to you about this,' she said, 'and lacking the courage. What you have so strangely set your heart on, Cousin Charlotte, can never be. I am not waiting for your son to ask me to marry him. Much as I like and admire George, never could I marry him. And I am engaged at the present moment to marry another man.'

There it is; baldly as she put it. My heart bleeds as I write it down. I thought at first I never could summon courage to write it to you.

Of course I have quarrelled with Hildred – or have tried to do so. You know from of old she is one of those intensely irritating people who won't quarrel.

I have hopes, my dear, that in time you will come to see she is not suited to you, on this account if on no other. If I have not mentioned it before I will mention now that I have of late found the irksomeness of living with a person who will not let herself go, who will give her thoughts no tongue. Emotions are not given to stagnate in us, unused. I thank the Gods, above all, for having given me the power of expression. Let us speak what is in us, I say; clear the air, and breathe the freer for it.

Perhaps I need not tell you that I said, in the pain and anger of the moment, as much if not more than I felt. I spared her not at all, George.

But in the end she cried and I cried; and when two women sit and weep together I suppose anger has died out of their hearts. I do not hate Hildred any longer, but I have not forgiven her. Forgive her, my dear George, I will not, till you can write to assure me the hurt after all is not a deadly one.

And, George dear, I beseech you, even in these first moments of your disappointment, do not be too unhappy. She is a beautiful woman, I admit, and a rich, and an amiable; but she is older by ten years than when you saw her last, and I begin to detect signs in her of a double chin. She told me, long ago, that her waist is two inches bigger than she wished it to be. I have not mentioned it before, but already, I assure you, she does not look so handsome in the morning as at night. With a uniform amiability I for one have small patience; and as for fortune – you will have enough.

And all this time I have not told you who the man is!

The curate-youth with the invalid mother she met at Cannes. He who crawled about on all fours, Nan on his back.

I remember having a suspicion from the first he did not grovel for Nan's favour alone.

What a fool she has made of herself! Neither money, nor position, nor even man's estate! – for he is years younger than she is. Nothing to recommend him, that I can hear of, but a pretended devotion to Nan!

But it seems he fell in love with Hildred on the first day he saw her, told her so on the second, and has been pestering her with the story of his adoration ever since. While you, my dear George, who have known her all her life, were too proud to lift a finger.

The more I see of Life – 'solitary, poor, nasty, brutish, short' – the more surely I perceive that personal dignity is a quality which puts a man out of the running for any goal in this vulgar, scrambling, hurly-burly of a world. You sit out there, among your tea-shrubs in Ceylon, and for the sake of some scruple best known to yourself, or for the innate delicacy of your nature, refrain from putting pen to paper to express the ardent desire of your soul; while this cub of a boy-curate, without a thought but to get what he wants, hammers away at the foolish woman's heart. In the result noise and clamour win as they always do.

It turns out now that it was in response to an appeal from his mother, brought back to die in her home in London, that Mrs. Valetta went up to town – not to see her solicitor! Amongst them this charming engagement was hatched up.

'It has made his poor mother very happy; and Nan will be pleased,' Hildred somewhat sheepishly declared.

I have small patience with such subterfuge.

'And do you suppose when he stands in the place of Nan's father he will crawl on all fours?' I asked her. 'Are you making this marriage, Hildred, solely because a dying woman wishes to arrange a satisfactory alliance for son, and your little girl enjoys romping with a boy? Or do you happen to be in love with the curate-creature himself?'

She turned away without any answer; but I had seen her face; it was suddenly ashamed, and ablaze; like the face of a girl of seventeen.

It all makes me so angry; and so sick at heart.

Oh, my dearest boy, I beseech you do not be too unhappy. It is, after all, the people who get what they want who have the bitterest griefs to bear. Better to lose and laugh than to win and weep.

It has been for years a dream of mine that my son and the woman I loved best in the world should marry. But an unfulfilled dream is better than a long regret. And remember –

But a woman is in a parlous state when she philosophizes. I leave off as I began with the words, 'I am very miserable; and very angry.'

To George

TO-DAY that wretched boy Clement's trial comes on at the Assizes.

It was confidently expected that he would get five years; the revengeful rustic mind even fixed it at fifteen, and for all I could discover would not have abated the sentence, or lessened one jot the sufferings of the whilom friend and neighbour. However, to the intense surprise of every one, and apparently to the acute disappointment of the boy's acquaintances, the sentence is six months, only.

Fearing the worst, I tried to prevent the mother from going to hear her son sentenced, but could only prevail on her to allow one of the other village women to accompany her.

It was Syers' wife, always ready for a jaunt, she whose house and garden are the picture of neatness and care, who spends her Saturday evenings dancing and singing at the public-house, who volunteered to bear the poor woman company. She came in to see me, this evening, on their return, and gave me her account of the trial.

Clemmy, it seems, by advice from the young lawyer who defended him, pleaded guilty, thus cutting the ground from beneath the feet of the mother, prepared to swear that her son never left her side all the day of the crime.

The officers of the court tried to prevent her appearance there, but she fought her way through them as she has fought it through life, and was only hindered by half-a-dozen policemen from storming the witness-box to give her false evidence.

'He'd got his new suit on, Clemmy had. 'Twas the navy suit he bought wi' th' suvreign he stole from poor Laura. Pale, he looked, from missin' th' sun, but smart enough; and after he'd said th' word "Guilty" to th' Judge he kep' a-smilin'-like, and his eyes a-wanderin' round.

'Th' Judge, he'd a right agrable sort o' way with 'm – more like an old lady I thought he looked then a old gen'leman, as they tell me, for sure, he is. Presently he lifted his eye from the paper what he was allust a-writin' on, 'steads o' mindin' what was a-goin' on around 'm, and he takes a long look at Clemmy, a-standin' up, so nate and smiling in 's bes' cloes! "Ain't there no man nor woman i' this here court to spake a word for this here lad," he say. Like as if he was wholly sorrerful to sen' sech an agrable-lookin' young man to prison.

'Eliza, she'd fought her way t'ro' the perlice, kickin' and scratchin' of 'em, me a-follerin' (seein' as you, ma'am, had giv me th' orders to stan' by her), to th' back o' th' witness-box, where th' Judge as he sat on his t'rone couldn't see her. "I'm here," she hollered out; "I'm his mother. I'll spake for him."

'So th' Judge he pointed with his pen to th' perlice, and they shoved her into th' witness-box, and shoved me out on't, a-hangin' on to her, accordin' to orders. Like a crazed woman Eliza looked, her hat o' one side, her necktie tore round to the back, and 'er cape unfastened at th' t'roat, t'rough a-scrimmagin' wi' th' perlice. She di'n't wait for no questions. "I'm his mother," says she, bold as a tiger, a-facin' th' Judge. Wholly done I felt when I see her there and heared her. 'What'll come o' this," says I to myself. "You're a lost woman, Eliza." "He never done it, my Lord. My Clemmy's a good lad. A good son. He never done it," says she.

' "Silence, my good woman!" the Judge, he say. "By this wi'lence you're a-injurin' your son's cause. Your son," he say, a-lookin' down at his papers again, "have admitted he done it. Have you," the Judge say, a-lookin' at 'er, and wholly gentle-like, "have you anything to say for the prisoner which may affect 's sentence," he say.

'Eliza, come to that, hadn't got nothin' to bring for'ard. "He's my son," she kep' a-sayin'. "He's my good lad. He's my son. He's my son."

'Come to think on't, tha's all she'd got ter say in Clemmy's favour; and she said it a-cryin' of it out; and a-shakin' her fist, as if 'twas a threat to 'em all.

'The Judge he beckoned to the perlice to take 'er away; he tarned 's eyes on Clemmy, a-smilin' round; he told 'm as how 'twas his mother who loved 'm what had seft 'm from warse, and he were allust to remember it. Then says he short and sharp, "Six mon's."

' "Good-bye, mother," Clemmy, he say; and down he went 'twixt the perlice; and Eliza (I was shamed on 'er) she took on orful, a-callin' out th' warst o' wards to th' Judge. But she'd ever an ill-tongue in 'er hid, my neighbour had, and you'd know it, ma'am, if you heared her a-goin' on when there ain't no sof' water i' th' rain-tub for washin'-day, or when th' smuts fr' th' chimbley falls on the sheets a-dryin' on th' guseberry bushes.'

Do not suppose my gardener's wife was kept to the subject in hand so straitly as is set down in the above report. She sighed and made a face for weeping over the glass of port with which I regaled her, and interrupted the thread of discourse often to tell me that she had overdone herself the day before, a-playin' of a neighbour's part; and that in spite of the fact that she ha'n't had a mite o' wittles inside 'er, bes' part o' th' day, suffin' fare to lay like a great ball on her chist.

These people love to consider themselves invalids. If you wish to ingratiate yourself with them you must comment on their delicacy of appearance. Listen to two women encountering on the way to the fields with their husbands' dinner, or meeting in the shop on the day they go to lay in their weekly stores:

'Yew look rare an' bad, bor. Wha's come to ye?'

160

'Thank ye, Mrs. Browne; yew ain't up to no matters yerself, this arternune, I'll lay a penny. Leastways you're a-lookin' fit to drop.'

To George

THE drought has broken up at last.

Hildred and I sat in the porch one evening in last week and watched the descent of the first gentle drops of rain. The earth, so unused to moisture, of late, forgot to imbibe; rivulets ran speedily over the hard gravel of the walks, while little pools formed on the parched lawn. But 'the patient rain went on raining,' and soon was soaking into a thirsty land which drank, and gasped for drink again.

Is there any sight more refreshing to eyes tired with watching for signs of a shower than the first downpour of steady, persisting rain? Each little rivulet running golden down the garden paths, each silver pool on the baked grass was a joy. We held out our hands to catch the welcome drops, put forth our heads to let them beat upon our faces.

But it seems to be ordained, this summer, that we are not to have enough of a good thing without having too much of it. Does the sun shine, it shines till the heavens are as brass and the earth iron-bound. Falls the rain at length, there is a deluge. When we had grown tired of watching from door and window the straight descent of the rain, we wished to walk abroad to see the flagging plants lift up their heads once more, to look upon the grass growing green again. But no! 'You wished for rain, now you shall have it,' the Clerk of the Weather seems to say; and, day after day, it comes down in sheets. The roses which bloomed through the drought luxuriantly are beaten down and lie with heavy heads draggled upon the earth, the buds decay on their stalks; the branches of my beech-trees hang dark and heavy and sullen with surfeit of wet. The barley which so badly wanted water is like to be drowned in it; the wheat and oats, where the crops were heavy, lie flat. The young turnips delaying so long to show their tops above ground, are getting washed out of it. 'As well be ruined by a drought as a deluge,' Mrs. Chisholm says, and pulls a long face.

The labourers sit at home when their homes are fit to sit in; sit in the public-house and drink away their already curtailed week's wage, when the wives are scolds or slovens.

Occasionally Syers passes the line of vision – we, tired of nothing but a drowning vegetation to look upon, welcoming the sight of him – wearing a sack over his shoulders tied with string across his chest. He is unusually attractive in this costume, perhaps, for Hildred going unexpectedly into the kitchen this morning finds the parlour-maid sitting on his knees.

The wet season has afforded the leisure which is one of Cupid's favourite expedients. Ethel is a pretty, dainty-looking girl, and Syers, besides the fact that he is a family man, either in or out of his sack is not an alluring figure.

Hildred, who is nothing of a prude, is yet inclined to be disgusted with the parlour-maid. But I remind her of the promptings of nature, and the limitations of Dulditch. A woman must have some one to love her, and if her Ferdinand does not appear, will sit on the gnarled, ugly knees of Caliban, as we have seen.

Nan is still staying with the blue Persian kitten and the Shetland ponies at Trench; and Hildred and I grow a little tired of each other's company, I fear. What have we in common now I can no longer speak of you, my dearest boy? or the past in which you always were; or the future in which I hoped you were to have been? She would like, perhaps, to talk to me of the curate; has indeed made an attempt once or twice which I have not encouraged. She has, I consider, behaved with an utter lack of feeling. To-day she told me that the young man would much like to run down for a few hours. He could not leave the mother (who is really dying now, it seems, and he is her only son) for longer. She mentioned that he was very desirous of making my acquaintance, and was a keen admirer of my books.

'The less he knows of their author, then, the better,' I told her. 'Make him my compliments and tell him I speak from experience. I have never liked a book the better through knowing its author; and often, I regret to say, I have liked it less.'

You see, I can't be nice to her, George. I can't, in my heart, forgive her. Not for her so keenly disappointing me, but for her hurting you. I begin to feel I can never forgive her.

To George

So, for more than a week we have looked out drearily upon the rain; or, with all the delightful ease of our former relations gone, we make 'company talk' and avoid each other's eyes.

'I know I'm not being nice to you. I know you are dying to get away from me; why don't you go?' I was impelled to say to her to-day.

She said quite gently she would not leave me while I would let her stay. That, more than in any spot on earth, where I was had always, from her babyhood, been in its best sense home to her – and so on.

In spite of her usually unemotional bearing, she dropped a tear as she said it. And I wanted in that moment to forgive her, and cry with her, and tell her how I, who had never known the joy of a daughter of my own, had always found one in her. But I thought of you, my dearest George, and held myself in. So we looked out at the rain again with sadness and anger and disappointment in our hearts.

Fortunately, perhaps, the continued wet weather has tried the patience of the Major too.

The desire to escape from his own company, to find some one upon whom to inflict his everlasting tales, has overcome the feeling of awkwardness he might have felt in our relations. Covered with a great blue golf cloak, he has appeared to-day for the first time since his absurd offer of marriage.

If he was at all embarrassed, a little uncertain of his reception, he did not show it. The impervious armour of his self-esteem has carried him through more dangerous places in his history, I am sure.

He should have been flattered by his reception. Hildred had been writing to her curate all the morning, and I suppose thinking about him all the afternoon, for she was hopelessly dull. As for me, I would have welcomed the devil if he had come with a human voice and the will to use it. I told him so.

There is a certain deference in his manner to me which I have never noticed before, and there is, I perceive, even a glimmer of interest and speculation in the gaze he turns on me from his small blue eyes. He was at last eager to gain information about my literary labours, hitherto by him ignored.

'How many hours a day do you write? How many books do you turn out in the year? Where do you get your ideas from?'

'I get some of them from you, Major,' I told him. 'Several of the things I have gleaned from you I shall treasure up and put in a book.'

He was not at all surprised. 'I have been often advised to take up with book-writing, myself,' he told us. 'But I have preferred to turn my attention to other things.'

Hildred and I in the same breath supposed – the pig? and laughed as we tripped over each other's question.

He reported on the pig a little coldly, and returned to the attack.

'I suppose that the writing of books and plays really pays nowadays?'

'It depends,' I told him. 'Write a good book and you probably starve; write the rubbish the public will read, and rich is the reward.'

'And you?'

Hildred dashed in with the answer: told him that I combined popularity with literary excellence – that sort of thing. 'She is the exception. Cheques flutter in on her by every post, thick as autumn leaves. One came this morning; I dare not tell you for how much. Into how many figures do you think her profits from her dramatized story already run – and they are likely to go on?'

I made a pretence of trying to stop her, but she would not be stopped, having heard, you may be sure, the history of the Major's wooing, and being bent on punishing him. I was amused to watch him as the story and the fortune grew. He forgot to snap the fingers poised tip to tip above his breast. The small cold eyes – it was Nan who discovered the poor Major's eyes were like his pig's, and declared she could not endure to look at them – were fixed in an unblinking stare upon Hildred's face.

'Why should I be quiet, you wicked woman?' Hildred inquired with as much heat as if she had believed me to be in earnest. 'You are here, as Miss Milgay said, on false pretences. You have chosen to live in this little place as a commonplace person with, say, five hundred a year, while, without counting the fortune your husband left you, you are making your annual thousands by your books. Why should the people of the neighbourhood be imposed on in such fashion? Allowed to waste their pity on you as a poor dear, every-day-to-be-met-with sort of widow with straitened means? It's not fair on them is it, Major Barkaway?'

The Major gave a slow shake of the head. 'It is misleading,' he acknowledged.

'It is never right to tell fibs,' Hildred went on, gravely reproving me. 'Authors are so used to making up stories and setting them forth as narratives of fact that their ideas of truth and untruth become confused, and they introduce their fiction into their daily existence.'

I laughed. 'As an instance I will tell you what one of the wicked creatures does whose secrets I know, for she is a friend of mine,' I said; for I also, you see, decided to make the old major's lesson complete. 'When a man makes her an offer of marriage – she is a widow, as I am – she tells him that her fortune goes from her on her remarriage. She does it as a test of the suitor's good faith, she tells me; for her fortune does nothing of the kind, any more than mine does.'

The poor old wretch stared at me for a minute in an absolute silence. I hope he felt, and will remember, that swashing blow. He was not at all talkative for the rest of his visit, which was short.

To George

I HAVE sat by my window to-day, watching, and listening to, the rain falling on my half-drowned garden, and I have been picturing to myself how it is falling, falling, falling, upon your father's grave. Does any one, besides just you and me, my dearest, in all the callous, forgetful world, give him a thought as he, good, even great man, only one year dead, lies there in his loneliness?

When I looked on his face in his coffin, I, who should have known better, could not but feel that all the world shared my grief. It was a shock to me, at first, to see smiles on the faces of those who had loved him; I resented the fact that people who had been his neighbours for twenty years went, chattering to each other, past the door which would never open to let him through again. The bitterest thing in his death has been the perception that his going left no gap.

On such a beneficent arrangement, ordained by Nature's law, I have moralized with my pen a hundred times. When your father died I felt as if I had come face to face with an astonishing fact for the first time.

For the first time too I felt the inevitableness of death.

Yes. You will laugh at my confession that it is only within the last year that I have begun to realize that I am mortal.

It is a truism that young people do not believe in death for themselves. Other people die – young and old and middle-aged – it is, in the scheme of things, reasonable and right that they should move on and move off. No young man believes it in his heart of himself. And I, by reason perhaps of an occupation that is absorbing and gives me pleasure, have preserved the spirit of youthfulness so far as to forget to look upon death. Death was lurking in the distance, but I was warm at heart, and how far off his terrors were! As far off as when I was a girl. Now, at times, I admit it, I feel the chill of his presence in my bones, and his shadows, I perceive, lie all around my feet.

I do not know why I have writ this dreary page, my dear George, except to show you why, with you so far away, I must cling to Hildred, whose affection warms my heart, and to my little Sunshine-Nan, in whose presence are no shadows.

I wish she would come back to me. The skies are all grey, and the rain is falling.

To George

NAN is back; bringing the blue Persian with her; bringing Etta Milgay.

'I've come to spend a long day,' she announced. 'It's wet and depressing, and Aunt Philippa has got a meeting on. Something about scullery-maids, in whom she is supposed for some reason to take a sudden interest. A lot of silly women, for the sake of getting into Aunt Philippa's drawing-room, are going to undertake to write to so many scullery-maids so many letters in the course of a year. An awful impertinence, I call it. Aunt Philippa is not the same person down here she is in town; where she is as worldly an old girl as the rest. Here she has been badgered into lending her name to all sorts of deadly things they call "movements," and poses as an out-and-out philanthropist. I told her I could not wink at such humbug, and came away.

'Charlotte Poole! Never have I had more than half an hour, uninterrupted, with you in my life, and I'm going to sit at your feet and talk to you about your books for six solid hours.'

I am happy to say that of course she didn't. She began duly on the books, but edged off on to her own writings and her love affairs. She is forty-five years old, but she always has a fresh love affair. It is generally on her side alone, a fact she makes no attempt to conceal, being an entirely truthful person. Generally, it is an actor about whom she raves – his voice, his smile, the fascinating fashion in which he moves his hands. It has been at various times a railway guard, a policeman, a certain royal prince.

'I've got a frightfully facile kind of passion, you see,' she explains. 'Just something – I can't tell what – stirs it. The outline of a jaw; that touch of rebellion in well-brushed down hair which makes it curve in *almost* imperceptible curls at the back of a man's ear; the modelling of a bony hand put up to remove a cigarette ash; the close-locking of a pair of lips you know could smile deliciously, could whisper tenderly. Just *anything* sends me off my head; and for a while I remain off. Isn't it a mercy I have never married, Charlotte Poole? Imagine me pretending to be true to the one vapid type I admired, perhaps, for a space, twenty years ago!

'How do women keep faithful? – imaginative women? impressionable, like me? I don't know how they do it; and of such women it ought not to be expected. How can they look up to a trousered thing with a great prominent stomach, perhaps, and pendulous cheeks, and his fat neck growing into his bald head above his collar? That is the sort of matrimonial misery for which a wife ought to be given a divorce, and given it cheaply.

'I grow old, I suppose – look at my grey hair – but my heart isn't old, and I am more susceptible than ever I was. I'm furiously in love at the present moment with a man in a shop in Regent Street. I won't tell you which shop, or you'll be going there, you naughty thing, and making fun, as you always do. He's got, oh, such a fascinating curve in his back – not a hump! no, you wicked woman! a curve the other way round. The voice in which he says, "This way, madam," has the most exquisite languor; he waves his hand to the counter with the gesture of a dethroned king –'

And so on.

As, in a moment of expansion, I had told her that Hildred was to be my daughter-in-law, I thought in this hour of disillusionment it was my duty to tell her she was not. She was very sympathetic, and called Hildred a fish, and a serpent, and a blockhead, and other uncomplimentary names.

'Imagine a woman losing the chance of having Charlotte Poole for a mother!' – that sort of thing.

But going into Hildred's room later, to wash her hands, she found there, by ill luck – for I had no wish to hear of it or see it – the photograph of the curate. Having obtained permission to bring it down with her, she sat on the floor, which is ever her favourite seat, by my chair, her long knees hugged up to her breast, and the photograph laid on the top of them. There she sat, and raved herself into rapture over the curate's boy's face.

'You don't mind my loving him, do you?' she inquired of Hildred. 'You aren't jealous?' Hildred reassured her with her absurd new blush; and I declare to you, George, that as she said the object of all this exaggerated adulation would be flattered, she simpered. She did indeed – Hildred! – although I know you won't believe it.

Presently the picture was held to me above Etta's head to call my attention to a cleft in the middle of the creature's chin. I tried not to look, but could not help seeing a portrait of a long young man in clerical dress, with smooth hair, and smug features, and a silly grin.

'Will you let me guess the colour of his eyes, Hildred?' Etta raved on. ('I may call you Hildred, I know, because Charlotte Poole's friends are my friends, and I will be Etta to you.) Grey, aren't they? I know I'm right. Grey flecked with green?'

Hildred, looking down her nose in the most silly way, acknowledged that they were; or green flecked with grey; or some absurd combination.

'And the eyelids! Now, see here, Charlotte Poole; the eyelids are cut just as a man's eyelids, let me tell you, should be cut. Not straight across; the whole eye bulging out when he looks at you like a button from a button-hole; but curved to the corner. See? And his eyes – grey, flecked with green – look as if he could laugh; does he?'

Hildred admitted ashamedly that he laughed a great deal.

'And when he laughs his mouth opens squarely, doesn't it? I see it does. Not just a gap –'

I will spare you, dear George; but there was much more of it. Nauseating in the extreme, I found it; but I gathered from it that Hildred's curate is a beauty-man – or beauty-boy, perhaps I should call him.

While the pair were still rhapsodizing Nan came in. She glanced at the photo on Etta's knee: 'Oh, it's Ernest,' she said indifferently. 'I wish he'd come, Mummy; I haven't got any one to play with here.'

'You Serpent's Tooth!' I addressed her.

'Well, you're an old woman, Gran. A little girl can't play *always* with just an old woman. I want Ernest to come, Mummy. He does just exactly every single thing I ask him to do. Which is most extremely agreeable, I think, of Ernest.'

168

To George

OH, my dearest boy, what a sinking of the heart I had when I found in the letter-box this morning a letter in your handwriting addressed to Hildred!

It was, I felt certain, in response to the entreaty to say something definite to her I had sent you, mail before last.

For a minute I had the impulse to send it back to you, unopened, to save you the humiliation of your pride, if not the wound to your heart. But while I stood with it in my hand, hesitating, Hildred came down.

I believe she divined my fear and shared it, for she turned quite pale as she saw the letter. She took it without a word from my reluctant fingers, and laid it beside her plate. The every morning task of coaxing, scolding, threatening, and finally bribing Nan to eat her porridge before she attacks her egg was performed perfunctorily and with a mind, it was easy to see, otherwise. Her own breakfast she ate with a preoccupied mien, as a duty expected of her, and obviously without relish. Behind the teapot I waited, treating her few remarks about the weather with the contempt I felt they merited; dreading to have the letter opened, yet angry to see it, in your dear handwriting, George, laid away as a thing of no importance, to await her leisure.

'My dear Hildred,' I was moved to say, at length, 'three times you have announced that it looked like rain, and three times I have patiently replied that it did not. The room is filled with sunshine. Through the gently waving branches of the creeper which frames the window you can see a cloudless sky. Do observe these patent manifestations of Nature, and say the day is fine, if you must speak of the weather. That letter by your plate is from my George, I think?'

She picked up the letter and examined it as if not quite sure of the fact.

'I am anxious for news of my dear son,' I reminded her.

'He has not written to you by this mail?' she asked; fingered the letter for a minute, laid it down by her plate again, helped herself to another triangle of toast.

Don't laugh at me, George, but I was roused.

'The letter won't *bite* you,' I said. 'Whatever my son has said to you in that letter, he has said, I will go bail for him, in a manly fashion. Whatever answer you may send him, he will accept, be assured, without any whining. I am waiting for news of my son. Unless you are afraid to do so, open his letter.'

'Gran, you look as if your eyes would fall out. You look like a startled buffalo,' from an unflattering, if observant, Nan.

'Cousin Charlotte!' from an offended Hildred.

But she hesitated no longer, and opened the letter. You know what she found within, my dear boy. Not the avowal of your undying love for her which I had expected, but the confession of your love for a sweet young girl to whom you are going to be married next month.

I have not yet recovered from the surprise of it, the – well, the shock –

But you know with what joy I read of your happiness, my own dear boy; how I long –

Perhaps you can guess a little of what I felt, seeing I had urged your making the fatal declaration I believed to be written there, as I sat opposite to her, and watched Hildred's face while she read your letter. Presently her face flushed crimson. Then she looked up at me; stared in my face; laughed. Laughed!

You remember, George, how even Moses – that meek man of God – spake once 'unadvisedly with his lips'?

'You are heartless, I know, but at least be decent,' I said to her, the words bursting from me.

She flew up, letter in hand, and dashed round the table, like any schoolgirl – our stately Hildred! – and flung her arms round me, and kissed me on my furious face.

'You dear, foolish, Cousin Charlotte!' she said. 'You glare at me. There is murder in your heart, I know it. You long to stick the butter-knife into me. Don't you think I can be trusted to know if a man is in love with me or no? That dear, old, silent George of yours was rid of his boy's fancy for me years and years ago. And now – and now – ! I am so glad I could sing for joy! – he has written – written to tell me – what do you think? I am to "break it to his mother, who may be disappointed"' – she had turned back to the letter, and was reading from it – '"she having set her heart upon a plan, you and I, Hildred, found to be impossible years and years ago."'

You remember in what words you set forth the news that she was to break to me, George.

To George

AT last the fact that she is to have that obliging quadruped, the curate, for her stepfather has been disclosed to Nan.

I was not present on the interesting occasion, having received an especial request from Hildred to absent myself; but I caught Nan as she issued from the interview, and asked her what she thought of the intelligence just imparted.

'Well, you see, I was most extremely disappointed,' she acknowledged. 'Mummy said she had something of great importance to tell me. So, of course, I thought that Lady Tatterbury had sent me the Shetland pony. I don't call just *Ernest* of great importance; do you, Gran?'

To George

HILDRED has plucked up courage to announce – what I suppose she has been longing to do for the last few weeks, but has feared to seem to desert me – that she must leave me and Dulditch, and go up to town to help her young man to nurse his dying mother.

All my love has come back for Hildred; but it is Nan, Nan, Nan; naughty, adorable, perverse, plaintive, fiendish, *angel* Nan that I shall miss!

Yet, I am not murmuring, dear George. Nothing has turned out as I expected, and wished and planned for; but I shall love your sweet young wife, I am sure; and all, I know, is for the best. And Hildred has promised Nan to me for a month when the marriage takes place.

So the pair of them go next week, and I shall be as lonely as before they came. More lonely, for I have had them.

Not even a Bertha Flatt will there be, to fall back on; for she and her missionary sail for their islands in a fortnight; not even 'that fat, round, oily man of God,' her brother; not even, if I can keep him at arm's length, Major Barkaway.

But there is the garden, there are the birds, the trees, the squirrel in the nut-bushes, which I have forbidden the bloodthirsty Syers to shoot, on pain of instant dismissal; there are the fields, spite of rain and drought, fears and doleful prognostications, grown ripe for harvest; there are the children who pass to and from school in their pinafores, or their funny wide trousers, adapted from the parent stock, and make their shy, but smiling 'obediences' or touch their caps to me as I lean to look for them upon the garden gate. There are the men and women of the labouring class with some few of whom I have succeeded in making friends. Do not think that I am murmuring or would have things otherwise.

To know that you and your Helen are coming to England to me for your honeymoon is sufficient joy.

But minds grow stiff, as joints do, with old age, and just at first it is difficult, and a little painful, to turn them from their long bent.

To George

LAST evening we went round the village to say to every one good-bye. For, at the last, dear George, I found I could not face the solitude without Hildred, or rejoice any more in the sunshine without my little Nan. Besides, we all think you and Helen will prefer to come to me in the old home in Harley Street, and that I can give you both a better time there.

And it is wiser to say farewell to Dulditch before the summer is quite over, that so I may retain a happier impression of the place.

When I sit by the fire, o' nights, and look back to the six months I have spent here, and the picture of the Cottage – its red bricks mellowed by the suns and storms of two hundred years, its garden made to blossom with beauty for my enjoyment by the obliging ministrations of t'other woman – I shall see it at its prettiest, as I left it. With the crimson creeper and that 'gadding vine,' the purple clematis clinging to its walls; with all the windows of its pleasant rooms open to air, and sunshine, and hum of insect, and song of bird; with Syers tying up the heavy heads of the dahlias, and staking the 'Lady hollyhock'; with the sun lying warm on the short dry grass of the lawn; and the birds – the dear, dear, friendly birds, starling and blackbird and thrush – holding high festival in the rowan-tree loaded with scarlet berries by the gate.

We found the Rector, poor man, uncomfortably conscious of the fact that he was but a worm in the eyes of the beholder. His cheeks, once fat and red, hung flabby and grey. He had really been fretting over his worminess, I believe. His hand shook as he held it out to

Hildred; he was nervous, and ill-at-ease. I was sorry for the Rector. He is but as he was made; who shall blame him?

We found him in his garden, and he at once led the way indoors. In a low voice as we went he asked as not to mention to his sister the voyage upon which she was to have started on the 30th of the month. At the last moment his friend the Reverend Pevensey Pryngge had decided that it would be better for Bertha to wait for him at home, and not face the dangers of the country and the climate, as she had generously consented to do. He had therefore sailed for the Fiji Isles alone.

The engagement was not broken off; but the marriage must of necessity be postponed for several years.

We were sorry for the poor, disappointed bride. She would have been quite content to run any risk, from climate, of assassination, of lifelong misery, by the side of the little, hardly known monkey-missionary she wished to marry.

We found her the Bertha Flatt of our earlier acquaintance. All the little airs, the smiles, the giggles, even, of a recaptured girlhood had dropped from her. She was frankly past her youth again, frankly plain, soured, embittered, peevish, once more. She expressed neither surprise nor sorrow at the object of our visit; what interest she felt in our going from Dulditch she took pains to conceal.

We made but a few minutes' stay. Nan was escorted by the Rector, glad to escape us, to the stables, to say good-bye to Greyman, the white pony.

'I have told about my new daddy, mummy,' she announced on her return. 'I am going to have Ernest for my daddy, did you know?' she inquired of poor Bertha, to whom we would have spared all mention of happy love affairs.

'I am most extremely glad,' the irrepressible one proceeded to inform the glum-looking Flatts, 'because now I think it is likely I may have a little brother and sister; which I extremely wish for.'

Poor Nan could not understand why, when we came away, her mother seemed displeased with her, refusing to let her hang all her weight on the parent arm, as is her custom when they walk together. 'I asked Mr. Flatt to give me just one more trot round on Greyman as he used to do; and he wouldn't. I think he is a selfish beast,' she remarked.

'You are not to use such expressions about people who have been kind to you – about any one,' Hildred scolded. 'Where do you pick up such words, pray?'

'It is what Ernest always called the old man who would sit in your chair in the garden at Cannes. If I mayn't pick up Ernest's words, who is going to be my new daddy, whose words may I pick up, then?'

'No one's. And don't ask questions.'

'You'd better have said you wanted a little deaf and dumb girl, mummy, when you were giving orders for me. It would have been much more extremely interesting for you.'

Then she came round, and transferred her weight to my arm, and whispered with a trembling lip that her mummy was not at all agreeable to-day; but that I was always an agreeable old lady, and she loved me best in the world.

Oh, George! I can't help thinking, if only it could have been! You know what I mean, dear – don't be vexed with me. We should so have loved Nan, you and I and Hildred!

'I suppose if we come back here in ten years' time we shall find them where we left them,' Hildred said, speaking of the pair to whom we had said good-bye. 'The trees and shrubs will have grown in the garden, the number of things which the Rector is certain it is dangerous, or derogatory, or unnecessary to meddle with will have grown. The Flatts will be older, stupider, more narrow –'

'Flatter.'

'– but they won't have grown. We can picture them walking those damp paths of theirs, beneath the overhanging branches, telling each other in whispers that some one has stolen three plums since yesterday from the tree by the back door; that Mrs. Chisholm must be offended at something, as she was not at church last Sunday; that they must ask her to tea to put her in a good temper. They'll be trembling at the nod of the Hobbleboys, still; still jealous of the number of times Major Barkaway lunches at the hall –'

'To people who take what comes in a forlorn stupidity, nothing comes,' I reminded her.

But, after all, isn't there something, in the world of change we know, to be said for the world in which you are sure to find your friends as you leave them? With us the leopard is always changing his spots; or concealing them with some new kind of artificial covering, so that with difficulty you recognize your leopard when you meet him.

We found Major Barkaway at a happy moment, the pig-sticker having come that morning and killed his pig. The companion of all these summer months, the object of such tender care, hung from a beam in the roof of one of the dirty outhouses. A stick had been passed through his hind legs, sticks extended the sides of his stomach, to exhibit its emptiness.

Nan was delighted at the opportunity to make a close study of the pig's anatomy. She was charmed with the new, unexpected rose and white of his inside and outside complexion:

'It's such a pity he can't be alive now he's dead,' she lamented. 'He's much more extremely pretty so.'

If there had been any embarrassment in the Major's mind over the awkwardness of our relations, he had forgotten it in the pleasant excitement of the occasion. He had depended on me, it seems, to buy from him a quarter of the animal; the other three quarters being disposed of to neighbours. Desirous as I naturally was to oblige him, I did not see the way to burden myself with such a portion of the Barkaway pig as luggage to be conveyed to town.

He almost forgot to express his regret at the prospect of our sudden departure in his eager efforts to impress on me what a boon to my household would be so many stones of pork; 'fed' as this pork had been fed; of such a delicious wholesomeness and superior quality. I believe he felt more hurt by my firm refusal so to benefit myself than he had done over the failure of his marriage scheme.

Determined that we should see all there now was to see of his pig, he led us into the stuffy little kitchen, where his housekeeper was in the act of dividing that mass of the animal's interior, known in its present condition as 'fry' – the heart, lungs, and so on, into parcels destined for disposal among the Major's intimates.

'I don't entertain,' he explained, 'being a bachelor. I have no means of showing gratitude for hospitality; but I always find such little attentions as these welcomed by my friends.'

I observed a parcel covered with a transparent veil of fat upon which lay a ticket with the word 'Poole' in the Major's handwriting.

'You will find it make an excellent supper-dish,' he assured me. 'I had intended carrying it to the Cottage myself, but shall now have to set about finding some one to buy the quarter I had made sure of your taking. Perhaps, therefore – ?'

With our share of the delicacy, bestowed in a minute basket which we were enjoined to return that evening without fail, we finally departed, the Major raised his cap, and bowed with a preoccupied air at the gate, easy in his mind about having discharged the debt for hospitality which social laws demanded, but his thoughts preoccupied with the disposal of the unsold portion of pork.

Before we left we made our way over the rubbish-heap he calls his garden. Here and there in the tangle of weeds a clump of tall lilies grows, a rose blooms, a few spilt packets of seeds have come to the flowering stage. In the sty, a successor to that dead hero hanging head downwards in the outhouse has been installed. A young successor, whose progress towards saleable 'quarters' the Major will watch with keenest interest every day; whose scaly back he will rub with his stick; out of whose intestines he will, by and by, in the fullness of time, make presents to his friends.

At the last moment as we came away he remembered to present us with a rose apiece from the Gloire-de-Dijon over the porch.

Farewell, Barkaway. Bertha, and Algernon Flatt, farewell. You and I, in all human probability, will never encounter again. In the end of all things there is a feeling of sadness; but I am sorry I cannot be more sorry in this moment of bidding you good-bye.

'To think,' said Hildred as we came away, 'that of that domain my dear Charlotte Poole might have been mistress; that she might have been in at the death of the pig, and herself dispensed little parcels of 'fry' round her social circle! To think that there is a man of some breeding, I suppose, and upbringing, endowed in the beginning with as large a mental capacity as many men who are talked of, and written about, and have made for themselves places in the world! This, my dear Cousin Charlotte, is what Dulditch has done for Major Barkaway.'

'But he is so extremely happy with his pig,' Nan reminded us.

To the Chisholms, too, we have said good-bye; roamed for the last time about their lovely garden, heard once more poor Mrs. Chisholm's regrets that she, a doctor's daughter, should have married a farmer. 'Not that I'd have looked at any other man; but I ought to have insisted on his taking up with another business,' she finished, as usual, the matter.

'The son from Cambridge, home for the long vacation, was playing a single at tennis with a college friend. He left off to make dashes after Nan, and to pretend not to be able to catch her, dodging him alluringly among the bushes. I put a question to him as to his future. He said he supposed he should have to take Holy Orders, as his mother wanted him to, but he looked upon the necessity as a beastly bore, and would far rather adopt his father's business, which offered the only life, to his thinking, worth living. But it cost more to put a man into a farm than to put him into the Church, and his mother was set on it, and so —'

'If I could live in a lovely old place like this, and shoot, and hunt, and play tennis all day, I'd never be saddled with the fag of preaching,' the friend said, who also was to embrace, we were told, preaching as a profession.

Poor Mr. Chisholm, sad-eyed, listened in silence, looking out over the blossoming garden, the park-like meadow, to the scant harvest field beyond; where the barley had only grown a foot high, and in some places had not been found worth the expense of cutting. What he thought we never knew; he had a still tongue, but the look of one who ruminated much, and not always happily.

Nora in her pink pinafore – busy with the turkeys in the orchard, gazed with wistful looks when we told her we were going back immediately to town.

'I shall see you always, in my dreams of Dulditch, young and fresh and peaceful, in this lovely old place,' I said to the girl.

'You may always picture me here, for I can never get away,' she said. 'It is a lovely place, but it chains us. The life is a pleasant one; that is why the people who lead it can never escape.'

I gazed over the beautifully ordered garden on which the afternoon sun lay like a benediction. There flowers bloomed, from the spruce-growing rows of ten-week stocks in the beds bordering the walk to the entrance gate, to the antirrhinums, yellow and crimson, growing and glowing on the buttresses of the old house itself, as flowers will bloom where people love and encourage them; hardly a leaf on the big trees stirred in the warm stillness; not a yard of the place but had been tended by loving hands for generations. If ever a place looked the abode of peace it was this.

But Discontent, I fear, does not eschew the quiet spots of the earth for a dwelling-place; even in the mind of the hermit Rebelliousness is to be found; and beasts sometimes eat the hearts of those who walk alone.

To George

THE really handsome sum I have paid Syers as compensation for short notice has failed, I find, to reconcile him to the loss of his situation.

'This here's a nice look on!' he accosted me with, this morning, when I made my farewell walk around the garden. 'You're a-takin' off, you tell me. Tha's all werry well, but what I want ter know is, wha's to become of *me*? T'other woman behaved well to me, she did. "I'm a-lavin', Syers," she say, "but I'll spake to any lady or gemman for ye; for well yew ha' done by me, Syers, bor, and yer garden's a credit to ye." Them was her wards; I mind 'em well; "Yer garden's a credit to ye."'

'She gave you a fair character, Syers. She told me you were of absolutely no use "under glass"; that you were very slow in wits, and inclined to shirk your work when not looked after. She omitted, however, to mention a few facts on which I also have hitherto kept silence: That although you are supposed to begin the day's work at six you do not arrive until nine; that you keep your own household stocked with coal from my store; and that, in spite of being a married man, you nurse the parlour-maid upon your knee.'

Syers was by no means abashed. 'Tha's all as ter may be,' he admitted. 'We don't want no argy-bargeying about wha's come and gone, and wholly done with. What I'm a sayin' is this here – is it fare to up and lave a man afore he's found a continyation of the job he done for ye? Is that, I'm a-askin' of ye, the ac' of a lady?'

Some extra sheets, towels, and a blanket or two, additions I had made to my original stock brought with me, I tied into a parcel which Hildred and I carried between us to Mrs. Moore's door.

Laura's baby, we found, was now promoted to crawling over the brick floor on its stomach. For Laura herself I had been instrumental in finding a situation as kitchen-maid with a friend of mine who takes a generous view of such histories. The tragic face of Mrs. Moore was bent above the wash-tub; she glared at us through its steam with the baleful gaze of hatred.

'Yew kin put it down,' she said, alluding to our burden; and, as its size was considerable, we thanked her in availing ourselves of the privilege.

I explained that to her large family a few extra sheets, &c., I hoped would not come amiss.

'I ain't a-sayin' as I couldn't ha' made shift without them,' said Mrs. Moore. 'Howoever, they'll mayhap come in handy-like when my Clemmy come home.'

With my incurable habit of attempting to manage other people's affairs, I advised the poor woman to get Clemmy a place outside the neighbourhood, in order to give him the chance to begin again, unhandicapped by the drawback of his history.

'That'll ha' ter be as Clemmy see fit,' his mother pronounced with dignity. 'If so be as Clemmy, when he come out, have a fancy to stop in his nat*ive*, there he kin' stop, I take it, askin' no one's lave.'

She went on to remark, as she dashed her linen violently up and down beneath the soap-suds, that she'd allust heared th' land was free, and a poor chap had as much right to breath the air in one spot as another. Clemmy, he'd had a misfortune, there weren't no denyin' of it, and now he was a-payin' for it. 'Come to th' bottom o' things, if so be as Clemmy ha'n't been tarned at a minute's notice off the job he took to oblige, he wouldn't ha' had th' occasion to git into no trouble.'

Hildred had picked up the baby from the floor. Mrs. Moore made a grudging apology for the condition of its pinafore – nothing else about it was dirty. 'While she crape 'tain't possible to kape her pinny clane,' she said.

I suppose poor Mrs. Moore is the most disagreeable person in Dulditch. I like her cleanliness, however, her stoutness of heart, her fighting powers. I told her that we had come to say good-bye, and that I was sorry I should not see her again.

'I heared you was a-goin',' said Mrs. Moore uncompromisingly, turning aside to wring a screw of counterpane in her red, steaming hands. 'Good arternune.'

To George

TO-MORROW I shall have turned my back on The Cottage, and on Dulditch. This evening I write for the last time, sitting at my sturdy oak table and beneath the fir-tree on the lawn. Hildred is consulting with Nan's Nurse, who has come down to make the journey with us, about some important matter of Nan's wardrobe. Through the open window their voices float down to me. When I pause to listen I can catch a word or two of what they say. It is warm to-night, but it may be chilly in the morning; Nan's white flannel coat is to be left out, as well as her silk one, I gather. Will Nurse remember to put new laces in her brown shoes?

The lamp is lit in the dining-room; I can, as I sit, catch glimpses of the servants moving about there, putting our frugal supper upon the table. Our last supper in Dulditch.

The great white owl we have watched, night after night, goes in heavy silence from his home in the hollow elm, across the bottom of the garden, on his nightly quest for food. The air is full of ineffable sweetness.

Ah, what a sweet procession of delicious scents I have inhaled as I have sat, each day as evening fell, filling my paper to send to you with any nonsense which came into my head. Scent of violets hidden in the grass, of wallflowers, honeysuckle, sweet-pea, carnation, heliotrope; whiffs from the white clover-field across the way, the bean-field further down the road, the sweet-briar hidden in the hedge, the new-mown hay – what a delicious feast of good things!

> *'Come, Summer, from the South, and blow apace until thy prime be reached,*
> *Then linger, linger, linger on the rose.'*

And now the time of roses is over, although, here and there, a dark deep-hearted Jacqueminot, heavy with sweetness, may be gathered still; a Caroline Testout smiles in delicate pink loveliness among its glossy leaves.

The beauty of the quiet place seems to reproach me to-night. Yet I have not 'thought scorn of the pleasant land.' There were times when I would have asked no better than to spend in this peaceful spot what remnant of life is mine. But, I confess it to you, George, there stirs within me a longing to be gone; to find myself once more in the haunts of men; to forsake, in a word, the vegetable for the animal kingdom.

I do not forget to be thankful, too, that I have the strength to go; that after sipping the narcotic with which Nature drugs her devotees, saturating myself in the beauty, the silence, the torpor of the place, steeping my senses in the sluggish stream of inertia which creeps through the flowery meadows, the rose-grown gardens of Dulditch, I have still spirit enough left in me to escape from the subtle, sweet influences; discernment enough to recognize that idleness is not always rest; that the peace of mind which is procured through the atrophy of the intellect is bought at too dear a price, and is by no means 'well.'

Here comes Hildred, seeking me, with preoccupied face, and mind divided between the joy of meeting again the Beauty-Boy Curate to-morrow and maternal cares as to Nan's welfare in travelling.

Nan, excited by the coming change, cannot sleep to-night. She is singing in her bed as her custom is until slumber drowns her voice, holding tucked beneath her pillow, I know well, the absurd china elephant wrapped in its bit of scarlet flannel.

Hildred stops under her open window, listens for a moment, calls softly, 'Go to sleep, darling.'

The song ceases instantly. 'Are you there, my most precious mummy?'

'Here, darling; looking up to your window.'

'Is Gran there, mummy?'

'She is writing at her table on the lawn.'

'Do the stars shine?'

'Just one. A tiny naughty one; he twinkles on one side of the chimney-pot, and tries to play bo-peep with me.'

'Mummy!'

'Yes, darling.'

'That little star. I suppose when you and me and Gran are gone away he'll always be there?'

'Yes, darling.'

'And everything just the same? The flowers, and the birds, and Mr. Chisholm's men walking behind the dear horses?'

'Just the same, Nan. Always.'

A long silence. Hildred, thinking sleep has fallen, is turning away, when the high, clear voice calls again:

'I'm glad we don't *live* in Dulditch where things are always the same, mummy. I am extremely fond of difference, you see.'

So Nan in a few words voices what I have been trying to explain to you, my dear George, in many. Dulditch is well in its way, but it is not the place of my rest.

Nor should it, for her soul's sake, be ever made the abode of one who is 'extremely fond of difference.'